WALTZ WITH A RAKE

"I don't regret interfering since it means I shall achieve a goal I have long held dear."

"And that is?"

"To dance the waltz with you, of course."

Althea bit her lip. Since she had not contradicted him when he'd said she was promised to him, she was trapped.

How, she wondered, *could I have allowed it to happen?*

She had always avoided dancing with Sir Valerian. She had not allowed him so much as a country-dance. And now, for no better reason than that the most arrogant bore in London had demanded she dance with him. She had allowed herself to be tricked into standing up with him.

And not merely a *dance.* A *waltz.* Silently, Althea admitted it was something she, too, wanted. Desperately wanted. . . .

Books by Jeanne Savery

THE WIDOW AND THE RAKE

A REFORMED RAKE

A CHRISTMAS TREASURE

A LADY'S DECEPTION

CUPID'S CHALLENGE

LADY STEPHANIE

A TIMELESS LOVE

A LADY'S LESSON

LORD GALVESTON AND THE GHOST

A LADY'S PROPOSAL

THE WIDOWED MISS MORDAUNT

A LOVE FOR LYDIA

TAMING LORD RENWICK

LADY SERENA'S SURRENDER

THE CHRISTMAS GIFT

THE PERFECT HUSBAND

A PERFECT MATCH

SMUGGLER'S HEART

MISS SELDON'S SUITORS

AN INDEPENDENT LADY

THE FAMILY MATCHMAKER

THE RELUCTANT RAKE

Published by Zebra Books

THE RELUCTANT RAKE

JEANNE SAVERY

ZEBRA BOOKS
KENSINGTON PUBLISHING CORP.
http://www.kensingtonbooks.com

ZEBRA BOOKS are published by

Kensington Publishing Corp.
850 Third Avenue
New York, NY 10022

All Kensington titles, imprints, and distributed lines are available at special quantity discounts for bulk purchases for sales
promotion, premiums, fund-raising, educational or institutional
use.

Special book excerpts or customized printings can also be
created to fit specific needs. For details, write or phone the
office of the Kensington Special Sales Manager: Kensington
Publishing Corp., 850 Third Avenue, New York, NY 10022.
Attn. Special Sales Department. Phone: 1-800-221-2647.

Zebra and the Z logo Reg. U.S. Pat. & TM Off.

First Printing: October 2003
10 9 8 7 6 5 4 3 2 1

Printed in the United States of America

With many thanks to
Jim Ozinga
for timely assistance

PROLOGUE

Canadian Interlude

"Are you certain?" asked the tall narrow-faced man with the steady eyes. "Could it not have been someone who looked like him?"

"Dressed like a prince, he was, but couldn't fool me. I checked. Surreptitious-like? There was the scar in the eyebrow and your ring on his thumb."

"My ring." Jared Emerson Andover stared at the rough bark of the undressed logs of which the fur station was constructed. "He's my half brother, Mac. I should be pleased to know where he is."

"Don't see that," objected the older man. "Bastard in name and bastard by nature. Would have done the world good if he were gone for good."

Jared ignored that. "What, I wonder, is he doing in London?"

"He couldn't very well stay here, could he? Not after thinking he'd killed you? And everyone suspicioning it? Couldn't wear your ring here either—which he'd want to do."

"But why England?"

The trader chuckled. "I thought you might want to know

that. Appears," he said on a sly note, "our old *friend* is *heir* to a mar-kiss. You never said you'd a *mar-kiss* in the family."

"The man was born that way, wasn't he? With the coronet around his brow? Never seemed a thing to be all that proud about," said Jared mildly—but his frown deepened. "I suppose the man is my uncle," he mused.

"Too young. Cousin, maybe." The fat man's belly jiggled with his roar of laughter. "That's one for the books. *You!* Maybe a mar-kiss someday!"

Jared cast the trader a look of horror.

Mac laughed another belly shaking guffaw. "So, Jared?" he asked when he could speak. "What will you do?"

Jared pushed his lower lip out, a grim look narrowing his eyes. "My half brother is not and never can be heir to a marquisate. I cannot allow him to perpetrate a fraud on my unknown relative," said the young man slowly. "Besides, given *my* experience, when all he wanted was our winter's take of furs, it is not unlikely that that same identical relative, a man who has far more, is in danger." He sighed. "Even a marquis shouldn't be murdered."

"Your republican tendencies are showing, Jared." The man chuckled again.

Jared, thinking deeply, didn't respond.

"So, then," asked the trader, "you'll write your mar-kiss?"

Jared ignored the question. "Did you see him?" asked Jared, curious. "My cousin?"

"Now where would the likes of me clap hands with a mar-kiss?"

Jared hadn't expected anything different. He turned back to finger the stock of the gun he thought of buying, but his mind wasn't on it. He pondered the unwelcome news concerning his older half brother.

Should I write my cousin? Warn him? Would that do? Would he believe me . . . ?

"Did see a cartoon of him, your mar-kiss," Macalister said in his most insinuating voice.

Jared tensed. His head came around and he stared.

"I bought it." The Scotsman's ready smile tightened his plump cheeks, laughter barely contained—but at Jared's expression the raucous knee-slapping chuckles rang out freely. "Yes, sir," gasped Mac. Then, in a falsely innocent manner, he added, "Thought it might be of interest to someone I knew. Now who might that a'been?"

"Mac, if you've got such a thing, I would appreciate seeing it."

"Oh I got it all right. Now where did I . . ." The laugh held a touch of chagrin this time when Jared formed a fist and studied it. "Oh very well, man. Put your smelliest sock in it. I'll stop my joshing and get the thing for you." He disappeared into living quarters at the back of the trading post, returning quickly.

Jared, the badly printed, two-penny-colored cartoon in hand, stared at a face very like his own. Thin, dark, bent at the waist and a trifle bemused, the caricatured figure of the Marquis of Lambert followed along behind the skirts of a demure woman who held a delicate chain—the end of which was attached to a ring through the Marquis' nose.

"Petticoat led?" asked Jared.

"He married unexpectedly after a very brief courtship— or so I was told by the biggest gossip in the City. He *may* be tied to her skirts, but I've doubts. If he *is*, it doesn't prevent him from being an important man in the government and spending so little time with his bride it's one them on ditty things." He corrected himself self consciously. "*Ou dit,* that is."

"Nonsense," said Jared sharply. "That he's important, I mean. If he were I'd have read about him. News from London may be months old when I get it, but I eventually read about what goes on in the world."

"Didn't mean he was First Minister or like that. He's an under-secretary or some such. My man said he works for the foreign office and the war office, a liaison. Seems he's the only one who can get the one to understand the other. And you know what that means. *He* does the work. The *politicians* get the glory."

"Hmm."

"Yep. I heard he works so hard that little wife of his doesn't see much of him. But not a word of scandal trails her petticoats. Probably," added Mac thoughtfully, "because she was reared in a vicarage and wouldn't know how to make herself a byword."

"You appear to have discovered a great deal while in London." Jared stared at his friend from under well-formed brows.

The twinkle commonly seen there, faded from the trader's eyes. "When I saw that low-down water rat wearing your ring I made it my business to discover what I could. Baron is pretending to be you, Jared. Only he's calling himself Emerson."

"My middle name." Jared's mouth firmed into a hard line. Then he grimaced. "That settles it. I cannot allow my name to be blackened by that scurrilous cur."

The trader looked at his fingernails and picked at a hangnail as, the suggestive tone back, he said, "There's a naval ship on the Hudson I hear. About ready to set off downriver." The trader raised his eyes to meet Jared's. Then he raised his thumb to his mouth, his chipped front teeth worrying at the roughened bit of skin but he stared steadily at the tall young man standing so straight and stern before him.

Finally Jared's gaze livened and he actually seemed to see that Macalister was studying him. "Thanks, Mac. I owe you," he said as he turned on his heel to return to his cabin. He'd things to do if he were to leave immediately for London for no one knew how long.

"You'll need to hurry," called the trader. "If you mean to catch that boat, I mean."

"Do one more thing for me, will you? Send a runner with word they are to wait for me."

"I'll do that. Oh, Jared. . . ."

Jared paused.

"My cartoon?" Mac's voice had a touch of the wheedling about it. "Can I have it back?"

Jared looked down at his fist where he'd grasped the rolled up page so tightly he'd very likely damaged it. Apologetically, he handed it back.

CHAPTER 1

Miss Althea Bronsen glared at the man who had just crossed to her from the far side of her mother's salon. "You had better have a truly excellent reason for this . . . this nonsense." She waved the calling card on which Sir Valerian Underwood had written a cryptic note.

A muscle in his jaw jumped. Impatiently, he stripped the gloves from his hands and took his hat off. He held both in his right hand, showing he meant to leave at once since he'd not handed them to the butler.

"It is true," said Sir Valerian. "Clair is in danger."

With great difficulty Althea kept her eyes from the scar marring the back and forefinger of Sir Valerian's left hand. She would not stare at that mark of shame.

"Nonsense," she said rather belatedly. "She has married a far better man than could possibly be expected of a mere vicarage miss. She is happy. Every letter she wrote me during the winter months rang with happiness. Except," she added thoughtfully, "for a few I received just after she and the dowager crossed the channel leaving his lordship behind."

"I do not deny she is happy." A muscle jumped in his jaw. "You have not been long in town. Have you visited her?"

Althea, frowning, shook her head.

"She does not make her own trouble, Althea—" He held up his hand palm forward in a fencer's gesture when she glared daggers. "—*Miss* Althea." With the addition of the honorific, there flashed a dark look of passionate derision, but it faded, his mission too important to allow interference from what was between them. "The danger comes from Lord Lambert's heir."

Althea frowned. "The man from our Canadian provinces? I met him during the little Season—a diffident soul, willing to please, a trifle like a roughly trained puppy that isn't certain of its welcome. But, for all that," she finished, "not lacking in charm."

"That might have described him before Lambert married Clair, Althea—*Miss* Althea."

Again that faint sneer that left Althea feeling guilty when she'd no reason to feel that way. It was only proper, after all, that a man unrelated to her not take liberties with her name. *Especially* a man of Sir Valerian's reputation.

"He changed," continued Val, drawing her attention away from thoughts better forgotten. "Andover changed even before the banns were read for the third time. Althea, he fears he'll be supplanted by an heir of Lambert's body."

"More foolishness. He can never have thought to inherit. Lord Lambert is far younger than Mr. Emerson Andover."

"By as much as a decade, I would think," agreed Sir Valerian in normal tones. He again lowered his voice so others would not hear their conversation. "Nevertheless, it is true. Clair needs all the protection we can give her. I cannot be with her at all times. There are places I cannot go. Althea, you must help."

Althea eyed him and wished he were not quite so tall, quite so dark, and, most of all, that he were not so dangerous to her peace of mind. She sighed. "This must be another of your irritating attempts to escape boredom, Sir Valerian," she said, making vague reference to the hours he spent teas-

ing her with light dalliance, breaking her heart, and making
it impossible that she accept marriage to any other man. She
drew in a deep breath, sweeping aside thoughts she wished
could be erased from her mind. "You tell a tale far too
Gothic to be believed," she insisted. "This is eighteen fourteen, not seventeen fourteen!" She watched him make a
great effort to find the patience to continue and, knowing
him well, was a trifle surprised when he actually managed
the trick.

"Whatever the century, there is evil in the world," he said
quietly. He grimaced at the odd sound she made, which was
neither a laugh nor a sob, but the gesture with which he ac-
companied it was definitely one of rejection. "I am not
bored," he said gently. "I am never bored, although you do
not believe it. Nor am I evil. Mr. Andover *is*."

"This *must* be nonsense."

Althea turned her back, unable to sustain that steady
look, unable to keep to the front of her mind that this was a
gazetted rake, a dangerous man when crossed—witness that
scar that everyone said was received in an illicit duel, im-
properly arranged and unwitnessed. Worst of all, he was the
man who had made game of her for three long years—the
three years since that summer interlude—pretending to woo
her, but, all the while, laughing at her. She bit her lip.

Once she was certain she had herself well under control,
she turned. Speaking in a cool tone that was worse than if it
were truly cold, she ordered, "Leave my presence, Sir Valerian.
I'll listen to no more of your fairy tales."

Sir Val sighed. "Call truce, Althea. I need your help."

Althea, whose pert nose had been nicely elevated when
she turned back to him, dropped the pose of outraged maiden-
hood she'd adopted with difficulty, and, instead, cast him a
look of disbelief. "You? *You* need *my* help? I am an eminently
respectable woman, Val Underwood, and I mean to retain
that reputation. What can you, a confirmed rake, possibly
have in mind that requires aid from such as I?"

"Cold," murmured Sir Val sadly. "So cold—but only toward me. You," he continued in normal tones, "do have a care for Clair, do you not?"

"I do not know how she bears you anywhere near her. She is such a sweet child."

Sir Valerian clenched his fists. "Devil take it! My cousin knows I mean her only good. I have done since she was an infant in her cradle."

Althea gasped.

"Hell and damnation," he said, his voice low but intense. "Althea, stop pretending you are stuffed full as you can hold with prunes and prisms." A brow arched. "Once you were not so stiff and prim." The reference to that certain episode in their past had Althea blushing rosily. Val ignored the rising color and continued. "I am deadly serious—*if only you will listen.*"

Althea frowned every so slightly. Considering all the bad things wrapped up in Sir Valerian's oh-so-seductive exterior, a lack of proper feeling toward the convention against swearing in the presence of the softer sex was not one of them. "You are truly upset about this, are you not? This is *not* another game to tease me to distraction?"

"I am truly upset." He spoke through gritted teeth.

Althea glanced around the salon. Her mother was not too far away and no one among Lady Bronsen's handful of guests appeared at all interested in the fact that the *ton*'s leading rake had accosted her. "Very well. I will listen. But do not make a long tale of it, Val, or I will walk away and never again trust you in any fashion or any place."

He sighed again. "You will never see that I love you and would do nothing to harm a hair on your head." He held up that long-fingered hand again, the scar hidden since his palm faced her. "Never mind. You do not wish to be *teased* with my love. We will talk of Clair who is in serious danger not only of losing her reputation but, if Andover's plans succeed, of being cast off by her husband, legally separated from him if not actually faced with divorce."

Althea blinked. Then, scornfully, she made an unladylike and very rude noise. "Clair, Lady Lambert, is a lovely well behaved young woman. She could never bring herself to do anything that courted the sort of disaster of which you speak."

"You are not listening. It is not what *she* would do, but what Lambert's bloody-minded heir will do to her. I have already saved her from more than one disaster and, so far, I've done so without it appearing that I have been on guard against his plots. But, as I said, I cannot be everywhere and I do not trust that man one inch."

"And what does Lord Lambert have to say about this?"

"Jason—" His voice was soft and low, but nevertheless, somehow, it carried to her ears with a harsh note. "—is so involved in his government work he hasn't time to say good morning to her, let alone see to her well being."

"But, Val, she knew he would be involved up to his ears when she wed him. Until the war ended. Of course, now it *is* ended," she added, scrupulously honest, "he discovered that, until the Peace is signed and all is once again well with our world, his work is *not* finished." Against her will, Althea found she was growing convinced that Sir Valerian believed a problem existed, believed that he was *not* playing another game. She relaxed slightly. "Clair wishes it were otherwise, but she understands his time is not his own."

"Of course she does, although he is a fool and a poltroon to treat her so. It is doubly unfortunate that his neglect gives Emerson Andover all too many opportunities to be in her company and carry out his plots to lead her astray. Althea, all I ask is that you spend as much time with her as you can, that you attend the same parties and, on any occasion where you can manage to wangle an invitation—which should not be difficult since you head her list of special friends—that you accompany her on her rounds of formal visits, go with her when she shops, walk and ride with her in the park, that sort of thing."

Althea frowned slightly, surprised he wasn't asking anything *outré* of her.

"And," he continued, "when the two are together do not let her out of your sight." A sudden thought lightened his expression. "Perhaps, since your mother does not truly enjoy the hustle and bustle of the Season, Lady Bronsen would agree to allowing Clair to chaperone you to parties?"

Althea swallowed a quick chuckle by hiding it in a cough. A quick flash of white teeth in his overly dark face, a look of understanding, made her heart beat hard against her breast.

"I know," he said with soft humor. "You are six years her elder and the chaperoning will be in quite the other direction, but that is good. She is unlikely to find herself in difficulties if you are with her. Can you not understand the need? Will you not oblige me? In *this*, at least?"

She tried once more to disbelieve him. "Are you absolutely certain you have not dreamed up this so-called plot because you need something absurdly dramatic to rouse you from one of your lethargies?"

"You disappoint me, Althea. I had thought you loved Clair as much as I do."

Althea had known Clair for very nearly as long as had Sir Valerian who, as he'd indicated, had first met their friend when she was a babe. Althea's lips compressed. "I do love her." Again she turned very slightly away from him. "I will attempt to be in her company whenever it is possible, but because I love her and enjoy her bright nature and *not* because I've any belief that Mr. Andover is a villain." Since she was no longer completely certain of that last, she bit her lip, but then, in a rush, wanting, *needing*, to believe the worst of Sir Valerian, she added, "Just because he grew up in the wilds of Canada and is a trifle rough around the edges, does not mean he has a black heart."

"It *needn't* mean that. One can grow up anywhere—right here in the midst of the *ton*, for instance, and have an evil heart." He named two elderly peers who were known to have belonged to the infamous Hellfire Club, a group of dissolute men who, in the last century, had gone to extreme lengths in their pursuit of illicit pleasure, if one could call such evil pleasure. "What *is* true is that *Andover's* is black as the pips on a deck of pasteboards and, as time passes, he grows more and more frantic to sunder Jason from our Clair." When Althea blinked, he added in a gentle voice, "Before an heir appears to replace him."

Althea's eyes narrowed and she stared across the room at nothing at all.

"You have thought of something."

She glanced up at him and then, with effort, tore her gaze from his. "Have I? Perhaps I have. Will you go away if I promise to do what I can? Within the bounds of propriety, of course?"

"It is all that I have asked, is it not?" he asked gently.

When she said no more, Sir Valerian bowed, straightened, and stared hungrily into her downcast face before turning away. When the Bronsen's butler had brought him word Althea would condescend to speak to him, he'd had every intention of leaving the moment he attained her aid. But instead, unable to leave her presence, he strolled across the room to where another old friend, this one as old as Althea was young, was seated in regal isolation. He asked, politely, if her ladyship would care for a fresh cup of tea.

Once Lady Elfreda Sinclair had her gently steaming tea, he settled beside her for a gossip, which, if the chuckles and rolling eyes were any indication, both enjoyed a great deal. Only when Althea, moving slowly from guest to guest, reached Lady Bronsen's side and bent to speak softly in her mother's ear did he look up. Althea excused herself with a melodious but carrying voice and Sir Valerian fell silent. He watched her departure.

"She'll have you in the end," murmured Elf.

Val turned a suspicious look toward his companion, but her ladyship merely sipped her tea making him wonder if he'd actually heard that soft murmur that barely reached his ears.

"Bah," she said glaring at her cup. "This is cold."

Lady Elfreda Sinclair, known as Elf to three generations, set cup and saucer on the small spindle-legged table at her side. She picked up her cane, and setting it before her, struggled to her feet.

"I believe," she said in a very slightly acid tone, "that this particular 'at home' has offered up all the entertainment it is likely to provide. Escort me, Sir Val, to my next destination and I will tell you a bit of gossip you may find of interest— given your interest in the Andover *ménage.*"

As Althea climbed the stairs to her room, two thoughts fought for dominance in her mind. When she closed her door, she found her maid brushing the habit she'd worn earlier that morning.

"Leave that," she said, "and fetch my new bonnet, please."

Memory of that never-to-be-forgotten kiss, shared in a bower behind the vicarage where Clair was raised, competed with Althea's growing fears for her young friend. Her thoughts and emotions were in such a whirl she found herself wishing *both* Sir Valerian and Clair to the devil!

"The matching *pelisse* as well? Are we walking out?"

Althea seated herself at her dressing table and leaned forward to peer at her face in an effort to regain some self-control. Unfortunately, that only added another problem to the mix already stirred up within her. All was not well with her normally smooth and fine textured skin.

Those are lines at my eyes, she thought, horrified.

"A *pelisse*?" she asked when her maid persisted. "The green one I think."

She tipped her head slightly to catch the light. Yes. Definitely. The faintest of lines radiated from the corners. She sighed. At twenty-eight she was too young to show lines, but there they were. Soon, if she did not manage to control her heart and discipline her mind and bring herself to accept an offer—any offer other than Val's insulting proposal—she'd be glued firmly to the proverbial shelf.

Assuming she were not already stuck to it.

"Where are we off to, Miss Althea?" asked the maid who returned from the dressing room with the required bonnet and *pelisse,* having donned her own. "Shall I inform a footman he should prepare himself to accompany us?"

Althea forced herself into a more rational frame of mind and, speaking firmly, said, "I mean to go no farther than the Lambert house in Grosvenor Square, Merrily. It is just down and around the corner so we need not take a footman from his work."

After leaving word with the Bronsens' butler as to her destination, Althea departed from number thirty North Audley and strolled down the pavement toward the square.

"I do hope Clair is in," she fretted.

Only now that she was on the way did it occur to her that the bride was likely to have a dozen destinations to which she might have gone. *Most likely had gone.*

"The *young* Lady Lambert?" Merrily had a great admiration for titles and loved using them whenever she'd an opportunity. Her only regret in life was that her mistress had turned down two noted titles, a viscount and an earl. "I spoke with Bitsy, her maid you know, only last evening. Lady Lambert has no plans for today. Bitsy said her ladyship feels guilty. She promised herself, you see, to finish the chair seats for the dining room at Andover Place before the Season ended and has completed only four of them. She means to work this morning."

"That sounds like our industrious little Clair," said Althea, smiling. "But, Merrily," she scolded, "you should not gossip with people's maids about their mistresses."

"You mean you are not pleased to know her ladyship'll be at home?" asked Merrily with a sly sideways look.

Althea's lips twitched. "I believe we'd best drop this topic before I find myself cornered." She turned into the square. "I will admit that I am glad that I've not abandoned my mother's 'at home' to attend to a fruitless errand."

Althea's determination to see Clair as soon as possible had firmed as she mused over Sir Valerian's words and recalled several humorous little tales from Clair's letters, wryly written news of her friend's doings. Unfortunately, the more she recalled, the less humorous they seemed.

Perhaps, just this once, Sir Valerian was truly concerned for another's welfare? Worse, perhaps he had *reason* to be concerned? However difficult it was to believe that such a care-for-nobody could worry about *anyone*, let alone a young woman who was no more to him than his cousin? And a married cousin at that. Or, as a rake, did he prefer married women?

Althea was admitted to Lambert House by the Lambert's stuffy butler. "Jimson, is it not?" asked Althea. "Is Lady Lambert at home to guests?"

"I shall ascertain her ladyship's wishes." He cleared his throat. "We are inquiring of the younger Lady Lambert, are we not?"

"Yes, Jimson. I should have made clear that I do not refer to the dowager," said Althea, her features totally bland. "I ask after Lord Lambert's *wife,* not his mother."

She suspected Jimson had not accepted that there was a new mistress in the household—or perhaps it was that the *dowager* had yet to accept the fact and had not turned the reins of government over to her successor, as was proper? Althea's frown deepened and had not disappeared when she was led into the small and cozy lady's parlor at the rear of the house, overlooking the long narrow back garden.

Clair rose to her feet as Althea entered and ran to her, her arms wide. Althea accepted the enthusiastic welcome—including an exceedingly Frenchified air-kiss near each cheek. She chuckled. "One can see you have only recently returned from France, my love." She looked over the shorter woman's shoulder and her fading frown reappeared. "But you entertain company!" she said.

"Company?" Clair swung around. "Oh! It is only Emerson. Have you met my husband's cousin?" asked Clair leading Althea across the room to where the Canadian lounged in an arm chair, long legs stretched out across the Axminster carpet and very much in the way. "Emerson, are you acquainted with my very oldest and dearest friend, Miss Bronsen?"

Insultingly slow, the man rose to his feet and bowed. "I had that privilege last fall at the Opera. My cousin did the honors, I believe?"

"He did," agreed Althea. She appraised the man's mannerisms and was displeased. This was not the diffident creature she'd met then. This was a brash and self-confident man, arrogant, and, she feared, uncaring. She suddenly realized she was being weighed in much the same fashion. Inwardly, she withdrew, consciously repressing a desire to physically cringe away from the cold, pale, blue eyes studying her.

"Emerson," said Clair, filling a silence she did not understand, "has suggested that while the weather is so cooperative we must organize a picnic expedition to Kew. A riding party. Would that not be delightful? And, of course, those who do not wish to ride so far could go by carriage. It seems an age since we were last in a bucolic setting," finished the young woman just a trifle wistfully.

Her husband's work had required his presence in London and they had spent only a very few weeks of their five months of married life in the country, Clair's preferred milieu.

"Later in the season I would find it a delightful plan," said Althea carefully. "So early in the year I fear that, before you could arrange the whole expedition, the weather would have returned to its usual wet and blustery self."

Clair sighed. "Yes. And so I said. But it is a wonderful idea and I would enjoy such a day to no end." She turned to her husband's cousin and heir. "I think perhaps we must wait. I would hate that our frolics were ruined by rain or cold and, besides, the gardens would not be at their best so early which would be a great shame after riding so far."

Emerson Andover, who had not reseated himself, bowed. As he did so he cast a glance toward Althea that she could not read but felt was inimical.

"As you think best, my lady," he said. "If you will excuse me, I must be getting on. I've a vague recollection I am to meet a friend at Tattersall's about now and am certain to be late. Such a bore," he said in a world-weary manner, "keeping strict accounting of time. There is a team about which he wishes my opinion before he bids on it, so I suppose I'd best be off."

"Ah!" said Althea and continued in a voice touched by seeming admiration. "You did a great deal of driving in Canada, I am sure."

Spots of red appeared on Emerson's cheekbones. "I am certain *you*, Miss Bronsen, are aware we haven't the roads for it," he retorted snappishly. He drew a rein on his tone. "However that may be, I seem to have a knack for judging horseflesh."

Althea allowed her eyes to widen in well-simulated surprise. "Did I insult you? Somehow? I am sorry for it." *The dratted man*, she thought, *is far quicker than I thought if he recognized my snide comment for what it was rather than the compliment I pretended*.

Althea had been startled to find Andover in her friend's company and displeased that there was nary a sign of a chaperone, but she knew she reacted badly. In actual fact, she had been surprised to see him with Clair under *any* circumstances, not wanting to believe that Sir Valerian's Gothic tale of evil cousins had a grain of truth in it. Unfortunately, Mr. Andover's lounging about in that overly relaxed manner in Clair's private sewing room gave a great deal of weight to Sir Val's accusations.

So, when she thought of it, did the plan for a long ride to

Kew and a picnic there. A great deal could happen in and around the gardens, and picnics were notoriously lax where the proprieties were concerned. She had never found them particularly entertaining herself and hoped this one would never come about, since her promise to Sir Valerian would require that she attend it.

Clair returned from seeing Mr. Andover on his way and said, "I've ordered a tray for us, Althea. You have surprised me, you know. Oh, a pleasant surprise, of course, but I had thought you were not arriving until next week."

"Did you? That explains why you did not visit while we settled in." She frowned. "But I wrote you the exact date, Clair. Perhaps my letter did not arrive?"

"I have had no recent letter from you." Clair, too, frowned. "It is strange. You are the second person to mention a letter I did not receive."

"Who was the other?"

"I fear I thought *her* claim a tarradiddle to make herself interesting." Clair grimaced and then blushed. "My father would be so displeased with me! I should not dislike the lady, but I cannot help myself. Althea, it was Lady Thomilson." Clair sighed. "She was insulted that I failed to respond to her missive, complained that my marriage had made me hoity-toity, ignoring old friends, which—" Clair looked insulted that anyone would think it of her. "—I never would." She frowned. "I think she did not believe I'd not received it. Her letter, I mean."

Althea blinked and Clair giggled at her friend's owlish expression. Althea found herself smiling at the infectious sound. "I had," she explained, "the notion the Thomilsons were not coming to London. I heard that Lord Thomilson had such reverses on 'Change that he meant to stay at home this season."

Clair's eyes widened. "But Althea, how can you possibly imagine our Lady Thomilson would survive without her nose in the very midst of every scandal to touch the *ton* this season? She prides herself she is always the first to *know* and to be forced to remain at home and hear everything second-hand? Or, worse, at thirdhand?"

Althea nodded. "But if the gossip *is* true then one must wonder how she means to keep up appearances." Althea realized that she had just indulged in exactly the sort of gossipy speculation she abhorred and instantly put aside all discussion of Lord Thomilson's finances. "Which *hopeful miss* did she bring to town this year?" she asked and then sighed. It seemed she was unable to speak of Lady Thomilson without saying, or at the least *implying*, something nasty. "Please believe I *wish* to know," she added.

"She brought both Elsmere and Julia. *And* her son. You know Morton Thomilson, do you not?"

"The pampered heir is too young to have come much my way." Althea grimaced that, once again, she was snide, but she didn't apologize.

"Althea," said Clair, a warning note in her tone, "you must not tease Julia. I *like* Julia."

"My dear, she is a featherhead of the worst sort."

"Yes, but occasionally it is quite relaxing to be in the company of a prattle-box. One need not think, you see," said Clair.

Althea smiled her understanding. *It cannot*, she thought, *have been at all easy for dear little Clair to come from the vicarage into the very midst of the ton. Especially that part of the ton responsible for government and military matters where so much of importance is discussed at every turn, whether at table or in a salon. Perhaps, knowing Lord Lambert, even when enjoying a tête-à-tête with one's new husband.*

The tray arrived and Clair occupied herself measuring the leaves and pouring the water and setting out cups and saucers. She relocked the tea caddy and set it aside. As her hands moved among the tea things she prattled about people who were already in town, those who had continued on to the continent, and then, when it had brewed and she lifted the teapot, she also lifted a worried gaze to meet Althea's. "*You* are not thinking of going off to Paris or Vienna, are you? You must *not*," she added before Althea could respond.

"*Must* not?"

Clair slumped, her shoulders drooping, and a frown marring her young brow. "Jason fears Napoleon will not remain on Elba. He has told me there are . . . are strong suspicions *something* is in the wind, but my dear Beast—" She spoke the insulting term with earnestness but an obvious fondness as well. "—will not allow me write to even our dearest friends that perhaps they should start for home. He said if I were to write even one, the information would come to the ears of those we do not wish to hear it and certain people would know England has sources of information she should not have, sources which must not be revealed." Clair bit her lip, her eyes widening. "Oh dear, even to you I should have said nothing!"

"I will not repeat it and you may be easy." No one wished to admit to the dishonor of supporting spies, but everyone who knew anything also admitted they were necessary. "Mother suggested a visit to Paris. She is torn between her dislike of foreigners and her yearning to once again see the city to which my father took her on their bridal trip. You need not concern yourself that it will happen, however, as we've no gentleman available for escort and she will not travel without one." Althea chuckled. "She reproaches me for remaining unwed, saying that if I had not been so selfish we'd *have* a suitable bear-leader!"

"That is an idiotic reason for wedding someone."

"So I told her." Althea smiled a sly smile, her eyes twinkling. "I also pointed out that she herself might have re-wed, a suggestion she did not appreciate, even though she has had the same cicisbeo for years and years. But, since neither of us obliged the other in this matter, we will not cross the channel."

Althea drew in a breath. Without her having to manipu-

late things in any fashion she had been offered a way to start
the conversation that, thanks to Sir Valerian, she was determined she and Clair must have.

"You wrote such deliciously *hinting* letters from Paris,
Clair. You must tell me more about *your* sojourn there. There
were many questions you did not answer to my satisfaction.
Including," she said, when Clair seemed to withdraw, "details concerning your new Paris wardrobe. Is that one of the
gowns?" she finished, knowing she could, with care, ask
about Emerson Andover's role in escorting them only when
Clair was fully relaxed.

Althea was feminine enough to find the details concerning Paris fashions interesting and didn't move on to what she
really wanted to know until they set aside their cups and
Clair returned to her stitchery.

Althea set herself to sorting her friend's yarns. She asked,
"You were going on to Vienna, were you not? I know you
wrote that that was her ladyship's intention so you can imagine my surprise when your next letter was posted somewhere
in the Low Countries."

"You will find it a great surprise to learn we were actually
on the road, somewhat east of Paris, when Mother Sarah
changed her orders to our driver."

"You would say it was a bolt from the blue?" Althea pretended shock. "But then, how did Lord Lambert know where
to find you? You did say he crossed over and came to you,
wherever it was?"

"A very pleasant *chateau* east of Brussels, actually. A
friend of Mother Sarah's youth had crossed the channel
when widowed as a young woman. She was left with *less*
than a mere competence you see, and it was cheaper to live
abroad. There she met the Comte." Clair giggled. When
Althea asked why, she added, "They've been *happy*. *Much* to
Mother Sarah's chagrin. She cannot understand how anyone
can be happily married to a foreigner and, still worse, happy
while living anywhere other than England."

"Yes, that sounds very like the dowager, but Clair, you do not say how Lord Lambert knew where to find you. I would have thought he'd have traveled on to Vienna when he discovered you gone from Paris. Or did Lady Lambert write him her intentions?"

"Yes, well, she did not—" Clair frowned, the faint lines unfortunately reminding Althea of those unwanted lines she'd discovered on her own face an hour previously. "—and when Lady Sarah gave the order, I would have sworn Emerson was as taken aback as I, but I must have been wrong. The fact is that Emerson left word with friends that we would be found in or near Brussels. I heard Jason thanking him for having done so."

"I wonder how he knew," mused Althea, watching her friend.

Clair shrugged one shoulder—another new and exceedingly French gesture. "Does it matter? I am merely glad that poor Jason did not run off to Vienna on a wild goose chase. We had a wonderful few days at Lady Lambert's friend's *chateau*. Oh, Althea—" Clair's eyes glowed and a subtle blush gave her cheeks a rosy glow. "—you can have no idea how very nice it was to have that time together, when Jason had no appointments, nothing about which he must worry, and no one bothering him to *do* something, adding still more to all the work he accomplishes as it is."

"I can imagine," said Althea blandly. And, in theory, she could. She had, after all, dreamed of living in just such a blissful haven with the man of her dreams.

Dreams. The man of her dreams existed *only* in those dreams. The *real* man, who *looked* like that rather piratical dream man, was another matter entirely and nothing like him. Not where important matters were concerned. He must *not* be allowed room in her head and must be discouraged from wandering freely in her dreams . . .

Unfortunately she thought sadly *it is too late to forbid him setting up housekeeping in my heart.*

CHAPTER 2

Althea was in a thoughtful mood as she returned from the Lambert townhouse. Each tale Clair related in her exceedingly droll fashion had brought laughter to Althea's lips—at the time. But when one counted up the near disasters that trailed Clair like Nemesis in a Greek tragedy, one could not help but wonder if this particular Nemesis wore a human name and a face.

Worst of all, one was forced to conclude that Sir Valerian might be correct in his assessment that Clair—dear sweet funny fun-loving Clair—was in danger. Real danger.

"At the least," murmured Althea, "she is not *enceinte*. He has no reason to fear immediate displacement."

"Did you say something, Miss Althea?" asked Merrily, skipping to catch up with her taller mistress' longer stride.

"What?" Althea berated herself for growing eccentric. Already she was talking aloud to herself. What would she be like in another decade if she continued on as she was going?

"Did you say something?" repeated her maid.

"Well, yes. I am forced to admit that I did—but for my ears alone. If you heard it you are to forget it. Immediately."

"Like I should forget that Bitsy doesn't like him?"

Althea stopped so abruptly that Merrily actually moved a pace or two ahead of her before she managed to stop and turn her anything but innocent face toward Althea.

"Bitsy doesn't like him?"

"That's what I said. She was glad you came and chased the creature away."

"*Why* does she dislike him?"

"Well, to begin with, he's the sort who pinches a maid's bottom, but it is more that his glib tongue leads Lady Clair into all sorts of difficulties. And it isn't enough that he claims he didn't know or that he didn't mean harm or that he is very sorry that something didn't work out as he thought it would, or that Lady Somebody-or-other led him wrong about a shop she'd recommended in some awkward part of town where who knows what might happen to one?"

"Merrily," asked Althea carefully, "are you suggesting that Lady Lambert has been in difficulty so often that her maid believes it is not accidental?"

Merrily's lower lip stuck out a trifle. "Don't know about *suggesting* . . ." she said.

Althea bit back a word she should not have known. "Are you *saying* . . . ?" she amended.

Merrily eyed her mistress. "Maybe. And what if I am?" She tossed her head in a pert manner. "Someone should say something," she finished with a faintly-to-be-heard belligerence.

Althea drew in a deep breath. "Yes. Definitely. Someone should. So why has Bitsy said nothing?"

"And just who would she tell? You tell me that!"

Althea debated scolding her maid for impertinence, but there was some reason for the girl's question, if not for the tone, and she gave it a moment's thought. It was true it would be difficult for a lady's maid to go to his lordship directly. A gentleman would be unlikely to pay much attention to his wife's maid—especially a maid so young and countrified as Bitsy, who was the vicarage housekeeper's granddaughter.

Jimson? she wondered—but put that thought aside as well. Jimson held himself very much up and was more likely to order Bitsy to desist from all attempts to make herself interesting than to listen to her, which was also true of the Lambert housekeeper, who was a bit of a martinet and thought Bitsy too ill-trained to be dresser to Lord Lambert's wife. So who . . . ?

"Lord Lambert's valet, perhaps?" asked Althea a trifle diffidently since she did not know the man and had no knowledge of how he would react.

Merrily's eyes widened. "Now why did we not think of that?"

"Once we reach home, I want you to run back and suggest that very thing to Bitsy. Will you do that?"

"Yes. Of course," said Merrily, nodding firmly. "We like Lady Clair. We don't, either of us, want anything to happen to her."

"You are afraid something will happen?"

Merrily nodded, her eyes wide open.

"Then I think there is something else I might do—if I dare," said Althea. After a moment's thought, she nodded. "Yes, I *will* do it."

The decision made, Althea continued home with a mannish stride that drew disapproving eyes from a dowager in a carriage just then passing in the street. The sharp-nosed old lady shook her head and suggested to her companion that Miss Althea should take care if she did not wish to gain the reputation of a hoyden. Rushing along in such an unladylike manner was surely a long step in that direction.

Which interesting fact, thought the down-trodden companion, *you, you old harridan, will gladly report to one and all.*

Later that day Sir Valerian eyed a twist of paper that lay on the table near his hand. He was seated at a long table in his favorite City coffeehouse reading the latest prospectus to come his way, a scheme purporting to double one's savings practically overnight.

The young man sipping coffee in the chair beside his was dressed in a servant's Sunday best. The fellow rose when finished and, as he did so, sort-of-by-accident it seemed, pushed the note nearer Sir Valerian. Val looked more closely at the servant.

"The Bronsens' youngest footman, by God," he muttered.

A sensation of mild shock swept through him that the very proper Althea would do anything so *improper* as send him a message, which was, he was nearly certain, what she *had* done. His hands trembled ever so slightly as he opened the twist, read his name and title primly written at the top and dropped his gaze to the bottom of the small piece of paper nearly filled with closely written lines—

Thank Heaven, she'd the sense not to sign it.

Val knew the handwriting, of course. Clair had passed him letters from Althea and there was no question but that this was written in Althea's angular and rather spiky script. He glanced around, but no one within the ranks of the *ton* who knew him happened, at that moment, to be in the low-ceilinged rather smoky room, so he turned back to the note.

C's maid spoke to mine today. B, the maid, is as worried as you are. She claims that all too often Mr. A . . . r has a hand in something happening that could hurt her mistress. I have suggested B speak to L.L . . . t's valet, retailing the list of near disasters. I would additionally suggest that your valet become acquainted with B and that some arrangement be made whereby she can get word to him so that he can then get word to you so that someone will know what to do

*if another such occasion arises. I assume you will
know how to go about this.*

Sir Valerian read the words twice more and grimaced at
the implication that he was capable of organizing any nefar-
ious dealing. On the other hand, it *was* an excellent plan.

He deviated from the direct route to the door, wandering
nearer the fireplace where a cheery blaze roared in the large
hearth. Reluctantly, wishing he dared keep it close to his
heart, he tossed the note into the fire, watched it curl, blacken,
and then fall into ashes before turning and leaving the coffeehouse.

Very likely, he thought sadly, *that is the only missive I will
ever receive from her, but it is never safe to keep such things . . .*

He wasn't allowed to dwell on the thought. A down-the-
road looking man had followed him from the coffee shop.

"I say." The stranger hurried to catch up with the taller Sir
Valerian's longer stride. "I say, there. What did you think of . . ."

"You take me for a flat, sir?" Sir Valerian stopped, turned,
and cast the fellow a sardonic glance.

"No, no, of course not," blustered the man, his small eyes
blinking rapidly.

"Then I wonder that you offered me this *opportunity* to
prove myself one. I suggest you not try this ploy on any pi-
geon frequenting the Old Hat." He gestured to the doorway
from which they'd just exited. "Most of the regulars are
friends of mine and I'd not like to hear any of them have
been talked into investing in such an obvious bubble."

"No, no. Wouldn't think of it . . ." The man blinked.
"Here now! *Not* a bubble!"

"Is it not? The only person likely to gain from this particular plan is *you*. Sheer off, man, before I inform the banks of
your existence. Bankers dislike it when their investors take
money from their accounts to put into faulty notions such as
this. Perhaps I *should* inform them . . . ?"

Sweat popped out on the fellow's forehead. He backed away. "Certainly *not*, My Lordship. I'll just be off, then. You won't say nothing?" he whined.

"Get away with you," sighed Sir Valerian.

The badly composed and cheaply printed flier was unlikely to gain anyone's support, but he disliked plausible villains. Foolish or *stupid* villains were worse. They provided comic relief, making one laugh, and one tended to forget the villainy.

Sir Valerian ruefully considered that he might be getting old. A few years ago he'd have held the man up for ridicule. Using his tongue, he'd have flayed the fellow in such a way he'd not dare to show his face in the City for years.

"Going soft," he told himself as he stalked on down the street.

Not above twenty minutes later he entered his rooms above a store dealing in Men's Best Linens that fronted onto St. James's not far from the best men's clubs.

"Loth." When his call got no response he added, "I need you. Now."

Val had leased the rather large accommodations just after coming down from Oxford. He'd moved in with several similarly wild friends who had, over the following several years, one after another, had reason to move out. Two married. One found Val growing boring as he lost a taste for wild doings and the other one resided in debtors' prison, unable to come up with the money to pay his massive debts. Val, liking the location, had kept the leasehold to the place he called home whenever he resided in London.

"Loth!"

Lothario Bitterhouse spoke from the back regions. "Just a blidy minute, your honor. Got to finish this sauce or there'll be hell to pay."

As the words drifted into the salon Val strolled across the room toward a sideboard that promised a choice in the matter of liquid refreshment. What he wanted, however, was not there.

As usual.

Why Loth would not obey his command to have available a pitcher of the tart lemonade that was his preferred libation, Val could not say. No matter how often the order was repeated, the pitcher was rarely found among the bottles, mugs, and goblets.

Val joined his valet-cum-man-of-all-work in the kitchen, where the savory smells led him to wonder why he didn't spend more time there. A smallish pantry opened off the dark and overheated area devoted to the heating of water for his shaving and baths and, on those occasions he ate in, the cooking of his meals. He stalked into the pantry. There was his lemonade. *There*, instead of in the sitting room where it was convenient to his hand whenever wanted.

He reached up onto the shelf above and chose a large goblet, filled it, and wandered back into the kitchen.

Loth eyed him. "Hadn't gotten around to taking it in yet. You're early."

"Yes and if I'd been late you'd still not have managed it. I've a job for you."

"Oh you have, have you? And will this one about get my throat cut too?"

"That was a long time ago, and I saved you didn't I?"

Loth glanced toward Val's left hand and had the grace to blush slightly. At least his ears turned a ruddier red around the hairs that stuck out of them and Val surmised that it was due to embarrassment. "So you did," he admitted. "Don't like it, mind, when you get me mixed up in one of your ven-dett-as. Always seems me that gets the short end of the stick." Another glance at the scar and his ears reddened still more. "Well, *most* often."

"All I want this time is that you brush up your acquaintance with Clair, Lady Lambert's maid Bitsy and, once you are in Bitsy's good graces, tell her you'll gladly get information to me any time she thinks I should know her mistress might be headed for trouble."

"And if I'm waiting around for her to hand me a message, then how am I to get my work done here?" blustered Loth, who had a pernicious tendency to disagree with any order, whatever it might be.

"Use your head. You'll hire a lad to run messages, of course. But this time, find someone with at least half a brain in his head, if you please, so that he'll use it to find one of us if we aren't right where he might expect us to be."

"Well!" Loth sputtered. "Can I help it if that one I hired last time was asleep on his feet?"

"You might have discovered that he was already doing one full-time job of work and couldn't very well work the other twelve hours of the day as well."

"Liked the boy," mumbled Loth.

"Yes, well, so did I," admitted Val. "I put him in the school, didn't I? And paid his fees?"

Loth sighed. "I don't know why I ever bother to argue with you. You always have an answer."

"Why I *allow* you to argue with me is the real question, is it not?" asked Val, frowning. "I wonder why I keep you on?"

Loth grinned, showing one missing tooth where he'd gotten the worst of a fight they'd been in—another situation in which he'd been of aid to Val. "Yes, well, *you* like *me* like *I* liked that *boy*—and I'm too old to stick in your blidy school."

Val couldn't help grinning in response. "Yes, but I'd like you a devil of a lot more if you'd only remember to put out my lemonade."

The ears, which had faded to a more normal pink, turned bright red.

"Yes?" asked Val gently.

"Blidy lady's drink."

"I am aware it is thought a lady's drink. But I *like* it. All right?"

Loth cast him a belligerent look. "No, it's not right. *I've* a thought to your reputation even if you don't."

"My *reputation* could use changing. *In the right direction, of course.*"

"Here now! Why'd you want to go and do a thing like that for?"

"Like what?"

At the stern look on Val's face, Loth backed down. "Like . . . like . . . have it known you like lemonade?"

"I hope," said Val, eyeing the man thoughtfully, "you have quite stopped relating tales of my misspent youth when you are drinking with your cronies."

"Who? Me?" Loth's eyes widened. "Now would I do such a thing?"

"I very much fear that you would. If I ask very politely this time, do you think you could bring yourself to desist?"

Loth sighed mightily. "You'd take all the fun out of life, you would."

"If it is that sort of vicarious *fun* for which you yearn, perhaps you would like to find a position with someone younger who is still green and foolish. You could collect a new pocketful of tales," suggested Val, overly politely.

"No. No," Loth shook his head sadly. "No," he said a third time, "can't do that. Afraid you're stuck with me. Can't see me breaking in a new master at my age. Don't think I've the patience for it."

"Then oblige me. When you are out of an evening we'll have no more of this blackening my reputation as you do every time you have a heavy wet at the corner inn. I'm tired of it."

"Why?"

Val drew in a deep breath. "Loth . . ."

"Why should you care, I mean?" In turn, Loth drew in the same sort of breath, his eyes bulging at a new thought. "Oh no!" Loth shook his head several times. "Don't do it."

"Don't do what?"

"Don't go and fall in love and spoil everything by bringing a blidy-minded woman into our lives who'll want more nonsense than that I keep blidy lemonade on the blidy buffet!"

"It is too late for the former, but, since the lady of my heart will not have me, I am unlikely to do the latter. Still," continued Val thoughtfully, "I think it is way beyond time that you stopped describing me as I was in my grass time and begin thinking of me as I am now."

Loth heaved another huge sigh. "Like I said," he said morosely. "You surely would go to taking all the fun out of life. Can't talk about how it used to be. Can't talk about how it is now . . ."

"Loth!"

"Well, your work for the government's a big stupid secret, isn't it?" He lifted the spoon and allowed the sauce to drip back into the pot. Satisfied, he pushed it to the back of the stove before he looked up. "Oh very well. I'll just sit mumchance, I will."

Val shook his head and returned to his parlor where he seated himself to mull over what he'd learned from Elf's man of business. He'd gone to the City directly after hearing Lady Elfreda's interesting bit of gossip, hearing her agent's story from his own lips. And then he'd gone to the coffeehouse where the Bronsen footman found him.

Once more he regretted burning the paper that his beloved had held in her hands. Even as he savored the clean sharp taste of lemon, a part of him, his cynical side, laughed at such sentimentality. In the usual way, he was not a sentimental man.

Putting it from his mind, his thoughts returned to what he'd learned and how he might learn more. Because, if there was any truth at all to what he'd been told, then Emerson Andover . . . wasn't Emerson Andover.

And, if he wasn't, then he wasn't Jason, Lord Lambert's heir. And if he were not Jason's heir, then his hopes of inheriting were based on something still more evil than previously assumed. Not only *Clair* was in danger, but *Jason's* life was worth perhaps as much as tuppence.

At most.

If he were lucky.

In fact, mused Val, *why is the villain playing games with Clair's reputation when it is obviously Jason he needs to be rid of?*

He let his mind drift over what he knew and guessed and finally grimaced at his confusion.

There is, it seems, more to Andover's—Val tipped his head but decided that the unknown man had to be called something—*plot than what is readily evident*.

The next day, early, Val entered the Lambert mansion and asked if the Dowager Lady Lambert was at home to guests. He handed over his card with the corner turned down indicating he had come in person and told Jimson that, if necessary, he'd wait.

The butler returned after only a few moments and asked Val to follow him, but Val was already on his way to the breakfast room from which the man had exited.

"I know my way, Jimson. No need to announce me," he said as he opened the door.

"Perhaps you will be so good as to tell me why my son employs a butler if it is *not* to announce guests?" asked the dowager in biting tones.

"To oversee the male servants, of course," said Val blandly as he shut the door in the outraged butler's face.

"Well, I wish you'd let him do his work. He's impossible when he feels he's been slighted," grumbled Lady Sarah. "Oh, get yourself a plate and sit down. I can't bear to have you hovering over me that way, you great hulking brute."

"My cousin," said Clair, "is not a brute."

"Is he not?" asked Sarah. She glanced to where Val stood

by the sideboard on which several salvers were kept warm on stands set above small candles. She eyed him and her features softened. "Well, well, perhaps you are correct. Why have you come so early?" she asked, her tone again abrupt to hide her brief instant of softening.

"For breakfast, obviously," he said, turning, his white teeth gleaming in his sun-darkened face.

"Never say so. Has that man of yours finally left for greener pastures?"

Val laughed. "I think," he said slyly, "that he is thinking of grazing in one rather closer to you, my lady."

"Close to me?" Sarah blinked.

"So *that* is the odd little man with hairy ears of whom Bitsy spoke last evening," said Clair. "You tell Lothario Bittersweet he is to leave my maid alone!"

"Since I told him to turn the chit up sweet, I don't think I'll do that."

"Why?" Clair turned a distressed look on her cousin. "Why would you do such a thing?"

He grinned. "Do you think he'll harm her? He won't. He wouldn't admit it to a soul, but there is a woman who has him tied up in such knots I suspect he had to report to her that I'd ordered him to get on Bitsy's good side before he dared make his first approach here."

"But Val, again I ask why?"

He sobered. "Because, my dear, I want to know what you are up to and I don't want to have to learn it by accident as I've been doing. I need an ally if I am to prevent you from falling into the briars and ruining yourself. And," he added thoughtfully, "Jason as well."

Clair frowned and the dowager made an indecipherable noise that might have been one of distress if one were generous—or a snort of derision if one were not.

"My dear child," continued Sir Valerian, "yesterday you gave Miss Althea chapter and verse of all the near disasters you've encountered since your marriage. Can you deny it? Come, Clair, admit you cannot be so unlucky that everything that has happened to you has simply *happened*."

"You are once again accusing Mr. Andover of playing an under game," said Clair, her frown deepening. "I wish you would not, Val. It is just that he is new to London, new to our ways, that he has so often fallen into error. He is always contrite, always apologetic. You cannot know what it is like for him, coming to England at his age after being reared in the backwoods and living rough all his life."

"Bah."

"What?" Clair turned toward her husband's mother. "What do you mean, Mother Sarah?"

"The man cannot have lived all that rough. He dances divinely, does he not? He dresses like a beau, which someone could not do if he was reared to wear nothing but skins or whatever it is they wear in the wilds. And he has sufficient funds he need not sponge off Jason—well, no more than a suitable allowance, which I am certain he finds very welcome." Her lecture done, she turned to her guest. "You would say, Sir Valerian, that Mr. Andover has been deliberately leading our Clair into potential disaster?"

"How did he prove his claims to be heir, Lady Lambert?" asked Val, sidestepping the question.

"You've only to look at him. Great Uncle Everett to the life. Well, nearly. His hair is darker and straighter."

"I don't doubt he is family. I too recognize the nose and that odd hairline. But there is family—and then there is family, my lady, so there is, one assumes, something more?"

Her brows arched. "If you must know, he had the signet ring that was replaced when the old one disappeared at the time my husband's brother left. I would guess it is the one thing the jinglebrain didn't sell when he reached the far side of the Atlantic."

"As I recall the story, your brother-in-law was *asked* to leave the country?"

"We don't speak of it," said Lady Lambert who had no intention of saying more.

"I suppose I must ask Jason."

"Fie! You did not answer me. Do you believe . . ."

". . . that Andover has deliberately led Clair into danger? Yes, I do. I have set up every means I can think of to keep her safe—and, my girl," he added when it appeared that Clair was about to explode, "you will accept with good grace that you are under guard and you will *not* do anything foolish."

Lady Sarah pursed her lips, staring unseeingly at a silver candlestick to the side of a low bowl of flowers. "Sir Valerian," she said, suddenly turning a sharp look his way, "is my son in danger?"

"I believe it possible," he said gently.

Her skin, which never saw the sun, was normally exceedingly pale. Although it seemed impossible, the dowager turned a still ashier shade. "What can we do?"

"I have an investigator sailing west on a speedy naval ship. It left its berth this morning to cross the Atlantic. Unfortunately it will be weeks, months perhaps, before the man can return with information concerning Emerson Andover."

Clair's growing outrage pushed her to her feet. "How dare you do anything so insulting to our relative without at least consulting with Jason as to whether you should?"

"My dear," said Val who was rapidly losing patience with Clair's tendency to excuse Andover, "I have done no more than Jason should have done the moment Andover arrived and claimed the position of heir."

Before Clair could do more than open her mouth, Lady Sarah spoke. "As much as I dislike approving such impertinence on your part, Sir Valerian, you *are* correct. I don't know why Jason has not set something of the sort in motion."

"Because," said a new voice, "I was busy and put it off

and then, frankly, I forgot." Jason Andover, the Marquis of Lambert, stood just within the doorway, which had opened so quietly that the others, involved in their argument, had not heard it. "That is, if I heard what I think I heard. Val, why have you bothered to do what I should have done when the man arrived on our doorstep?"

"Where to begin!" said Val, who, his eye on a steaming Clair, had begun to worry that his impetuous and loving cousin would do something foolish in her determination to defend the poor maligned—as she saw it—stray from the provinces.

"Good morning," said still another voice, coming from someone hidden by Jason's form.

This time Jimson managed to clear his throat and announce, "Miss Althea Bronsen," before backing from the room and closing the door.

"Have I come at a sorry time?" she asked, looking from face to face.

"Althea, do choose something to eat and come sit beside me and help me. Val has taken it into his head that poor Emerson is a villain and it is too bad of him," said Lady Clair.

Althea opened her mouth to admit that she tended to agree with that assessment when Val interrupted with a bored drawl. "You too, Althea? You would defend the underdog against my obviously superior powers of analysis and observation?" His languid tone brought her gaze to meet his and, his holding firm and steady, she guessed his intention.

"What nonsense," she responded brightly. "Clair, do let us put our heads together and determine how we may confound him."

Clair giggled, drawing smiles from everyone but Val who closed his eyes in relief at Althea's quick wits, the intelligence that allowed her to guess he wanted Clair to assume she had an ally.

"Why have you come so early? Not that you are unwelcome, of course." Even as she spoke to Althea, Clair's eyes spoke volumes, silently, to her well-loved husband—and her turned shoulder, equally eloquent, told Val how she felt about him at that particular moment.

"I came, Clair," said Althea, "to see if you had heard of the arrival of a new shipment of silks at our favorite warehouse. Mother and I mean to indulge ourselves and if you and Lady Sarah would care to join us we would be happy to take you up. Mother will stop here for me since it is on the way."

"I, at least, would very much like to go," said Lady Sarah, wiping her lips with her napkin after taking one last quick swallow of tea. "I shan't be more than a moment," she added.

Since she was still partially in dishabille, Althea doubted she'd be all *that* quick. "Clair?" she asked.

"Can you wait until I change? I will be as quick as I can," said the younger Lady Lambert. She glanced at her husband. "I won't buy anything but—" Clair's life as a vicar's daughter had trained her to go on in a thrifty manner and she was still shocked by the extravagance she saw around her. "—it is such fun to look at so much beauty."

"Two lengths for new evening gowns. *Three* would be better," Jason responded promptly. "And a heavier silk for a walking out ensemble. No arguments, Love. I know you believe you've far more than you need—and that is true if one thinks in terms of what is *strictly* necessary—but you have not got near so much as you *should* have as my very lovely wife. Especially," he added with a mischievous look, "if you are to return to the continent when I am sent there in quite the near future."

Clair rose from the table and rounded it. "You will be sent with the delegation to The Hague?"

"It is almost certain," he said nodding, "and although I am somewhat reluctant to take you into what may become dangerous territory—assuming what we fear occurs—I can bear even less to leave you behind. Will you come?" he asked softly.

"Need you ask?" she asked just as softly.

Althea looked at Val and discovered he was staring at her with a sad longing that tore at her heart until, sternly, she reminded herself that acting a part was the rake's stock in trade. She was *not* to allow herself to believe her eyes—however much it would mean to her if he were her *dream* man and not this *real* man who must not be trusted for a moment.

The two men and Althea remained in the breakfast room. Jason seated himself before a full plate. Val refilled his so Althea, to be sociable, took a sweet bun and nibbled at it, especially those portions where she could see a currant poking out.

Abruptly, with no introduction, Val said, "Andover's an impostor, Jason. I haven't any proof, but I've talked to Lady Elf's man in the city. He is not only a land agent, but deals with several Canadian fur traders, one of whom was here a few months ago. The trader saw Andover and claims the ring your purported heir wears was not only stolen, but that the owner is alive and well—although it was believed for some months that he was dead. He is named Jared Emerson Andover—our fraud's half brother. He is legitimate, which this man is *not*."

Jason, Lord Lambert, sighed. "Damn."

"Precisely."

Jason mouthed a silent apology to Althea for swearing. "It will," he said, "be embarrassing, getting rid of him."

"He might, hmm, be induced to leave the country, returning home, as it were."

"Why would he be willing?"

Val sighed. "He won't—until we've proof of his villainy."

"Proof you believe will return with your man?"

"Yes."

"And in the meantime?"

"Frankly, Jason, I am worried for both you and Clair. I was told there is no way our Andover could have possessed the ring legally, that the real owner would not have passed it over voluntarily. My guess is that our Andover believes the real heir is dead."

Althea made a small noise of distress. "But that makes him a murderer."

"Attempted murder, if my source has his story straight."

"Will the trader have taken word back to my unknown cousin?" asked Jason.

Val nodded. "Assuming they see each other. A man can be lost in the wilds for months. Nor can we know if, this spring, he'll take his furs to this particular trader. If they do see each other I am sure the fur trader who saw the false Emerson here in London will give word of it to your cousin."

"His looks alone prove this one is a cousin," said Jason slowly, "but you suggest from the wrong side of the blanket. My uncle was the sort, of course, to have produced any number of bastards. The surprising thing, from what I know, is that there is a legitimate heir."

"It is all so horrible," said Althea, looking distressed. "Yes. It is."

An hour later the four women left and Jason and Val stood in the Lambert's front hall pulling on their gloves in preparation for their own departure. A knock sounded and the footman crossed the parquet to open the door to the man they had decided they must continue calling Emerson Andover.

"My lord, Sir Valerian," said the fraud, looking from one to the other and bowing.

Val, thanks to a history that had given him more experience of the world than he cared to think about, controlled his features easily. "Morning, Andover," he said, nodding his head.

Jason, despite long years in the government, had a trifle more difficulty. "Cousin," he said just a trifle abruptly. "You arrive on my doorstep at rather an early hour, do you not? Is there a problem with which I may help you?"

"No, no, nothing of the sort. I had merely hoped to escort your lovely wife for a ride in the park. I know she likes the exercise and it is far more pleasant for a woman if she may dispense with her groom, I am sure."

"I hope my wife refrains from dispensing with a groom even when riding in a party," said Jason. He cast a look toward Jimson who nodded portentously. "If she ever does, I must have a few words with her on proper behavior for ladies residing in London."

Val hoped Jimson would see to it that Clair always rode with a groom in future and as he was thinking that, Jason, now having himself well in hand, added, "It is thoughtful of you, coming to escort her, but she'll not be riding this morning. She departed perhaps so much as half an hour ago. She and my mother mean to spend the day shopping with friends."

"Ah well, another time," said Andover. He made his adieus.

When the door closed, Jason, speaking with seeming idleness, asked, "Jimson, how often is that man in my wife's company?"

"For more often than necessary," said Jimson promptly and with none of the starch most people thought inherent in his nature.

"I see," said Jason. "Perhaps you will see that it is, in the future, no more than, er, necessary?"

"I will do my best," said Jimson, returning to his normal pompous manner—but with a satisfied little smile that indicated to Val that the butler also had reservations about Andover.

CHAPTER 3

Late that afternoon, Clair was seated with the dowager Lady Lambert in the small back salon when the door opened and Sir Valerian Underwood strode into the room, once again speaking over his shoulder, "Thank you, Jimson. I know the way."

"Again? However knowing you may be, Sir Valerian," barked Lady Lambert, "Jimson is paid to announce guests and he is right to feel aggrieved that you do not allow him to do so."

Val's eyes gleamed. "Should I return to the hall and pretend I have not yet entered your delightful presence?"

Her ladyship raised her hand and covered a smile. "You are a rogue and a rake, but are, nevertheless, delightful company. Why are you here?"

"I thought to take my cousin for a drive in the park." He turned a grin toward Clair, his very white even teeth gleaming against his unfashionably weathered skin.

"And how did you know we had arrived back from our shopping?" asked Clair with an abruptness that indicated she had not quite forgiven him his rudeness toward Emerson Andover.

His brows arched. "It is getting on for the hour of the promenade. Of course you have returned. Everyone must know it."

"We have been in this house for, at most, half an hour," said Clair. "I find it difficult to believe that *everyone* knows we have returned."

The doors opened and Jimson, in his usual sonorous voice, announced, "Lady Thomilson, Miss Thomilson, Miss Julia Thomilson, Mr. Morton Thomilson." He glanced at Lady Lambert who lifted her hand slightly as if holding a cup of tea. The butler nodded and backed from the room, closing the doors as he did so.

"As I said," said Val, his voice dry as dust. "Everyone." He bowed over Lady Thomilson's hand as he said proper hellos to the three Thomilson ladies, nodded toward young Thomilson, and then went to where Clair sat slightly apart at her tambour frame. He studied her work and shook his head. "That blue will never do, my dear."

Clair glanced up at him. "In the bird's wing? I feared it."

"Go get your bonnet, child," he said softly. "A *pelisse* as well since there is a chilly little breeze. The park awaits us."

"As do your horses?" Clair dithered. But, guiltily wishing to avoid Lady Thomilson, she nodded, hesitated. Still—to leave company? "Val," she said, lowering her voice, "I should *not* leave when Lady Thomilson has only just arrived."

"She knows you never miss the promenade if you can help it. I will make your excuses. My horses, of course, are being walked." He held out a strong well-formed hand and she, after a glance toward her mother-in-law who nodded, put hers into it. She then put a hand on his arm and, exerting a trifling pressure, turned him toward the ladies.

"You are looking very well," she said to Miss Julia Thomilson who was very nearly her own age and had had her coming out in the same little Season.

"I warned Mama that you would not wish company since Sir Valerian had come to call but she insisted we come in and discover all the gossip from Paris from whence you, Clair, have—" There was an interrogative note in her voice. "—just returned?"

"We went from Paris to Brussels where an old friend of Mother Sarah's lives. I fear I heard little that would interest you while in Paris."

"But you will describe the fashions, will you not? Oh—" Miss Julia turned bright red after an embarrassed glance at the obviously bored Sir Val. "—but not right this instant, of course."

"Why," said Clair kindly, "do you not come tomorrow morning and I will show you the gowns I had made up while in Paris."

Julia's eyes glowed. "Oh yes. Please."

"Tomorrow then." Clair moved to where Lady Thomilson was attempting, without much success to discover every detail of their recent journey to the Continent. She said all that was proper to Elsmere Thomilson, to Lady Thomilson, and, finally, with a quiet word to Sarah, Lady Lambert, she left to retrieve her bonnet and *pelisse*.

Sir Valerian was not allowed to escape so easily. Lady Thomilson turned her expertise onto him. "And did you also enjoy Paris?" she asked brightly, her eyes darting from him to the dowager.

"I have not left London in the past month, my lady. You will have to discover some other source of scandal, will you not?"

Lady Sarah coughed, hiding what had been an irrepressible chuckle. "You, Sir Valerian, are a rogue."

"Careful, my lady. You repeat yourself. You will become a dead bore if you are not careful and I will be forced to find my entertainment in another drawing room. I will have a care of my cousin," he added, bowed, and with general adieus, exited the room.

"I have known that man forever, Lady Sarah. He is not a . . . a *good* man. You should caution Lady Lambert against him," scolded Lady Thomilson once the door closed behind him. "I certainly would not allow either of my daughters to be seen with him."

"Yes, but your daughters are not closely related to him. Nor have they, either one, a husband—" This, as the dowager knew, was a low blow. "—who is the baronet's very good friend," she added as a means of softening what had been an insult. "Sir Valerian will not harm Clair in any way."

"You are very certain of that. She is a lovely girl and he a gazetted rake. How do you dare allow them such freedom?"

"She has known him from the cradle and he treats her as a sister. A rake he may be, but he is not perverted."

This plain speaking had Miss Thomilson blushing rosily. "My lady!" she said, shocked into speech.

Lady Sarah stared down her nose at the overly thin young woman who was known for her sharp tongue and catty remarks. "Have I said something more than what you've thought? Or perhaps it is that you are jealous of our Clair, that Sir Val has never so much as asked you to stand up for a country-dance?"

"He only dances with married ladies or those well past the first blush of youth. As you know," said Lady Thomilson hurriedly, uneasily aware that her elder daughter's temper was not to be trusted.

Julia spoke equally hastily. "My lady, you are such a jokesmith. As if either of us would wish him to cast his gaze our way. So much as a look and we would be ruined, would we not? The gossips have such a nasty way of taking the most innocent situation and making of it an interesting story for the credulous, have they not?"

Lady Sarah turned a curious look on the younger Miss Thomilson. "As," she said slowly, carefully *not* looking at the chit's mother, "*you* would know."

Julia digested that and then, blushing, rose to join her brother who stared out the window. She spoke softly, her eyes on her mother. "Her ladyship was wrong that Elsmere or I might be jealous, but *you* are, are you not?" She made a faint gesture to where Val helped Clair up onto the seat of his high perch phaeton. "Is it the horses or the lady?" she asked, slyly.

Morton didn't remove his gaze from the scene below them. "Perhaps, my dearly beloved sister, it is both!"

"You do not deny jealousy?"

"No. Only one man is not at least faintly jealous of Underwood's freedom to come and go in this house and that is because he too has the *entrée*."

"She has many lovers?"

"Nonsense. None at all. She is an angel and would not." He cast an impatient glance her way. "You don't even know of what you speak." He turned back to where Sir Valerian was leaning down to give his tiger orders. The lad nodded, stepped back, and the high-stepping well-matched blacks leaned into the harness and disappeared around the corner.

"He has everything, does he not?" she said softly.

"Everything any man could want."

She heard bitterness in his voice. "I am sorry, Morton. I should not tease you."

"I know you do not do it with conscious viciousness as Elsmere does. Why do you not accept Ralston's offer and escape our family?" he asked, a question which had been burning inside him ever since he'd discovered the well-heeled baron had offered and been refused.

Julia glanced toward the others. "I—don't quite know." She looked thoughtful. "Perhaps it has to do with the frying pan and the fire?"

Morton choked back a laugh, losing for a moment his morose look. "You feel it would be no improvement, living under Ralston's mother's thumb?"

"She is terrible," said Julia with a shudder.

"You like Ralston, do you not?"

"I have always liked Stewart, but . . ."

"But he does not make your blood sing?" asked her brother, a faint leer marring his even, rather undefined features.

She turned a reproachful look his way.

He pressed his lips together for a moment. "I apologize. That was outside enough."

She smiled. "Morton, one of the things I most like about you is that you will admit when you are in the wrong."

They were called just then to take tea with the others but, upon reaching Lady Sarah's side, Morton excused himself and departed.

Clair and Val were silent while he threaded his way through rather heavy traffic, but when they reached the park, he pulled his team to an easy walk and turned slightly to look down at her. "That is an exceedingly delightful bonnet . . . " he said.

She tipped her head to look at him.

". . . but that," he continued, "is *much* better. The overly broad brim hides your lovely face and I do not like it."

"It has to be wide, Val. It is all the crack in Paris. Surely you wish me to be right up to the knocker, do you not?"

Val ignored her use of mild slang terms for stylish clothes. "Not," he said sternly, "when it means I cannot watch your expressions."

"You would say I've a face which reveals my thoughts?"

"You do to me, but only because I have known you forever. I doubt anyone who has not would see the little signs which I find revealing." She didn't respond and after a moment he added, "So, since you are too intelligent not to believe me when I say others cannot read you, what worries you?"

She sighed. "You have always seen into me, have you not?"

"I have and I will. And as always, I wish to help you, little cousin."

She smiled a trifle wistfully. "Val, something horrid has happened."

"Hmm?" He cast a surprised glance down at her. Surely Andover could have achieved nothing since this morning. "What sort of horrid?"

"There was a man from the foreign office awaiting Jason when we returned from the Continent the other day. He has looked like a thundercloud ever since. Have you not noticed? You will recall what we said in the breakfast room about a delegation to The Hague? Something awful happened," she said quietly.

"Shall I attempt to discover the truth of it for you?"

"But I *know*. Secret word has arrived that we must expect the ogre to leave his little island and return to France."

Val was silent for a long moment. "I was unaware you knew." He glanced around and forced a grin. Speaking through his teeth, he said, "It is something about which you must not speak however. Especially *now*, while riding behind—" He changed voice and expression to something nearer to normal. "—my excellent new team—which, dear heart, you have yet to comment upon! Clair—" He cast a smile that was just short of a leer toward an old flirt. "—we must not be seen to be so serious. I am after all enjoying a drive with a lovely woman up beside me."

"No flummery, Val. I am not in the mood."

He cast her a look of feigned disbelief. "Is not one always in the mood for, er, flummery?"

"No."

He laughed. Again he glanced around. "I see it is true, but it would be a great deal better, my dear—" He once again spoke in that odd through-the-teeth fashion. "—if you were to pretend. You are showing a very long face to far too many observers. They will wonder what I have been saying to you and, before the day is done, will very likely have made up a whole conversation for us. Or worse, they will suggest Lambert dragged you back from the Continent against your will and it will be remembered that Mr. Andover escorted you, which makes a far better story."

Clair roused from her abstraction. She saw Lady Jersey casting her a speculative look, managed to smile and wave, and, when her ladyship beckoned, indicated to Val that they must stop.

"You have returned from Paris," said Lady Jersey.

Clair nodded. "It was a most interesting journey, but rather tiring. Do you mean to cross the channel, my lady?"

"We have considered it. No decision has yet been reached. Lord Jersey is not convinced it is safe," her ladyship admitted, making a *moue*. "He claims Elba is far too near the French coast and that Napoleon will be tempted to try his luck again."

"What a horrid thought," said Clair—and instantly cast an alarmed glance toward her cousin. "Val?"

"Nothing is impossible," he said smoothly, "but surely the French have tired of constant warfare and will not have him even if he does attempt to return?" Val patted her arm. "I will discover what I can so you need not worry yourself to death," he added in a teasing tone.

Clair nodded, knowing he'd understood she feared that Jason's secret reason for having gone, at once, to the foreign office was already known. "I noticed," said Clair slowly, "that many Frenchmen were not happy to have so many English in Paris. Their officers were particularly rude and ... and ... nasty?"

"We have heard tales of duels?" suggested Lady Jersey, turning her bright curious gaze from one to the other.

Val nodded. "I too have heard that it is not uncommon for a French officer to press a duel upon an Englishman. Very likely it is to prove that although they were beaten on the battlefield they are not down?"

"So unnecessary," said Clair. "No one believes the French cowardly! Why, they were only one country against so many and yet, for years, Napoleon fought battle after battle and won them all."

"A man may know one thing in his mind but feel in his heart another," said Val quietly.

Lady Jersey frowned slightly at his tone before turning her gaze toward Clair. "I will visit and you will tell me all about the very latest fashions," she said.

"I shall tell Lady Sarah we are to expect you," said Clair and, when her ladyship stepped back a pace on the pavement, she settled in her seat. When they were beyond Lady Jersey's excellent hearing she said, "Surely it is not possible. Surely Napoleon is still on Elba and will remain there."

"Jason has told you no details?"

She shook her head. "Only his fears."

Val knew his sensible cousin's ability to deal with reality even while he deplored her inability to think badly of anyone until evil intent was proven beyond a doubt. He said, "I will discover what I can and will tell you. Now, you put on a face to match that delightful bonnet or you will have all the old tabbies meowing and yowling. Did you, by the way, notice Silence Jersey studying your bonnet? Even when discussing the possibility of war, she could not keep her eyes off it. I will lay you a little bet that she owns one very like it before the week is out."

"Very well. If I win I get our sixpence back. You keep it if you win."

He chuckled. "What a very odd bet that I gain nothing by winning."

"Do not tease me. *Val* . . ."

"Yes?" he asked when she did not continue.

"Nothing."

"It is not a nothing. You are not one to grow morose over trifles."

"It is just that Jason . . ." Again she did not continue. Eyes forward, she clasped her hands tightly.

"You are worried about Jason," he said a trifle harshly. "You were a fool to fall in love with him. I warned you how it would be."

"He is worth the loving," she said quietly.

"Jason is a good man, I give you that. And he is my friend—but he does not treat you well."

"Val, I would not love him so dearly if he loved duty less." A cross expression turned her mouth down. "I had hoped this war was *over*."

"You believe you can win him when it is?"

"There have been occasions when—" She blushed slightly. "—I have wondered if he is not already won, but will not, for reasons I do not understand, allow himself to admit it."

Sir Valerian cast her a scandalized look, decided she was not referring to what went on in their marriage bed, and relaxed. "You mean soft looks and gentle touches?"

"Yes. And unexpected gifts for no reason at all."

"So you think that when he has time he will admit it?"

"Yes."

"My dear, life for a marquis is not the same as life for a villager. He will not wear his heart on his sleeve, whatever the occasion and whatever he may feel."

"Duties differ in different levels of society, but people, I have discovered, are much the same everywhere, especially when alone together. Some are good, some bad. Some are hateful and some worthy of admiration and . . . and love," she finished quietly.

"I suppose it is too late now in any case. You have allowed him room in your heart and once that occurs all is lost. We will have to see that he remains worthy of your admiration . . . and your love."

"Do not sound sarcastic when you speak of love, Val," she said quietly. "Someday you will understand."

"I hope not," he said, biting off the words. "I am too much the hedonist, my dear, to suffer as you suffer—as the poets would have it all lovers suffer. Bah. A waste of energy. A waste of time."

Not for the world would he admit to his cousin how he already suffered—and had for three long years.

"Now, I order you!" he continued. "Look about you and enjoy the sun and blue sky since we will have very few more days like it until spring does more than put her toe across the threshold of the season."

Clair, recognizing that her cousin was seriously disturbed, turned her mind to their stay in Paris and allowed her lips to form the words others had wished to hear, telling him the gossip she'd not revealed for the Ladies Jersey and Thomilson.

Val tucked every bit of it away to pour into Althea's ears when he next had access to them. Finding tidbits to interest Althea was among the more important of his daily efforts—for only if he had something new to impart would she allow him near her. Val wondered if he would ever climb up from those depths to which the poets predicted lovers sink and in which he was mired. Being near Althea was something he desired above all else. Even the safety of his cousin.

As if fate took a hand, Althea appeared, walking with her maid along the pavement.

"Val, there is Althea. Hire a boy to hold your horses and let us walk with her."

Others soon joined them. Young matrons, who had not seen her since her return from France, surrounded Clair. This allowed Val to offer his arm to Althea. She caught and held his gaze. He tipped his head. She sighed, shrugged, and accepted his escort, trailing along behind Clair and the others.

"Has something new occurred?" she asked.

"Regarding Clair? Not to my knowledge. She suggested we stop and walk with you. I doubt she anticipated becoming the lion of the hour," he added in a droll tone, nodding toward the excited group of ladies who tossed questions, one after another, at Clair.

Against her will, Althea chuckled. *It is too bad I cannot control myself*, she thought, chiding herself, *since I do not wish him to know he amuses me*. And then, to further her chagrin, she made a mild jest herself. "She *is* having to *roar*, is she not?"

"In order to be heard over the chirping and chattering of such busy little birds," he agreed. Val dropped his bantering style and, serious again, asked, "Althea, have you any way of convincing her she must not put so much trust in Emerson Andover?"

"Knowing Clair as I do, I cannot think how."

"I dropped a hint in Lady Lambert's ear, but I do not know if it will answer."

Althea cast him a startled look. "You think the dowager will do nothing?"

"She will, I think, keep a closer eye on Clair's engagements, but beyond that I fear she, too, is unconvinced that Andover is a real threat." He frowned thoughtfully. "She did ask if I thought Jason in danger and, at that instant, believed me when I said yes. Unfortunately, she is the sort who prefers life to be comfortable and will, somehow, manage to talk herself into believing it all a hum."

"You are certain he *is* in danger?"

"Are not you?"

Althea sighed. "I wish I could say I am not."

"But you cannot." He was silent for some paces. "Althea, you always think the worst of me, but where Clair is concerned, will you not believe that I love her as dearly as I'd have loved a sister if I'd been so lucky as to have one, that I would not see her hurt in any way?"

Althea nodded. "I have accepted that that is true, Sir Valerian. But," she scolded, realizing their mutual concern for her friend was drawing them into far too much intimacy, "you must not use my name!"

Val felt a muscle twitch in his jaw. She would not give an inch. Not half an inch. He felt despair building, a black mood he'd experienced before and knew how debilitating it could be. "I suppose I must feel some relief that you believe me capable of love for Clair—even if you do not believe that capacity extends to loving you."

"Enough!" She cast a sharp look around and was relieved that no one appeared to have any interest in them. Not while Clair continued to hold forth on French fashion!

Emerson Andover joined Morton Thomilson about the time Sir Valerian stopped so that Clair could speak to Lady Jersey. Morton didn't notice. He simply stood there on the path beside the carriageway, his heart in eyes that stared at Clair, Lady Lambert.

"She has an odd way of endearing herself to one and all, does she not? I had thought—" Emerson cast a sly sideways glance at Morton. "—that Sir Valerian was impervious to the more sentimental womanly lures."

"Sir Valerian is Lady Clair's very good friend."

"I suppose she told you so?" With difficulty Emerson repressed even a hint of a sneer.

"Yes."

It was a simple response simply said, but convinced Emerson that he had found a suitable vehicle for his latest plot. Morton's dog-like devotion to Clair had become something of a joke among his cronies—and more than a joke to Emerson. He cleared his throat. "You would like to spend more time in her company, would you not?"

"How could I not wish it?"

"Then why do you not?"

"I . . . am not made particularly welcome at Andover House. Oh," he disclaimed, "it is not that anyone is rude to me, but the dowager ignores me and I very much fear I bore Lady Clair. Not that she is unkind or anything of that nature. It is just a feeling. I will not impose myself upon her when she does not wish it."

"Very noble of you. But your sister—your *younger* sister—is Clair's very good friend, is she not?"

"Yes. Julia and she are great together. I have that excuse to see her more often than I otherwise might. I escort Julia to visit her, you see."

Emerson allowed a pause to stretch out before suggesting, "If you were to invent an entertainment for your sister, then you might ask Clair, Lady Lambert, as one of the guests, might you not?"

Morton raised his cane to his mouth, turning slightly so he could stare after the carriage which was moving away from Lady Jersey and on down the carriage way. "What?" he asked when he could no longer see the feather bobbing above Clair's new bonnet. "Did you say something?"

Emerson, gritting his teeth in vexation, relaxed his jaw and repeated himself.

"An entertainment? For Julia? But I have never done such a thing for one of my sisters. Would she not think it strange?"

"You might be honest with her, might tell her it is an excuse to be in her ladyship's company?" When Morton merely frowned, Emerson added, "Surely your sister would wish to help you?"

Morton looked undecided. "But . . . what would we do?"

Emerson realized he must do more than plant the seed of the idea. He must water it to make it grow. "If it were warmer—" He spoke in an offhand manner. "—you might take a party to Vauxhall Gardens."

"Yes . . ." Morton looked dreamy for a moment and then, his expression turning dreary, added, "But it is *not* warm."

"Perhaps . . . a theater party?" Emerson cast a glance at his prey and, in the lightest possible way, added, "With a little supper party arranged for after?"

Morton's eyes lighted up at the notion of the theater, but once again the glow faded as the full plan registered. "A supper. In a public inn? I *could* not." He shook his head. "Even if I dared, our mother would not allow Julia to attend it."

"You need not invite *Julia*. Or others of your party, whomever they may be. Just . . . Clair," finished Emerson softly, insinuatingly.

Again Morton's eyes glowed. He was not, after all, totally without imagination. But still again the glow faded. "She would not go."

"She need not know it is for her alone."

Emerson had a keen understanding of others' weaknesses, which was not surprising, perhaps, since he existed more by his wits than by hard work. He had had to be constantly on the alert against enemies in Canada and came to England at least partially because he feared some one of those he'd duped might . . . object. Strenuously. Not that he really understood why people felt irritated at him. He was too self-centered to enter into another's feelings to that degree. So, once he verified that Emerson Andover was heir to the marquisate, he irrationally expected to come into his cousin's title and estates in the not too distant future.

One way or another.

Jason's marriage came as an unpleasant surprise—but it had not taken Emerson long to see exactly what was happening within that oddly arranged *ménage*. And, slyboots that he was, he saw how he could use Lord Lambert's preoccupation with duty to his own advantage.

The *"another"* way it would be.

It was easy enough to plan particular ways and means to his particular end. That all was not progressing as rapidly as he'd have liked was, in part, because he must be so very careful. There must be no hint that he himself was involved in bringing about his cousin's demise—his ultimate goal.

His most complicated plot to date, the journey across the channel, a notion carefully planted in the dowager's mind, had irritated Lord Lambert a good deal but it should have annoyed him more. Lady Sarah's impulsive change of plan, turning aside from the route to Vienna, had made it a pin-prick rather than a deep gash leading to the couple's separation.

Separating them was essential if his *complete* plan was to work.

But, thought Andover, *this new ploy will add another straw to the pile. A large straw—perhaps a whole forkful. When I manage enough straw then all will go up in a conflagration of lost tempers and irrational behavior and they will part. Forever. Only then may I proceed to the second and more important step.*

Dreaming up single straws, in the form of small irritations, had been easy enough—although less useful than expected in forwarding his cause. Still, each carried some weight.

Unfortunately *this* particular sheaf of wheat, in the form of Morton Thomilson, was taking a great deal of threshing. It required a lot of cajoling and the spilling of devious drivel, shrewd gibes, unwarranted compliments, and, of course, the planting of further suggestions. It was nearly as difficult as bringing the dowager to a decision to journey to the Continent—with himself their courier since, of course, Lord Lambert could not be asked to leave his work.

As time passed, Andover fumed. He had discovered the young man believed a Thomilson must behave honorably, a complication he'd not foreseen. But in the end, as he'd expected, Morton fell into the trap set for him. The lad agreed not only to the arranging of the theater party, but also to the intimate little party which was to follow with the love of his life.

Andover returned to his rooms in a building on St. James's with a little cat-smile playing about his lips, one that would warn anyone who knew him that he was up to mischief. Sir Valerian did see him. And Valerian knew him—which set him to wondering what the creature was up to now.

If it had to do with Clair—as most of Emerson's plots did—then he must expect another tiring and fretting time of it, assuring that his cousin came to no harm.

Not only Clair had personal reasons to wish Jason's work to the devil. Val did, too. He, who felt little or nothing for most of the world—excepting Althea and a few good friends—had somehow, from first seeing Clair in her cradle, experienced a deep and abiding sense that he was responsible for his little cousin's happiness, her health, and her safety. It had not, of course, involved much effort before the chit's marriage. Her life in the vicarage had been mildly pleasant and had not led to a great number of adventures—but ever since the child wedded his old friend, Val had found it an ongoing and exceedingly tiresome necessity to keep a careful eye on her.

If Lambert were not so involved in the renewed war effort, he'd see to his wife himself—but until his friend was free to do so, Val knew it was up to himself to take care of her. *So*, he wondered, *what is that fool Andover plotting now*?

He hoped, if he did not discover it for himself, Clair's maid would get word to Loth and Loth would reach him—and that all of them would act in time to prevent disaster.

CHAPTER 4

"She what?"

"She joined a theater party organized by Morton Thomilson in honor of his sister Julia's natal day," repeated the dowager Lady Lambert, her eyes wide in astonishment at Sir Valerian's explosive question. "What could possibly be more innocent than that?"

"If Thomilson has ever before remembered one of his sisters has a natal day, I'd be surprised."

"Nonsense. He asked me, quite properly, if it would do. I could see no harm in it."

Val glared at his friend's mother and then, relaxing tense shoulders, sighed. "No, of course you would see no harm. What play did they mean to see?"

Lady Lambert opened her mouth. She closed it and, after a moment tried again. "I haven't a notion," she admitted reluctantly. "I presume whatever is playing at Covent Garden, but I made no attempt to ascertain that that is true."

"That what is true?" asked another voice.

Val swung around. "Good. You are needed. Your wife, my friend, has gone off racketing about town with that ridicu-

lous pup, Morton Thomilson, who has, or so he told your
mother, got up a theater party to entertain his sister."

"You've reason to think he didn't mean to take his sister
and a party to the theater?"

Val hesitated. It was all guesswork. That satisfied smirk
on Emerson Andover's face. The memory of the two men in
the park where, obviously, Emerson urged something upon a
reluctant Morton. His suspicion that Morton held warmer
feelings for Clair than were suitable . . .

"Val?"

"I've merely a strong suspicion but—" His eyes went to
Jason's, caught his friend's gaze, and held it. "—that itch I
occasionally feel up my spine? It is driving me like a whip
across my shoulders!"

Jason had reason to understand exactly what Val meant
by that itch—it had, after all, saved his life once when he
was set on by thieves and Val hurried to his rescue. He
sobered. "What should we do?"

Seeing that Jason was ready to follow his lead without argument, Val relaxed. "You go to Covent Garden. If they are
not there, continue to—" A rueful look crossed his face.
"—wherever you think best! Drury Lane, perhaps? You
know the theater was never of particular interest to me—"

"Except for the greenrooms?" inserted Lady Lambert with
a tartness partially caused by her concern for her son's marriage and partially irritation that she had not suspected a plot.

"—whereas you once knew them all very well—"

Lady Lambert cast a surprised glance toward her son
who, noticing it, felt heat in his ears.

"—so," continued Val, "give me a list of the lesser possibilities and I'll start there."

"Where will I find you if I find them and discover all is
well?"

"You won't. But if all is *not* as it should be, then once the
theaters let out meet me at—" He thought for half a moment.
"—the Red Lion. Near the front door. We'll lay new plans."

Val turned on his heel and left the room with Jason on his heels.

"Jason!" called his mother.

"Yes?" he asked impatiently.

"What did Sir Valerian mean by an itch like a whip driving him?"

"Half a dozen times in his life he has felt it—and it always means trouble," he added when he saw her open her mouth, ready to demand more information. Before she could, he left the room and hurried out to find a hackney to take him to his first destination.

Val had ridden. The lad he'd hired to hold his horse outside the Lambert house looked at the coin in his hand in disbelief and half started after the nob who tossed such *largesse*. Man and horse had already turned out of the square. There was nothing he could do to correct what must have been an error. Whistling cheerily, the boy set off to enjoy one of the most carefree evenings of his life—to say nothing of a feast fit for kings, which he remembered long after he forgot the high jinks he got up to that night.

Later, Val entered still another third-rate theater, scanned the benches and the balcony, waved at one man he knew vaguely from the old days, and walked out. He stood for a long moment, his hand on his horse's neck. Then, shaking his head, he abandoned the remainder of the theaters and went to a hotel that had private rooms for late night parties. They had never heard of Morton Thomilson. Nor had the next or the next. The theaters let out so he rode to the Red Lion where he found a worried looking Jason.

"I've tried several places where the cub might have arranged for a supper after the theater. He hasn't been heard of at any of them."

"Where can he have taken her? Val, do you think he actually had a party at all? Could he have . . . have abducted . . ."

Val interrupted. "He had a party. Jimson reported two carriages. Julia looked out the window of the first, the one

into which Morton handed Clair. Jason, I'm going to check
out more of the smaller inns where a young man might better afford a private room and a little supper—you know the
thing."

Jason nodded. Without a touch of sarcasm he said, "You'd
be far more likely to know where those might be found than
I would. What should I do?"

"Go home. Wait."

"Hard," said Jason, his jaw clenching. "Let me come with
you."

"Better if I find her by accident, do you not agree?"

Jason sighed. "If you've been asking after her all over
town, I don't think we've a hope of keeping this quiet."

"Ask after *her*? Nonsense. You think I'd do something to
hurt our Clair?" asked Val, worry giving his tone an edge.
"You go home, Jason. I'll find her. I promise."

As he left the Red Lion and retrieved his horse, the grim
thought crossed his mind that it was a promise he hoped he
could keep. He immediately put all thought of failure from
his mind. He hadn't time to worry about anything other than
complete success so, instead of fretting, calculated a route
that would cover as much of London as possible as quickly
as possible. The first three places he stopped no one had
heard of Morton. The fourth host to whom he spoke pokered
up, the expression fading not-quite-instantly into a bland
caricature of unconcern.

"Oh yes," said the innkeeper in a would-be offhand manner. "The young gentleman comes here occasionally." He
acted like someone who wouldn't lie, but had no desire to
discuss the topic either.

"Has he been here recently?"

"Only last evening," was the prompt and obviously sincere response. This was followed, quickly, by an addition
that rang true but without quite the same sincerity. "I don't
often see him more than once a week. If that." The man fiddled with a mug that had a chip out of the rim.

"You don't expect him then?"

"This evening? Didn't I say he's rarely here more than once a week?"

Evasion. Val eyed the man. He tossed a coach wheel, caught the coin, flipped it again . . .

The innkeeper eyed it briefly, but then, regretfully, looked away. "I run an honest inn here, I do. I don't know what you want with the lad, but you just be on your way."

"You serve up what is paid for, certainly," said Val.

The man bowed. There was a call from the other end of the bar and, visibly relieved by the interruption, he threw his towel over his shoulder and walked off.

Val was uncertain what to do. The innkeeper's behavior was such as to make him suspicious, but that might be merely that he *was* an honest man and upset at someone asking questions about a customer to whom he felt a certain loyalty. Val was frowning when he pushed open the low door to the street.

Ducking his head in order to keep from bumping it on the lintel, he stepped out—only to find his way blocked by a carriage. He straightened and found himself staring into his cousin's surprised and, obviously, relieved face.

Clair hurriedly pushed open her door. "Val!"

"Clair?" The frown marring his forehead smoothed out and then reappeared as he remembered he had a role to play. He peered beyond her into the carriage. "What in the name of all that is precious," he asked, "are you doing here? And with that halfling?"

"Never mind that. Do you have your carriage?"

"I fear I do not."

"Then join us—after you order Mr. Thomilson's driver to carry us to Grosvenor Square."

"You asked Thomilson to do so and he *refused*?"

The danger in his tone had Morton sliding to the far side of the carriage, sweat popping out on his forehead. He opened that door. "You take the carriage. I will ride home with the

Hampsons. After—" He spoke with bravado since he was certain Sir Valerian, at least, would not be deceived. "—we've had our little supper."

Suddenly he was gone, the door shut behind him.

Clair leaned back against the swabs and shut her eyes. "I don't know how you happened to be here just when I needed you, Val, but I am very glad you were. I was beginning to wonder if Mr. Thomilson had lost his mind."

"Not his mind. His heart." The carriage rocked slightly as Val, who had tied his mount to the back and had had a word with the driver, entered and seated himself on the backward facing seat.

"Nonsense. He is, at most, infatuated with the notion of being in love."

"The emotion is, for all its being temporary and a part of growing up, very real while it lasts. You should feel sorry for the boy."

"I might if he were attempting to abduct someone else." She tipped her head, thoughtfully. "No. I would feel far sorrier for the lady involved."

Val chuckled. "You sound cross. Did Thomilson mention the Hampsons? The Hampsons who live near your father's village? Did that ramshackle family have the gall to join Thomilson's party?"

"They were *invited* to it," she said bitingly. "Mrs. Hampson was supposed to chaperone our group of young people, but I fear she was more prone to joining in their high spirits than to having a care for anyone's reputation. Poor Julia. She will feel very out of place, riding to the inn with that party of wild things."

"Your Julia grew up with all of them running in and out of each other's houses so very likely she knows exactly how they behave and will expect nothing different." When Clair turned her head away, he added, "You would say she did *not* join in when things got a trifle out of hand?" He did not give her time to respond—not when he saw that she was biting her lip. "Where, by the way, were you, that you felt your friends did not behave in a properly decorous manner?"

"Mr. Thomilson took us to Astley's. I have not been since I was a child and would have enjoyed it very much if—" She spoke with a certain wistfulness. "—I had been there with another sort of party."

"Astley's. I thought of everything but Astley's," muttered Val.

"What did you say?"

"Hmm? Oh. Nothing you need worry your head about."

"You *knew* something was wrong, did you not? You were searching for me." There was an accusing note to her tone, but then she must have remembered how pleased she'd been to see him, because she continued in a more normal voice. "That is why you were frowning when I first saw you."

"It is my belief that Andover talked Thomilson into this evening's debacle," said Val. "Since you will not have it that Emerson wishes you ill, there is no use discussing it."

"Val, he is Jason's cousin and has become my friend. Friends do not endanger each other and, besides, surely he would not wish to embarrass Jason in any way."

"You are overly innocent, Clair. He is Jason's cousin, but he is also Jason's heir. Do you think he delights in the prospect of being supplanted by your son?"

"Oh—" Clair turned a startled if embarrassed glance his way. "—but he has always known . . ."

"Your Jason was never much in the petticoat line. At least not among tonnish misses—" Val realized that was an infelicitous admission to make to a young bride and hurried on. "—so he surprised the whole of the *ton* when he swept you off your feet and wed so quickly. On the other hand, no one was particularly surprised when, immediately after saying his vows, he returned to long hours at the foreign office and ignored you as if he had never met you, let alone wed you. Jason, as much as I admire him, has an odd kick to his gallop that leads others to erroneous and ridiculous conclusions. In this case, their error is in thinking that having wed you, he wished he had not."

"That is not true!"

"Of course not. It is merely that his behavior induces that conclusion."

"He explained to me how, until the war against Napoleon ended and peace returns, he would be unable to spend much time with me," said Clair thoughtfully, "but he did not tell the world? I see how others might not understand." She sighed. "I hoped that when Napoleon was exiled to Elba things would be different between us, but it cannot be. Not until the Congress in Vienna finishes its work. Jason says that if Castlereigh cannot manage to push through our program, then it is not unlikely that a new war will start within only a few short years. He says that the powers in Europe must balance so that none feels it has the upper hand. He says that it is *imbalance* among governments that leads to war."

Val was amazed that any man would waste time teaching his brand new wife political philosophy when he had only brief intervals when he could be alone with her. Nevertheless, he agreed. "Jason is correct in his thinking," he said, "but it is not his responsibility to see that all is done properly. He *should* see to other responsibilities."

"Other responsibilities?" Clair frowned prettily. "His estates, you mean? But they are in the very good hands of Mr. Singleton and . . ."

"I do not refer to his estates."

After a moment Clair touched the clenched fist that rested on Val's knee. "Why are you angry?"

"He, not I, should be seeing that you do not fall into the briars, Clair."

"But I have explained to you . . . Val, is it that you are tired of looking after me?"

He laughed and, with the laughter, relaxed. "No of course not. I could never be tired of it, child, but it would help—" Something of his former chiding tone returned. "—if you

would admit that it is not normal to find yourself in difficul-
ies quite so often as you have since your marriage, that it is
not *merely* that you did not grow up in this level of society
and are prone, therefore, to fall into scrapes. *If* you admitted
hat much, *then* you would also admit that your problems are
not of your making, but are traps set to snare your feet. And
if you admitted *that*, then you might be more wary of falling
into the next one. I am not pretending you could avoid them
all, dear child, because you did *not* grow up within the *ton*
and you have no idea of all the various ways in which you
can become a cropper. Nevertheless, if you were even a trifle
more wary, you might not so continually play into the hands
of your enemy. Clair, you've a wet eel by the tail."

Clair, who had been growing slowly more angry at Val's
insistence Emerson was her enemy, blinked. She laughed an
embarrassed little laugh. "I've a *what*?"

"A wet eel by the tail." Val grimaced. "A friend, a Captain
Snowden who is a naval captain, used the expression once.
He said it means you've a slippery person with whom you
must deal."

"I wish I could convince you how wrong you are. I told
you that when we left Paris, Emerson left word for Jason that
we would be found in Brussels. If he had not, then Jason
would have gone off to Vienna, thinking that was where we
were. I believe I'd told several people that that was Lady
Lambert's intention."

Val sighed. Once again he had failed to convince his soft-
hearted cousin that evil walked the world and that she was
not immune to it. "Tell me about your evening," he said, deciding not to make further attempts to change her mind.

She brightened. "I would have enjoyed it so much if I had
been allowed to view it properly," she said. "But the Hampsons
were so loud and boisterous and, well, that sort of humor—"

Val heard in her voice that she was embarrassed.

"—was a sort with which I am . . . unfamiliar?" She hurried on. "I could not like it. Worst of all, when the program

ended, Mr. Thomilson and I became separated from the rest of the party. I do not understand how it came about that I allowed Morton to maneuver me into his carriage alone with him." She waved a hand, impatiently. "Well, of course I assumed that Julia would join us for the ride to the inn where Mr. Thomilson had arranged for a supper to be served before we continued home but that is no excuse. I should have refused to go when I realized we'd be alone."

"I suppose you should have done, but then what would you do? You would have made a scene and had no way home, would you not?"

Clair cast him a grateful look that, thanks to a lamp hanging just beyond his window, he saw.

"When did you become suspicious, Clair?"

"We had crossed the river when I looked out the back window and discovered the Hampson carriage was not behind us. At first I worried only about Julia, left to Mrs. Hampson's care, you know, but Mr. Thomilson was unconcerned, insisting the lady would see to his sister. When I asked where they were, he suggested that they knew another route—but he said it in a strange sort of tone. It was almost a question rather than a comment."

"So?"

"So I accused him of playing a game with me and I told him I would be very angry if he were. And then . . ."

Once again she turned away. And again Val guessed that she was embarrassed. "Did that pup attempt to make love to you?" He should not have used such blunt words and realized his error instantly, but it was too late.

"No," she lied, using the prim little voice that always gave her attempts at a tarradiddle away. "Of course he would not do such a thing."

"If he managed to do more than kiss you, I will call him out!"

"Val, no!" She turned back, obviously horrified at the thought. "It would be such a *scandal*. And, besides, he didn't even manage that," she admitted. She straightened and looked at him. They had reached a better part of town and there were gaslights along the way. In their dim glow he could see how very confused she was. "Val, he seemed convinced I had *feelings* for him, that I *returned* his love. I do not understand how he could have come to such a nonsensical view."

Val, convinced that Emerson had had a hand in that bit of misinformation, knew he'd never convince Clair. "My dear, the boy is in love with you. It takes no particular reason for one in the midst of suffering through his first love to convince himself he sees that love returned."

Soon after they entered the house and Jimsen actually turned a look of approval onto Sir Valerian. "This way. My lady and my lord await you in the sewing parlor."

"An odd choice," murmured Val.

Clair whispered, "It is our favorite room, Val."

They were announced in the manner of a man offering a great treat and Jason, who had been staring at his wife's embroidery, jerked erect and around. He opened his arms and Clair ran into them.

Val looked away. A sudden and unwanted bleakness filled him, fueled by jealousy. Althea would never run to him as Clair had run to Jason, would never feel free to turn to him in affection . . . in love . . .

"I asked," repeated the elder Lady Lambert breaking into his growing black mood, "where you found her."

"Pardon me," said Val smoothly. Briefly, he told his story and then, excusing himself, he left the Lamberts to their own devices, saying he'd just recalled that he'd promised to meet a friend at the Arrowville's *musicale* and, if he left immediately, perhaps he'd not be late.

"Tell Althea hello for me, will you please?" asked Clair absently. "At least I believe she said she meant to attend the *musicale*."

Jason, looking over his wife's head, cast a sardonic smile toward Val. Val answered with a grimace.

The dowager, noting the exchange of looks, rather slyly suggested that Val tell Althea hello from herself as well—and Lady Bronsen, as well. Val bowed and, before their teasing got more out of hand and he was embarrassed beyond bearing, he departed.

CHAPTER 5

The very last piece was ending as Sir Valerian entered the Arrowvilles' music room. He saw Althea seated with her mother in the front row of seats, and, unable to get near her while she remained there, looked for a convenient pillar against which to lean. It appeared that other men, coerced into attending an evening of mediocre music, already occupied all the more comfortable architectural devices. Val shrugged and moved to where one of his oldest friends stood waiting for his wife who was an amateur musician of note. They suffered through many such evenings under the mistaken belief that young musicians needed encouraging.

"What? You here, Val?" asked his friend, grinning at him.

"I have been searching for someone. This was my last hope and I cannot see my quarry," lied Val. He heaved a sigh as if it had been a wasted evening altogether. "Your lady is in looks tonight."

"My lady is always in looks." Val's friend looked thoughtful. "Did I ever thank you for introducing us?"

"I can't recall and it isn't important."

"To me it is."

Val glanced at the shorter man, who, his heart in his eyes,

stared at his wife's profile. Once again Val felt that descending blanket of debilitating bleakness. He lifted his gaze and, surprised, met Althea staring back at him across the heads of those between them. The music had ended and, very unlike herself, Miss Bronsen, was instantly on her feet and moving around the still applauding audience.

Althea made straight for Sir Valerian, intent on discovering if anything had gone wrong with Clair's evening at the theater. Fear that it had was the only reason she'd come up with to explain why Val had not kept to his intention to speak with her at the Westermacks' ball which she and her mother attended earlier in the evening.

At the last moment Althea lost her nerve. She could not accost Sir Valerian. The rake. The man all young women were warned against when first brought on the town. The man to whom she'd lost her silly heart so long ago she could not remember when she had not loved him. Instead of coming up to him, she passed him, nose in the air—but with one sidelong look that flicked across his gaze and then away.

A very few minutes later Val coughed. He coughed again, a dry hacking sort of sound. "Blast," he said. Coughed. "Must get something to drink . . ." he muttered, and quickly made his way from the room and into the dining room where he was certain to find a supper spread out, complete with wines and orgeat and other of the milder forms of beverage.

He indicated a desire for tea and glanced around as it was poured for him. Althea stood in one of the alcoves. Seemingly with no thought, he looked still farther around, discovered they were the first to have left the music room from which the sound of chatter drifted down the hall. They were alone so he moved to join her.

"*Was* there trouble?" asked Althea before he could even say hello.

"There might have been, but through pure luck I found her in time to prevent a scandal."

"From the state of your boots, I suspect it was a bit more than mere luck," said Althea dryly.

She didn't give him time to do more than glance down at his boots, which were sadly in need of a polish and, indeed, had a nasty scratch across one toe. Boots, moreover, he should not have worn to an evening engagement.

"You will come tomorrow and tell me the whole story? Not too early. I mean to go with Clair to the glovers first thing but we should have returned in time for nuncheon."

His dark spirits lightened at the invitation. "I will merely pass on Clair and Lady Lambert's wishes that I tell you hello for them and then I am off. Sleep well, my beauty," he added softly and, with one last soft look, left her side, leaving the room just as the first of Lady Arrowville's other guests arrived there.

Althea watched him cross the room. Moodily she stared at nothing at all—until she saw her mother enter the room on the arm of her cicisbeo. She joined them. Sir Robert offered to bring her supper as well as her mother's, seated the two women at a small table, and moved on to the buffet.

"You left in such a rush," whispered Lady Bronsen. "Was something the matter? Are you ill?"

"I believe it was the heat. I stood near that open window for a few minutes and felt much better," said Althea, wishing she need not lie to her mother. She only wished she knew what had caused her to rise to her feet the instant the music ended, what made her glance quickly around until her gaze fell upon Val. It was as if she had known he was there—when she *hadn't* known. How *could* she have known?

Except that she always seemed to know . . .

And she would see him again tomorrow. Her heart soared. And then it fell. She was to see him to discover what had occurred concerning Clair. Clair. She must *not* forget that Clair was the reason she meant to allow herself speech with the man. She *must* not.

"My dear child," whispered Lady Bronsen, kicking her daughter in the shin, "do stop behaving as if you were about to go to sleep right there where you sit! I see we've been going about too much. We will not do so tomorrow evening, but will remain quietly at home where we belong."

Althea opened her mouth to object—and then realized her mother had happily discovered what she felt was a legitimate reason for doing what she preferred to do. She closed it. It also occurred to her that her mother's decision was a reason for discovering if Clair and Lady Lambert meant to attend Almack's, which was likely, and ask, as Sir Valerian had requested of her, that they take her up.

And it will be one evening, thought Althea virtuously, *that I am unlikely to meet Sir Valerian. He will surely avoid Almack's.* She smiled, thinking of how bland a *milieu* Almack's would be for a rake! *How excellent that I need not worry that I will see him.*

And, having decided *not* seeing him was good, she felt as if she were already suffering extreme tedium. Almack's, indeed *any* entertainment, was boring when Val—Sir Valerian!—was not in attendance.

"We will depart as soon as we have eaten," decided Lady Bronsen, giving her daughter a thoughtful stare.

The stare did what her mother's words could not. Althea could admit to no one just how obsessed she was with Sir Valerian Underwood. Especially, she could not admit it to her mother who, she was certain, would *never* understand how anyone could find a rake a man to whom one dared give one's heart.

Sir Robert returned with a footman following behind, several small plates resting on his tray along with a glass of wine and two cups of tea. Althea, eying the wine, wished it were two glasses and one cup, but, well-trained, did no more than murmur her thanks for the refreshments brought to her. She also remained silent, only half listening, to the banter between her mother and her mother's long-time friend.

When they were in the carriage and headed back to North Audley Street, it occurred to Althea to ask why her mother did not wed her cicisbeo who, Althea was certain, had asked for her mother's hand more than once. Indeed, once she had walked in on a proposal, embarrassing not only herself, but her mother and the gentleman as well.

"Re-wed? Oh, my dear, I could not."

"But why not? You enjoy Sir Robert's company so much. The two of you deal so well together."

Lady Bronsen bit her lip. A sideways glance slid Althea's way, which she'd have missed if she had not been half turned and looking at her mother. Finally, her ladyship said, "I thought you were very much against supplanting your father with another man."

"You what? But, why? What did I ever do to make you think such a thing?"

Lady Bronsen squeezed her eyes tight shut. She sighed. "It was a very long time ago. And, I suppose, not so very long after your father died . . ."

"Oh dear. Lord Tarrant!"

Lady Bronsen chuckled. "Yes. Lord Tarrant. It is just as well you took against him, of course. Just think where he is today!"

"A debtors' prison, is it not? Ah! But perhaps the love of a good woman would have . . . ?"

Lady Bronsen reached across the space between them and tapped Althea's arm with her fan. "There would have been no love, would there? At least, on my part."

"Then I do not regret my interference. But surely you know that I am no longer that spoiled young thing missing an overindulgent father, do you not?"

"I suppose I do. I suppose it is, in part, that I am lazy and that everything is so very comfortable just as it is. I've no reason to change, you see? Now, if you were to wed . . . well, then things would be different and it is not unlikely that I might accept Robert."

"I think you should," said Althea after a moment. "Even if I do not wed."

"My dear!"

"I truly think you should. As you know, I have dreamed of travel to foreign parts, something you hold in abhorrence—although that must not be so completely true as I once believed, since you have expressed a mild interest in crossing the channel now Boney is enisled." Althea drew in a deep breath. "However that may be, if you were married, I would be free to hire a companion and a courier and go to all those places I have read about. See all the sights I have wished to see . . ."

"My dear!"

"Do you think it terribly fast of me? But there is so *much* about which I have only read . . ."

"Not *fast*, my dear—or perhaps, yes, that too—but you cannot have thought! All those foreigners! All very well to see cathedrals and displays of art and even, perhaps—" Lady Bronsen looked less than convinced at her next thought. "—to try strange foods, but, Althea, to do so, you would have to deal with *strangers*. *Foreign* strangers."

"Some of whom," retorted Althea, "might actually be interesting."

Lady Bronsen shook her head. "Such a changeling I have reared! I do not know where you get your adventurous spirit! It has always been so. I will never forget the day you disappeared and we found you sitting at the feet of that awful old beldame who was known by one and all to be a witch—even if no one ever spoke of it."

"But she had such fascinating tales." Althea had never told her mother—and never would—that, for years, she had stolen away to visit Old Granny. She had learned a great deal from the old lady, much of which her mother would very likely not like her knowing.

Althea missed those visits which had ended with the woman's death. There had been only one more surreptitious trip to the cottage. Althea had had to retrieve Granny's book. The old woman had shown it to her not long before she died, revealing the hiding place, so that someone she trusted would have access to the old receipts and remedies for which Granny had become famous.

Or, thinking of *some* of those receipts, perhaps one should say infamous?

The next morning Althea strolled around to Grosvenor Square to join Clair for their trip to the glove maker's establishment. She arrived just as Lady Jersey descended from her carriage. The lady, known as Silence Jersey to one and all, immediately began talking and was still speaking as they were shown into the Ladies Lamberts' presence.

". . . so, of course, I was forced to tell her—" Her ladyship broke off without saying what she told her greatest enemy and greeted her hostess. "—good day to the both of you and a very good day it is. Dear Lady Clair has promised to show me all the fashions she brought back from Paris, but it occurred to me, Lady Lambert—" She spoke to the dowager. "—that you too will have brought home much of interest." The Jersey eyed the at-home gowns worn by the Andover women. "I do like what the French are doing to the hemlines, do you not?"

The discussion turned on fashion and it was some time before Althea was able to quietly discover that Clair had decided to postpone her shopping so she asked if they meant to attend Almack's that evening.

"We all go," said Clair and blushed rosily with happiness. "Dear Jason is free this evening. Is it not wonderful?"

Free, assuming nothing comes up in the meantime, thought Althea with more acid than she would normally put into such a thought. She had grown deeply worried about Clair and the worry made her cross. She forced herself to relax. "Would you mind taking me up in your carriage, Clair?

Mother made noises about staying in this evening. I think *she* is tired of our gadding about, although she persists in saying it is *I* that is in need of an early evening."

Clair chuckled. "Of course we will take you up." She turned as the door opened and Sir Valerian strolled in, Jason on his heels.

"Ladies," said Lord Lambert, looking very slightly taken aback at the number of women populating his drawing room.

Reading him correctly, Lady Jersey revealed a tact for which she was not well known. She made her adieus and Lord Lambert made no secret of the fact he was pleased.

"Good," he said when the door shut behind her. "I have asked Val to dinner this evening. Miss Bronsen, why do you not return in time to dine with us and we will go on to Almack's as a party? It is not one of your mother's happiest milieus so I'll not extend the invitation to her. Since my mother will have a care for your reputation she need not put herself out."

Val eyed Althea, his eyelids half lowered in a sleepy look that set her insides to roiling—although he could not know that. His thought was that she looked a trifle agitated. Obviously, he concluded, she hadn't a notion how to refuse an invitation which included himself.

"Perhaps," he suggested harshly, "it would be better if I go elsewhere once dinner is finished."

He could not bring himself to give up all association with his love, but feared she would not allow herself to accept the invitation at all if he were included in more than the small dinner party Jason suggested.

"I have already asked Althea to go with us to Almack's and it is a wonderful notion that she come to dinner first." Clair rose to her feet. "But if we are to have company for dinner, then I must consult Cook!" She disappeared out the door, her feet fairly twinkling as she left the room.

Val caught Althea's gaze, holding it, daring her to deny

them both the pleasure of a meal at the same table. She found she could not do it.

Carried away by bravado, she not only accepted but added, ". . . and I see no reason my reputation should suffer merely because I arrive at Almack's in the company of the Lambert ladies while you, Sir Valerian, come with Lord Lambert."

"No, of course there is no reason," he said, teasing. He grinned, a flash of white teeth that was immediately hidden, but inside a bubbling lightness grew to bursting. "Will you also give me the supper dance, Al—Miss Althea?"

"I will not," she said, her flashing eyes warning him he was not to tease her further, that she had given in to just as much as she dared.

"Ah well. One must accept the boons fate hands one—and not be too downcast at those denied."

The dowager turned from one to the other and then back again. She opened her mouth, encountered her son's gaze and shaking head, and shut it again. But that did not stop her from wondering what was between her son's friend and his wife's friend. Something. That much was clear. She would watch. If she saw what she thought she'd see, then, she decided, it behooved her to take Althea aside and tell the story of how Val had saved Jason's life, endangering his own to do so.

"I've an interesting bit of news," said Jason, breaking into what had become a slightly embarrassing silence.

Althea instantly assumed his news would be of a political nature, and was surprised when it was not.

"I had a note from Morton Thomilson this morning. He is leaving London for the family estate where he says he is needed. He wished to apologize for embarrassing Lady Lambert last evening."

"I suppose it was necessary to send the note to you. He could hardly send it to your wife," said Val.

"I am glad he is leaving town," said Althea. "He will be much happier in the country where, someday, he will marry a woman reared to country life. In the meantime he will be pleasantly occupied learning his role in the community."

Val looked at Althea and nodded. "I believe you are correct." Again he grinned that flashing grin. "Would you care to lay a wager that the woman will be one of the Hampson brood?"

Everyone laughed and soon after parted until later in the day when they would meet for dinner.

Lord Lambert's drawing room was softly lit that evening by the new gas lighting which his lordship had had installed only that winter. The soft hiss and occasional sputter were the only sounds as Sir Valerian entered. He moved with his usual cat-soft tread toward the fireplace in which a footman had kindled a neat fire.

There was a chill to the air that evening and he had walked from his rooms, allowing his mind to wander freely over the unexpected joy of having his Althea near him in a very nearly intimate setting. Now he spread his hands to the fire, enjoying the warmth . . . and heard the softest of gasps. He turned.

"My love!" he said, joy spreading across his dark features.

"No. You must not!" Althea seemed to cringe back into her chair.

Val sighed. "I would not, except that I have been thinking of you and seeing you so unexpectedly—I apologize," he finished.

They stared at each other, his eyes devouring her and she incapable of looking away from the face and form that haunted her.

"Can you not forgive me?"

Still she said nothing.

"Please?"

She sighed. "You would charm the birds from the trees to your hand, would you not? But then, charm must be expected in a rake."

"So bitter? Must I apologize for my wild youth?"

"Your *youth*?" She cast him a look of disbelief and he sighed.

"The stories told of me have been outrageously embroidered—and yet people still believe, as is obvious, since you are one of them." It was his turn for a touch of bitterness.

Althea drew in a deep breath. This would not do. They were guests in another's home and must not brangle. "If I cannot forget and forgive your reputation, Sir Valerian, perhaps it is because I have reason? What I *can* do," she hurried on, "is offer a truce. For this evening. While we are guests of Lord Lambert and his wife."

The door opened and, from Althea's point of view, none too soon. Many more moments in the rake's sole company and she was likely to forget her pride, her self-control, and give in to the urge to throw herself into his embrace, demanding that he kiss her as he had that never-to-be-forgotten summer evening in the vicar's gazebo.

"Jimsen said you'd arrived, Val," said Lord Lambert from just inside the room. "Are you early or am I late?"

Val, after a quick glance at Althea's pink cheeks, strode toward Jason, his hand out. "Another last minute demand from your masters?" he asked.

To Althea's ear his humor sounded forced but she could not but be glad when, a hand on his friend's arm, Val led Jason from the room. She heard his voice as he moved toward Jason's study across the entryway, words which were cut off as the door closed behind the two men.

"Why," asked another voice, "do you deny him when you love him so very much?"

Althea clutched the arms of her chair, a gasp escaping her.

"Tut-tut—" The voice was cross as crabs. "—it is only I."

Elf limped into view and took the chair beside Althea.

"How long have you been there?" asked Althea and then realized how rude that sounded. "I mean, I thought there was no one here when I arrived."

"I may have dozed off," admitted the old lady, a trifle ruefully. "It is a fault of my age. But," she added, hiding embarrassment behind a stern tone, "you do not answer. You two have loved each other forever and yet you, Miss Althea, will not admit it. Why?"

Tension stiffened Althea's spine. Her shoulders and hands ached with it. "You ask exceedingly impertinent questions, my lady."

Elf chuckled. "Impertinence is a *privilege* of age, my dear. The faults of age are many, and the privileges few, so I cherish those I have. Come now," she coaxed. "Admit it. You love him."

"I love the man he could be. Not the man he is."

"Are you so very certain you know the man he is?"

"Everyone knows."

"Oh, no. Everyone knows the tales told of him. Very few of those tales are based on more than the desire to be thought in-the-know and those that are based in fact have become exaggerated. As he said. I do not accept that you are such a one who takes in all gossip and spews it out again with nary a thought to whether it may or may not be true."

"I abhor gossip."

"Yet you have listened, have you not, to each and every word spoken of Sir Valerian?"

Althea hesitated. Had she been so unfair? Had she judged him solely by what was said of him? *Yes she had.* She found she could not sit still, and rose to her feet. She moved away and then returned. "Lady Elfreda, how else may I judge him?"

"You might allow him to talk to you, ask him questions."

"How can I trust him to the point we may indulge such conversation? *He is a rake.*"

"He *was* a rake. In his grass time. Later, as he he matured, he took a mistress and maintained her—as do many unmarried men. Those who can afford such! His mistress was given her *congé* three or four years ago." Elf tipped her head. "But you do not believe me. When you *know* I've a reputation for hearing everything worth hearing?"

Althea managed to reseat herself but only because she used every ounce of will power to contain her agitation.

"I like the boy," continued Lady Elf. "Miss Bronsen, I assure you, he has had nothing to do with the muslin company for years. Can you tell me why a man, used to his comfort, has abstained from that most comforting of all relationships for four long years?" Her ladyship, scrupulously honest, amended that. "Three, at the least?"

Althea felt as if she were bright red from her toes to the top of her head. "You speak of things about which I can know nothing."

"Bah. Your mealy-mouthed generation isn't worth tuppence." Lady Elfreda crossed her arms and glared. The glare faded as the door once again opened and, this time, Clair walked in.

"Oh dear. Guests here and no one to greet you? I am sorry that my toilet was delayed."

"Your husband home early, hmm?" asked Elfreda, irritable because her lecture to Althea seemed to have fallen on fallow ground.

Althea, her own blush fading, was almost glad to see color rising up her friend's neck and into her ears.

Clair, already standing with a properly straight spine, seemed to grow taller. "My lady, you are impertinent."

Elf harrumphed. "Mealy-mouthed I said and mealy-mouthed I meant. Each and every one of you." She struggled to her feet and returned to the high-backed chair in which she'd been sitting when Althea arrived. Settling herself, she appeared to drift off to sleep once again.

Althea, watching her, was not certain she was asleep, but Clair seemed to have no such thoughts. "The old witch," she said softly. "How can she have known? I am *so* embarrassed." She gasped. "Oh dear. I should not have said that."

"That you are embarrassed?" asked Althea, smiling.

"No, of course not. That bit about her knowing. I shouldn't speak of such things. Not to you. You are not married."

Althea swallowed a laugh and, after another glance toward the old lady, said, "But my dear, who was it explained to you what you were to expect in your marriage bed? And how you should behave?"

That conversation had been based on what Granny had taught her. Despite Granny's assurance that, the experience was pleasurable, she still wondered how anything so embarrassing could possibly be pleasurable. In any case, she had passed on information that Granny insisted should be known by every new bride.

Clair was silent for a long moment. "Althea, may I ask a very personal question?"

"Of course. I can always refuse to answer, can I not?"

"How did you know?"

Althea chuckled. "I had an excellent source for such information. Old Granny taught me a great deal my governess would have thought unsuitable for the ears of a young girl." *It isn't as if I really know*, she thought. *It does sound the most embarrassing of situations in which to find oneself.*

"Granny?" asked Clair after a moment. "That witch who lived by the stream through your woods?"

"I spent many a rainy afternoon with her when I was supposed to be shut in my room thinking over my faults. I suspect I deliberately courted that particular punishment as often as I dared."

"But if you were locked in your room . . . ?"

"Everyone has forgotten the old servants' stairs hidden in

the wall, Clair. I left the house whenever I wished with no one the wiser. Sometimes in the middle of the night I'd rise and visit Granny."

"I don't know how you dared. A witch, after all."

"Granny was no more a witch than I am. Merely a very wise old woman to whom secrets had been passed, from mother to child, to the next, each generation learning a bit more, each adding a bit to the healing lore."

"But Granny had no child."

"Oh, but she had three. Her son was pressed and taken to sea and never seen again. Her older daughter died in childbed and her younger—" Sadness enveloped Althea for a moment. "—her younger worked at her side during a cholera outbreak long before I was born. She caught the disease. She too died."

"Did she . . . did Granny teach you other things than . . . than . . ."

"Than how a woman should be womanly for her husband?" Although she spoke lightly, Althea gritted her teeth. It was not a subject about which she could think without a certain agitation.

"Yes," said Clair, curious.

"Oh, yes. Many things. None of them, however, of much interest to you, I am sure."

"You mean her potions for the croup and that sort of thing," said Clair wisely.

"Exactly," said Althea, thinking of lessons in midwifery and certain potions about which she wished she had never heard—even if they did make life easier when there were more mouths to feed than a poor family could support.

The dowager, her son, and Sir Val entered the room and Lady Elfreda "woke up," returning to a place near the fire. Conversation became general—mostly concerning the late war and Jason's fears for its renewal. When they moved to the table, the dowager insisted they discuss more pleasurable topics and the talk veered toward gossip—the Regent's doings, for instance—and to a proposed race between two noted whips.

Concerning the latter subject, Lord Lambert said, "Val, you should enter your new team. They've a turn of speed I've not often seen and you told me of their remarkable stamina, which is often more necessary than mere speed when one races."

"My racing days are done, Jason. I sold my racing curricle."

"You didn't! Why, it was built to your design, Val."

"It was a good design, but better will come out of other heads. Tell me," he said, turning the subject, "about this meeting you will attend next week. The one to be held somewhere in Oxfordshire.

"How the devil did you learn of that?" asked Jason, half starting from his seat.

Val frowned. "It is the talk of the city. Should it not be?"

Jason shook his head in despair. "No. It should *not*. It is the most secret of meetings. Or was supposed to be."

"Word has been on the streets for more than a week, Jason," said Val quietly.

"So we have another in our midst who cannot keep his mouth shut. It is a wonder that we ever manage to keep any information from the enemy."

Lady Elfreda harrumphed, drawing the men's attention. "Recently took on Sumpter's pup, did they not? At the Horse Guards?"

"Yes," said Jason, his eyebrows rising.

"Get rid of him," said her ladyship and turned back her attention to her slice of roast fowl. "Excellent cook, Lady Lambert. I congratulate you on ridding yourself of that harridan that ruled your predecessor's kitchen—" She cast a quick look toward the dowager who stiffened at the insult. "—and on the courage it took to send her on her way."

Clair flushed. "Not courage. Ignorance. I didn't *know* she was dangerous. Poor woman," she added. "Although I understand she is quite happy in her new, er, home, ruling the kitchens there as she used to do here."

"So she should be. Happy, I mean," said Lord Lambert, a rueful smile lighting his eyes as he gazed fondly upon his wife. "Keeping her in food for the inhabitants of that place is costing me the earth. You, my dear, will ruin me with your charitable heart."

"But we have so much," said the young Lady Lambert earnestly. "Surely you do not begrudge . . ."

"No," said Jason. "I don't begrudge a penny of it. After all, it was seeing you buy a meat pie for that beggar child and watching that she ate it that opened up my heart to you at my very first sight of you."

"*Did* you see that?" asked Althea, drawing attention from Clair's rosy complexion. "My poor mother didn't know where to look and when Clair returned to our carriage and told Mother that it really did no good to give such children money since an older child or even some adult would only take it from them, but giving them something to eat, then you knew you had, for that day, helped."

Lady Elfreda cackled. "Your poor mother!"

Althea cast an amused look at her ladyship. "I see you know exactly how it was. But do you know what happened? I have, since then, seen Mother give fruit to several children. Clair is good for us. She reminds us that although charity is right and proper, it should also be practical."

"Like your school," said Lady Elf slyly while looking at Val.

"School? I haven't a notion what you mean," said Val blandly.

"Secret is it? Afraid it might polish your tarnished reputation if it were known you founded and support a school for poor lads?"

"Elf—" Val frowned. "—we will have a falling out if you are not careful."

"So cross you sound! I shake in my little shoes," said Elf, her voice dry.

Val glanced at Althea who was frowning at him. He sighed. "Why is it so difficult to keep secrets in this town?"

"Then it is *true*?" asked Althea softly.

His lips compressed and there was a slightly strained look about his eyes. "It is not something of which I speak."

"But it exists. You support this school, which you founded."

It was not a question and Althea's expression gave away nothing of her thoughts. Val could only hope they were turned in a direction he wished them to go—or at least that she looked over her shoulder in that direction. If not, he'd be doubly angry that Elfreda had revealed something he'd thought a very private thing indeed.

CHAPTER 6

Almack's that particular evening was more crowded than usual. Althea thought it to be expected. After all, she had arrived in a party that included the *ton*'s most notorious rake, so *of course* the whole world was there to see it and comment.

Worse yet, Lady Jersey gave her that look that meant she had concocted a complete drama in her head and was considering with whom she might discuss the interesting possibilities—which conversation would be repeated and repeated again and would, by the time it was repeated for the third time no longer be mere speculation, but a fact. It would be said that the *ton* must expect an interesting announcement in the near future. Althea sighed.

"We might confound them all by having the announcement inserted in tomorrow's papers. You only need say the word," said Val in her ear.

"You cannot have read my mind."

"Can I not?" He looked thoughtful for a moment. "Too late to complain, my dear. I have known how to manage that trick ever since that never-to-be-forgo—"

Althea walked off and heard him chuckle softly. She was

too angry to blush although she'd not be at all surprised to learn that her skin was flushed by temper. How dare he embarrass her so in public? Come to that, how dare he embarrass her at all? She smiled a small rueful smile that she hid behind her fan. Sir Valerian Underwood would dare anything.

A long-time friend approached and asked if she was free to join the next set. She agreed, happy to have her thoughts distracted—and then found his first question anything but helpful.

"I see Sir Valerian is with Lord Lambert this evening. Do you know if he too will join the forthcoming working party I have heard is to meet somewhere in Oxfordshire? I know he has added to such business occasionally, although I understand he doesn't like his participation known."

Althea was about to ask her friend to change the subject when a question of her own arose. "Where did you hear of that meeting, Denton?"

"Hear of it? I don't know . . . yes I do. I believe Lambert's heir was asking questions about it, wanting to understand how things are done, don't you know?"

"I wonder where *he* heard of it . . ."

"From Lambert, I would suppose." He was jostled slightly by a couple leaving the dance floor. "Ah! This set has finished. Shall we take our places for the next?"

Althea realized she was about to say something that would rouse Denton to curiosity—if she had not already done so—and was relieved she'd been prevented from being still more indiscreet. She took his arm and walked out onto the floor for the set. When it was over, she returned to the dowager's side and managed to say all that was proper to her partner and dismiss him before Lord Lambert led his wife up to join his mother and Althea.

"A word with you, Lord Lambert," she said softly when the dowager demanded Clair tell her all about an unknown young lady sitting demurely beside an old friend. Althea told Jason of her conversation with Denton and he frowned.

"I have never discussed politics with Emerson. I wonder how he discovered it . . ."

"My lord, did Clair ever mention that some of her letters have gone astray? She should have received one from me shortly before Mother and I returned to London and she was all but accused of lying when she told Lady Thomilson she'd not received one from that lady. I haven't a notion if there were others."

"You think Andover had a hand in it?" Lord Lambert's lips formed a hard line. "Clair didn't mention it, but she would not have thought it important. I begin to think Val correct in his distressing notion that something is very wrong and that my cousin is, very likely, at the core of it. I will have Jimson take greater care to see that Emerson Andover does not make himself free with my study or lay sticky fingers on the post."

Lambert's eyes followed his laughing wife as she went down the next set. The couple reached their place and Clair said something. Not only her partner chuckled, but also those beside them. Althea wondered what had roused such humor.

Althea glanced around and stiffened. "Speak of the devil," she murmured.

When Lord Lambert glanced down at her, she pointed behind her fan. Lambert moved in a slow circle, taking in the whole of the room as he did so—including, part way around, a newly arrived group standing just within the entrance. Emerson Andover laughed with the brother of one of the *ton*'s most courted heiresses.

"The devil indeed," muttered his lordship. "I wonder how he gained an *entrée* to that particular house."

Althea hated gossip, but sometimes it was useful. "Have I heard," she asked, "that that young man is something of a gambler?"

"I believe it is rumored . . ."

"He is," said Sir Valerian from just behind them. "I would guess it was at the baize-covered table that Andover won a *card* of *entrée*." He frowned. "The chit is closely protected in the normal way. How much must the fool have lost that he agreed to introduce Andover to her notice."

"Which means you tried your luck?" asked Althea and was appalled that the question came not from a wish to tease him but from a fierce jealousy.

"You know very well I have not. And *why*," returned Val so calmly that, against her will, she believed him. He turned to Jason. "Should we do something?"

"What can we do? We've no *proof* . . ." Jason's expression grew distinctly worried.

Rather hesitantly, Althea suggested, "Perhaps you could inform her father that inquiries are in progress, checking Mr. Andover's antecedents?"

"I should have thought of that," said Jason, relaxing. "It says nothing but that we are waiting to confirm his claim before making a formal announcement of our relationship. Is it not fortunate that we have not done so?"

Althea thought it more than fortunate but just then a man she disliked accosted her. When he asked for the next dance in the arrogant manner of one conferring a choice treat upon the honored woman, she could not prevent herself from recoiling ever so slightly.

"The lady is promised to me," said Sir Val, responding for her.

"Ah. Perhaps another time," said Lord Bradford. He glanced from Val to Althea and back again. His brow rose, but he said nothing as he strolled languidly on to where one of the stodgier patronesses stood talking to a second very nearly as starched-up lady.

"I wish you had not," murmured Althea.

"You wished to dance the waltz with him?"

"No, but I am perfectly capable of turning a man down and doing so tactfully."

"*That man?*"

Althea felt herself blushing. "He is difficult. I am not above lying if I must."

"Then I saved you from perjury, did I not?" He chuckled. "And I don't regret interfering since it means I shall achieve a goal I have long held dear."

"And that is?"

"To dance the waltz with you, of course."

Althea bit her lip. Since she had not contradicted him when he'd said she was promised to him, she was trapped.

How, she wondered, *could I have allowed it to happen?*

She had always avoided dancing with Sir Valerian. She had not allowed him so much as a country-dance. And now, for no better reason than that the most arrogant bore in London had demanded she dance with him. She had allowed herself to be tricked into standing up with him.

And not merely a *dance*. A *waltz*. Silently, Althea admitted it was something she, too, wanted. Desperately wanted.

That night, all night, Althea waltzed through her dreams in Val's arms. His sleepy gaze held hers, his faintly cynical expression softened in a way she had never before seen. His hold was perfectly proper, his steps light, drawing her around the room as if they had danced together for years. And she had felt protected, warmed by affection, friendship . . . love.

She woke, frightened out of her wits.

"It isn't true," she said out loud to her bedpost.

"What isn't true?" asked Merrily who was laying out her riding habit, moving in the silent way all good dressers know.

"There I go again!"

"Go? Where?" Holding Althea's pert little shako, the hat

worn when riding, Merrily turned. "You *do* mean to ride this morning, do you not?"

"No, no."

Merrily stood arms akimbo, the hat tucked into her fist. "No? No you do not ride or no you . . . you . . ." She frowned. "I forget what I meant to say."

Althea chuckled. "I ride."

"Good." Merrily eyed her mistress. "You are awake early."

"Hmm."

Awake and worried. If she had loved Sir Valerian before that waltz, she now loved him ten times more. But it was all wrong. He was a practiced rake. Of course he knew how to make a woman melt at his feet, crave his every touch and . . .

". . . and why," she muttered, another thought breaking through her distraction, "did Denton ask if Val would be going with Lord Lambert to this meeting about which they spoke?"

"I don't know. Who is Denton?"

"Lord Saltwyn." Althea waved her hand, a gesture indicative of the unimportance of his lordship. "Why would anyone think Sir Valerian a part of some very important and supposedly secret government meeting?"

"Because he has done work now and again for the foreign office?"

Althea stared at her maid. "What do you mean?"

Merrily frowned slightly. "You do not know?"

"I do not know. What is it *you* know?"

"More than once, or so says the servants' grapevine, he has uncovered French spies and stopped their work."

Althea's eyes widened. "But that is dangerous!"

"Yes. It is said he was wounded. Maybe more than once."

Althea thought of the scar on the back of his left hand and for the first time wondered if the rumors she'd heard of an infamous duel had begun as speculation and become fact in the re-telling. She sighed. Was she to learn that everything she believed was wrong?

"He is a rake," she said, reminding herself.

"Sir Valerian?" Merrily shrugged. "He is a man."

Althea had no response to that.

"Why are you wondering about Sir Valerian?" asked Merrily.

Relieved she had somehow managed to keep from the one person who was likely to know all her secrets that she was hopelessly in love with Sir Valerian Underwood, Althea scrambled for a believable answer. "He was in the Lambert party last night. I actually waltzed with him!"

"And enjoyed it, too, is my guess!"

"So I did." Althea flipped the covers to one side and climbed out of her old-fashioned high bed. "Is it very early?"

"If you are asking if it is too early for breakfast, I fear it is."

"I will ride first and return for breakfast after," decided Althea. "While I wash, go order up my mare and a groom to escort me."

Merrily swirled away out of the room and Althea glimpsed a touch of lace below her hem. She shook her head. The girl would never save anything for her old age that way, buying such nonsense as lace. And then she remembered she herself had given her maid the lace on the chit's natal day. She hoped her mother's housekeeper did not notice that Merrily wore it during a working day. For Sunday or her day out it might be acceptable, but for everyday? No. The girl faced a reprimand.

But perhaps she will think it worth it . . .

Althea put the maid and her fancy petticoat from her mind as her thoughts returned to Sir Valerian. If Val were working for the government in the dangerous position of spy-catcher, then perhaps his reputation as a rake had been exaggerated, even encouraged, to make him seem less like the sort of man who would do anything of importance. Could that be possible?

And if it is, wondered Althea, *how do I discover the truth of it?*

And then her thoughts came to a screeching halt. "What am I doing? Am I *trying* to find reasons why I could give in to my love for him? But even if it is true that he has done these things, falling into his arms, into his bed—" Althea blushed at the images filling her mind. "—is not possible. Not at all possible."

"What isn't possible? Here now! You have not washed!" Merrily closed the door and hurried across the room to the stand. She poured water into the bowl and dipped in the cloth, soaped it, and turned, holding it out to Althea who, all the while giving herself a stern lecture on the nature of rakes, took it and disappeared behind the screen where she made her morning ablutions.

Half an hour later Althea felt her heart leap in her chest at the sight of the two men riding toward her and her groom. Or rather, at seeing *one* of those men. Sir Valerian rode a tall black with one white stocking. He himself sat tall and well back as men tended to ride. He looked as if he and the horse were one and Althea thought of pictures she'd seen of centaurs, their classic physiques revealed to her curious gaze. Would Sir Valerian have such a broad chest? So well formed? Would his arms be hard and rounded with muscle?

Realizing where her thoughts headed, Althea bit her lip. She slowed and found the men doing the same. They came up to one another.

"Good morning, Miss Bronsen," said the man at whom she'd yet to look.

"Good morning, my lord," she said, recognizing the voice. Her blush deepened as she realized she still had not turned to him. She did so. "I have not seen you around town yet this spring. Have you just arrived?"

The social chatter continued for a bit and then Lord

Conners excused himself. "The world will not go away just because I've the opportunity to flirt with a pretty lady." Conners sighed soulfully. "I must attend the First Minister in only fifteen minutes. It is a terrible burden, this necessity to leave your bright self, Miss Bronsen."

"Perhaps we will see each other at the Hartstones' this evening."

His lordship's eyes sparkled. "Ah yes! Do save me the supper dance."

"I fear it is already promised," said Althea. "Perhaps the first waltz?" she suggested daringly.

"I will look forward to it," said Lord Conners sincerely. "Coming, Val?"

Sir Valerian said he would ride with Miss Bronsen and that he would catch up with his lordship later in the day so Conners rode off alone. "Miss Althea," said Val courteously after a brief glance at her groom, "perhaps I should have asked first if you would have me as escort."

"Of course I will. You are my dearest friend's cousin. Why would I not ride with you?" She knew at once it was a stupid question and, biting her lip, tipped a glance his way.

CHAPTER 7

Val quirked a brow but refrained from teasing her. Instead, he said, "You are out early this morning."

She closed her eyes for an instant, realizing how she had feared his response to her provocative comment and, still worse, *how disappointed* that he had not taken the opening given him. "Yes," she said. "I could not sleep. Sir Valerian," she said, taking a big breath, "someone told me you have been involved in spy catching for the government. Why is something so much to your credit a secret?"

Val scowled. "Someone has a big mouth. I hope word hasn't spread far and wide."

"I don't understand."

"Of course you do. Of what use would I be if every French sympathizer knew I was on the side of the angels?"

Althea nodded. "When you point it out, it is obvious. Worse, it is known. My maid heard it on the servants' grapevine." She heard him swearing softly. "But . . ."

Drawing in a deep breath he asked, "But?"

"Surely it is no longer important. The war is over."

"Is it?"

Althea pulled up.

Val did the same and turned his mount so that they faced each other. "My dear, surely Clair has told you there is reason to believe that Napoleon plots to leave Elba and return to France?"

"She has . . . suggested something of the sort."

"She hinted did she?" Val grimaced. "Ah well, you are her dearest friend. As to Napoleon, if he has not already landed, he will soon."

"It is that certain?"

"It is."

She stared at him. "I see. And your reputation. It is of advantage to such work?"

"It *was*." He grimaced. "I hoped you had forgotten where this discussion began."

"I could not forget."

His expression softened. "My dear, will you not accept that I am no longer that silly lad who was accused of misdeeds perpetrated by another? A ridiculous boy too proud to deny the charges, convinced no one could possibly believe such things of him? And then, when it *was* believed, decided to show the world that if it would believe the worst for no reason, he'd *give* them reason?" He drew in a deep breath. "Althea, I grew up. I am no longer that fool, thumbing his nose at the world. It is years since I was so immature. A fair number of years before I fell in love with you, actually," he finished almost as an afterthought.

Althea hung her head. "I wish to believe you."

"But you do not." He sighed.

She hesitated. Did she? No. Not entirely. He was a rake. Rakes had to be plausible. "No."

"Is there nothing I can do to prove to you that I am yours and yours alone?"

The sound of approaching hooves drew their attention.

"Ah," he exclaimed, obviously irritated. "My love, this is neither the time nor the place for this conversation, but do not think it ended. Good morning," he called to approaching friends. He lifted his hat to Althea, said that they'd meet again that evening and, at the firm hand on his reins, his gelding reared and turned in one smooth movement. He cantered off to join the men that had just passed by with waves and a few mildly ribald comments.

Althea smiled a wistful smile. "No longer a lad?" she murmured. "But that was a very boyish trick, was it not?"

Emerson Andover stood down a side path. Very nearly hidden, he had watched the scene between Miss Bronsen and Sir Valerian. Andover had searched for, but found no weakness in the baronet, a man he believed to be his enemy. But Sir Valerian was in love with Miss Bronsen. Deeply in love.

He had found a lever that would pry the baronet off his back.

Emerson constructed the final turn in the maze of his latest plot to rid himself of his cousin's wife. Once the chit was ruined he could take the *next* step and rid himself of his fine lordship. Once Lambert was forced to cast off his beloved wife, no one would suspect his "suicide" was really murder. Not when it had been noticed by one and all how downcast, how unhappy his lordship was that his marriage was in shambles.

There must be no suspicion whatsoever that the current Lord Lambert died by anything but his own hand. Unfortunately, his cousin's character was such it would require great motivation for his suicide to be believed. Andover worried that it was taking far too long to give his lordship the need to leave this life.

And—Andover frowned—it was Sir Valerian Underwood's interference that upset so many well-laid plans.

But not this time.

* * *

"Yes, I mean to hire a box and have great hopes that you and my cousin will join my party." Andover hid a sour smile at Clair's hesitation. "I mean to ask Lady Bronsen and your friend, Miss Bronsen, as well," he added before she could deny him on the grounds that Lord Lambert would be from home. He felt satisfaction when she relaxed at hearing the Bronsens would accompany them.

"Mother Lambert? Would you enjoy an evening at the theater?" Clair turned toward her *belle-mère*, her brows arched.

"You forget, my dear, that that is my evening among my oldest friends. Now if Mr. Andover would change the night . . .?"

Andover adopted a chagrined expression. "I fear it was the only night on which I could hire the box. It is a particularly popular play and newly mounted. I do not wish to postpone the date, perhaps for weeks . . . ?"

The dowager Lady Lambert bit her lip. Her monthly visit with the handful of friends remaining from her youth was important to her. The idea of denying herself was repugnant. She glanced at her husband's cousin. "The Bronsens are to attend?" she asked.

"I have not yet invited them but mean to do so once I've your agreement. It is, after all, a sort of thank-you for all you have done to ease my way into a *milieu* utterly foreign to me."

The dowager relaxed. "I see nothing wrong with your attending Clair, assuming, of course, that Lady Bronsen is among the guests to act as chaperone. If she and Althea *cannot* join the party, then I think you, too, must refuse."

Andover rose to his feet. "So-be-it. I will go immediately to see if they are free." He made his adieus and departed.

Emerson Andover rounded the corner into North Audley Street just as Sir Valerian was admitted to the Bronsen's house. His step faltered but then he shrugged. Sir Valerian would know of the invitation soon enough. He might as well know immediately.

Emerson made himself agreeable to Lady Bronsen, but, surreptitiously, watched Sir Valerian and Miss Bronsen as they conferred over the lady's needlework. When they finished and moved back into the circle of chairs near her ladyship, he cleared his throat.

"I have come with an invitation," he began and explained about the theater box and his desire to thank his cousin and his family for all they'd done for him. "I hope that you, my lady, and your daughter will join the party. You too, of course," he added with a glance toward Val.

"You know, of course," said Val, "that Jason is away from London? I also believe it is the evening the dowager saves for her monthly *tête-à-tête* with her bosom bows."

"Unfortunately," said Andover smoothly, "it is the only evening in the near future when I can rent a box and I would not dream of asking a party to sit elsewhere." He turned back to Lady Bronsen. "I believe I heard that it is a play you are particularly interested in viewing?"

"It is," said her ladyship, nodding. "Althea? Did you not also express a wish to see it?"

Althea hesitated but only briefly. If she and her mother joined Clair, and if Val were to be of the party, what possible danger could there be? "I would like to see it," she said.

"That is settled then," said Andover, smiling broadly.

"Sir Valerian?" asked Althea, turning to him. "You will join us, will you not?"

"Much to my regret, I've accepted another invitation for that particular evening." Val spoke with the faintest of sneers. His tone implied he did not so much have another invitation as that he would not accept one from Emerson Andover. The insult was perceived and, as intended, stung Andover into indiscretion.

"You mean to attend the Cyprian's Ball, of course," said Andover, his eyes narrowed, burning into Val's. He turned quickly when his words elicited a gasp from Lady Bronsen.

"I have not attended that particular function for some

years now," responded Val calmly, but that ever so faint sneer doubled. "Allow me," he continued, his voice silken, "to give you a hint. This is not a subject with which a gentleman sullies a lady's ears."

"Ah," responded Emerson quickly. "Another of the many traps for the feet of the unwary," he added, seemingly contrite.

"It is, perhaps, a topic you would discuss before the women you know in our colony across the water?" asked Althea innocently. "The *decent* women?"

For the first time in a great many years Andover felt heat in his neck. "No, of course not. I apologize," he said, biting off his words as if they were vinegar in his mouth. He bowed first to Lady Bronsen and then to Althea. "Do forgive me."

"Of course."

"Well." A muscle jumped in his jaw and he looked from one to another. Val's look of contempt turned dislike into hate. He thought of his most recent plan and decided here was another reason for carrying it through. As if he needed more reason.

Hiding his feelings, he bowed again, first to one woman and then to the other. "I will return to my cousin's house and inform Lady Clair you have joined my party," he said, bowed once again, and left the room.

CHAPTER 8

Althea waited until the door was firmly closed behind Emerson before she strolled with Val to the pianoforte where she said she had new music to show him.

"Sir Valerian," she said, "I admit I only agreed to go because I assumed you would join us. Do you think we'll be safe?"

Val hesitated. "My dear, I suspect our man has some scheme in mind. I do *not* think it entirely safe. Because of that, I must be free to save you if, or should I say *when*, it becomes necessary."

"What can he have planned?"

"If I knew that . . ." Val shook his head and sighed. "You must believe I'll not allow you to be harmed. I can say no more than that."

"I wish Lord Lambert had not left London for that meeting," fretted Althea.

"I notice," said Val, adopting a lighter note, "that you do not refer to it as a secret meeting."

"When something is known from one end of London to the other, one cannot call it secret," she said, bitingly.

He chuckled. "Very true. My dear, I will not be far from you on the evening. I'll have done everything I can to counteract any plan the man has made. Do you trust me?"

"In this, yes."

He smiled, but there was a sad look in his eyes. "I must, I suppose, be satisfied with that."

She nodded.

"For now," he added and was given a view of her shock when her eyes rose to meet his gaze.

His faintly sardonic smile, the promise in his sleepy gaze, his seeming assurance that, one day, she would give him all he wanted from her, automatically stiffened Althea's spine to repulse him. "We will see."

He nodded. "Yes. We will."

She thought he did not mean the exact same thing she'd meant, but forbore continuing what was a fruitless argument. Besides, she was reminded that she now questioned whether he *was* the villain she had always believed him to be.

And if he were not such a villain? Her heart raced with an unexpected sense of excitement . . . which, as she replaced her music on the stand, she firmly repressed. When she said no more, he bowed and returned to Lady Bronsen's side where he said all that was proper and, with only one brief look toward Althea, left the room and the house.

Half an hour later he opened his own door and called, "Loth! I need you." He stalked toward the buffet, swore when he saw no pitcher, and turned sharply. He was halfway across the room when Lothario entered, carrying the despised drink.

"Knew you'd be all in a lather. But—" Loth passed a narrow-eyed look over Sir Valerian. "—that's not why you yelled, is it?" He filled a glass and handed it to Sir Valerian.

"Andover has invited not only my cousin, but Lady and Miss Bronsen to the theater the night of the Cyprian's Ball. I cannot help but make a connection. Still—" He frowned

darkly. "—I cannot, for the life of me, see how he will manage it with Lady Bronsen along for the treat. Not and keep
his part in it secret."

"You want I should hire some bully boys for guard dogs?"

Val sipped and then clinked the glass lightly against his
teeth. "I . . . don't know. Blast it! I wish Jason would realize
his wife's safety is more important than any contribution he
may make to plans for returning an army to the field."

"You don't mean that!" said Loth, scandalized.

Val sighed. "Yes I do. There are many men available for
the work Jason does, but he is Clair's only husband."

"So I should hope!"

Val frowned, thought about what he had just said, and a
bark of laughter escaped him. "Well, yes. One husband is all
that is allowed, is it not?" The frown, which had not totally
faded, returned. "You know what I meant." After a moment
he nodded. Once. "You'd better hire a couple of men. I mean
to follow Andover's carriage from the moment he sets off to
pick up his guests, so I'll be near, but have a man stationed at
each house, just to assure me that nothing unexpected occurs
at their doors. If it does not, and I think it will not, then have
them fall in behind so as to be available when we need them.
You too, of course."

Emerson, a satisfied expression clear in the gaslight from
the lamp hanging beside the Bronsen's front door, climbed
into the carriage after assisting her ladyship and her daughter into it. He took his place between Althea and Clair on the
backward facing seat, facing the elder ladies. The dowager
had decided, at Val's urging, to join the party.

Emerson laughed lightly. "I am so pleased we could do
this," he said.

Oh yes. Very pleased.

Even if he suffered a mild beating, one that would leave
his face marked as proof of his innocence, it would be worth

it. His men were well paid to do no more damage than was absolutely necessary, of course.

Ah, but I must not gloat just yet. Not until my plan reaches fruition.

As the carriage moved away from the Bronsen's house he began a droll story from his years in Canada and soon had everyone laughing. He kept them laughing—and their minds off the route taken by his carriage until, suddenly, it pulled to a halt.

The doors on either side opened and masked men reached in, pulling the young women from their seats. Miss Bronsen screamed. Clair, her mouth covered by a rough, disgustingly dirty palm, could not.

Behind her, as she was carried off, Clair heard Emerson's outraged voice, heard the beginnings of a fight, heard Althea scream again and still again and then, suddenly, struggle as she would, she was within doors, the sounds cut off.

"Now my pretty," said a wickedly oily voice in her ear, "let us see what prize we've gained." He set her on her feet but did not release her wrist. "Oh yes. Very pretty indeed. But a smile would make you ever so much nicer. Smile, my pretty. *Smile.*"

Clair opened her mouth and screamed.

The man who had captured her laughed. It was not a nice laugh. "No, no. You must *smile.*" He slapped her.

Val felt a *frisson* climb his spine as Clair was carried off, but, his jaw clenched, he followed the man carrying a squirming and fighting Althea. His love must be saved. He must trust Loth and the men to see that Clair came to no harm.

Shoving through the crowd that laughed and encouraged the villain, Val caught up with them. He clutched the man's shoulder, swinging him around. Althea was dropped. He heard her outraged o-oof from somewhere near his feet, felt her scramble away, but, facing an angry man, dared not look to see if all was well with her.

Suddenly, Val faced a knife, the situation far more dangerous. The crowd, perceiving it, stilled. Althea was helped to her feet. He could hear her urging someone, *anyone* to interfere, to *do* something, but he put even that, her beloved voice, from his mind, concentrating on the man crouched, circling, watching for an opening.

Val's opponent snarled. "Come on, then. Come on, my beauty. We'll see, won't we?" There was something evil in the low-voiced words.

"How much did he pay you to kill me?" asked Val conversationally.

For just an instant the accusation caused the villain to lose his concentration. It was enough. Val caught the man's wrist, twisted, turning the fellow as he did so. He squeezed and the knife dropped. Val kicked it away and Althea picked it up. Holding the man in an inescapable grip, Val glanced around and chanced to see a man who owed him a favor.

"You," he ordered. "take this animal to Bow Street. Tell them I'll be in later to make charges."

Val shoved his captive toward the burly man to whom he'd spoken. The chap caught the captive, got a good grip on him, and doffed his hat. Val nodded.

He turned and his expression softened. "Were you hurt?" he asked, catching and holding Althea's gaze. He noted the white encircling her mouth, the tension holding her rigid. "Everything is fine now. The man cannot hurt you. Come, Miss—" About to use her name, he refrained. "—I will return you to your carriage."

He took her arm and supported her first steps. The crowd parted to allow them to move back to where the carriage still stood, the driver gone and Lady Bronsen's screams still splitting the air. Lady Lambert stood on the paving dabbing at Andover's eye, a sour expression on her face but her spine rigid.

"You might have been killed," breathed Althea before they reached the others.

"It didn't happen. Forget it," he said.

"He meant to *kill* you," she insisted.

"Perhaps. *It didn't happen*," he repeated.

"But if he tried once—"

Val realized Althea was not referring to the man with the knife, but to Emerson Andover.

"—will he not try again?"

"I am alerted to the danger. I won't be caught by any tricks our friend may try."

"Please . . ."

"Please don't mouth platitudes? My dear," he said softly, "I have too much living to do to allow a rat, any rat, to shorten it by one second. I promise you."

Althea glared at him and he chuckled.

"You cannot make such a promise," she said. "You cannot know."

He sobered. "You will not be jollied out of your moroseness. Perhaps it is as well. You must face the villain and not give away that we know he is one. No, Althea, you must allow me to know best. And I've no time to argue. Loth went after Clair, but—" Val had been scanning the scene before them. "—they have not returned. I must go discover what happened."

Inside, the slap swung Clair's head to the side. It wasn't a particularly vicious slap, but it stung. Unused to such treatment, shock stilled Clair.

"That's better, my pretty," he said in a satisfied tone. "Now show a man your smile."

Clair, her eyes wide with fear, made a sudden twist to her wrist that hurt far worse then the slap had. But, by it, she freed herself. She ran, ducking in and out among the revelers. Unfortunately, she hadn't a notion where she was or where to go and the noisy throng, clad in fancy dress or dominos, confused her.

Because she was small and could slide through the crowd, she achieved her first goal, that of eluding her captor.

But that was only her first problem. To escape altogether was a pressing predicament. Realizing she must not be recognized, she pulled pins from her hair and let it fall around her face, the only way she knew to hide herself and, as she did so, she reached a wall. She slithered along it behind men's backs, frantically searching for a door to the outside, to a hall, someplace where she would be free of the hectic noise, the nauseating mixture of smells that included too-cheap perfumes mixed with the terrifying odors of unwashed bodies and foul breath.

Twice she freed herself from clutching hands. Twice she continued onward, unknowing of where she was or where she was going, but moving, moving, hoping that somehow she'd escape the nightmare in which she found herself.

And then, suddenly, she was confronted by a masked man who clutched at both her arms. "What the devil are *you* doing here?"

Even through her terror she felt she knew that voice. "I don't know. I was pulled from our carriage and carried inside. I escaped that man, but now . . . I am so frightened. If you know me, then please, please, take me home." Clair blinked rapidly, fighting to keep the tears from falling.

"Pulled from your carriage!"

"Yes. Oh dear. So was Miss . . . my friend." Clair, somehow, knew she should not name names. Whatever was happening to her, to Althea, it could not be good. So, if there was any chance of retaining a stitch of reputation, then names should not be mentioned. "My friend! Oh good heavens! What is happening to her? What *is* this place? Where are we?"

The almost-stranger barked a laugh. "The Cyprian's Ball, that's where. And it isn't a place such as you belong. Damn.

Look, if I take you away, will you refrain from telling anyone you saw me here?"

"The Cyprian's Ball! Oh dear, it is worse than I thought."

"You won't reveal my presence, then?" he asked even more insistently.

"Since," she said bitingly, "I've no desire to have it known *I* was here, then I surely won't talk about *your* presence!"

"There's that," he conceded. "No, go away. I found her first!" he said to another man. As he spoke, he turned her so her face was toward the wall near which they stood.

The drunken man didn't wish to go away, however, and Clair realized this was someone else she should know. Neither man was a close acquaintance and both were men she had thought to be upright and honorable, so she couldn't understand why either of them was to be found at an entertainment such as this.

"Want a dance," insisted the sot, his voice slurred and an inane smile on his face. He bowed . . . and nearly fell on his face.

Clair desperately hoped he'd not remember any of this on the morrow. "Please," she said quietly to the first man. "Take me out of this."

"Want a dance," insisted the drunk, reaching for her . . . but he was suddenly lifted off his feet and set down facing another woman entirely.

In his place stood Val. "You, my child, should be put on leading reins. Thank you, Hawick. I'll take her home. I saw it, you know. Jason's cousin had invited a party to the theater. The driver had been replaced and he stopped outside." As he spoke he draped a domino around Clair, shrouding her from others' eyes. "Rogues opened the carriage doors on both sides and pulled the ladies out and brought them in. Your friend is on her way home, my dear," he said to Clair. "And so are you. Goodnight, Hawick."

As he led her away, she heard the drunk pleading with still another woman for a dance.

"I heard a fight," said Clair in a low voice. "Was Emerson badly hurt?"

"He'll have a black eye, but the look of satisfaction on his face when I brought our friend back to the carriage was one I'll not forget in a hurry. He *paid* for that black eye, Clair, along with everything else. I don't know how I'll prove it, though."

Val thought of the man his acquaintance had taken off to Bow Street. With any luck they would get the truth from him, but it was not impossible the villain would keep mum.

"Will my reputation be ruined, do you think?" asked Clair in a small voice.

"I doubt it. You haven't been inside long and you had the good sense to let your hair down so that it hid your face pretty well. I'd suggest, however, that you get rid of that really delightful gown. Someone might be sober enough to remember seeing *it* even if they didn't recognize *you*. If they see it at a proper ball, they might guess who wore it here."

They reached the doors and Val gave a shrill whistle that he repeated twice more. His carriage arrived and, after making certain that it was *his* driver on the box, Val bundled Clair inside. He closed the door, caught the step, and climbed up to the driver's seat as the rig pulled into the heavy traffic that always clogged these streets but was worse on a night such as this.

It wouldn't do for someone to see him *inside* a closed carriage alone with Clair. Saving her from one disaster only to be the cause of another would be outside of enough. So Val took the reins, to excuse his being on the box. He'd be seen. If someone recognized Clair, at least no one could pretend *he'd* been inside.

They arrived back at Lambert house to find Emerson in the salon going over and over with Lady Lambert just how it had happened that they had lost Clair and Althea. Jimson was painting arnica around his eye as they entered and finished in time to look up.

Clair was surprised to see her husband's butler relax at sight of her and that a look of satisfaction crossed his face before he composed it to his usual disdainful expression. She had thought he disliked her and was surprised to discover, if she could believe that look, that he'd been worried about her.

"Ah, my dear. We were about to mount a rescue," drawled Lady Lambert. "I am very glad that you happened to meet up with Sir Val. It is so distressing to find oneself without transport when one wishes to return home. I believe we will dispense with your presence, Mr. Andover. My son's wife looks a trifle haggard with her hair undone that way. She will not care to be in company in that condition. Jimson, I believe we need a tea tray. Or perhaps we require something a trifle stronger. The sherry and a bottle of good brandy, do you think?"

Jimson nodded and strode in stately fashion to the door—which he held open with an inquiring look at Emerson Andover who had said not one word from the moment Clair and Sir Val entered the room. Now he bowed a quick, almost insulting bow, and his lips still locked in a down-turning arc, he left.

"As soon as you have repaired the damage, Clair, Sir Valerian will escort us to the Morningsides' ball," said the dowager. She spoke in a tone that would not be denied. "It would be well for you to be seen elsewhere *and at once*," she added, her eyes narrowed. "While you are above stairs repairing the damage, Sir Val will tell me the tale and we will decide how much we must fear exposure—and what we will do about it."

"Val?"

"Lady Lambert is correct, my dear. Go fix your hair. Quickly. *And remember to change that gown!*"

"I most definitely will. I never want to see it again."

Lady Lambert cast the gown a look of regret—it was one of the Paris creations—but she didn't ask why Clair wished to be rid of it. "Don't give it to your maid, Clair," she warned. "We'll send it out in the ragbag. Someone will be very pleased to find such a windfall."

"No," said Val. "Bundle it up and give it to me. I know just who should have it—and who will wear it late this evening. She has—to a trifling degree—the look of you. I will take you and Lady Lambert to the ball, stop long enough for one, at most two, dances, and then deliver the dress with the, er, lady wearing it, to the Cyprian's Ball. If she and I are seen there we should slide through this whole escapade with no harm done."

Lady Lambert laughed. "You, Sir Val, are a complete hand. *Lady*, indeed. We know what sort of lady you mean, sir. We are not fooled."

Jimson, entering just then with his tray, relaxed still more. If her ladyship could laugh like that, then it was unlikely anything really dreadful had happened. Nevertheless, he was glad it was he himself who waited on her ladyship and Lord Lambert's heir when they arrived. It would not do for the footmen to have overheard Mr. Andover's prattling. It was too good a tale for any but a man as loyal to the family as he was himself to refrain from passing it on over an evening's stout or heavy wet.

Althea's mother had reached the same conclusion that the dowager reached and, despite Althea's objections, insisted they attend the Morningside ball. Now, seeing the Lambert party arrive, seeing Sir Val in attendance, Althea backed farther into the draperies against which she'd pressed when a jesting group of young men passed too near her.

No matter that it was not her fault, she'd found herself in a situation from which she needed rescuing. No matter that Sir Valerian had been on hand to rescue her. The Cyprian's Ball, for Heaven's sake! Utterly outrageous and very possibly ruinous. If it were *not* she must lay that fact at the feet of the *ton*'s best-known rake.

She could not face him. *It is*, thought Althea, moving

completely into the shallow alcove behind the draperies, *too utterly embarrassing for words*.

Sir Val, who had seen Althea standing before the window, paused near it, and frowning ever so slightly, looked around. Where had she gone? Unhappy to have missed her, he ducked his head to hide his expression. And smiled. The toes of her little pink slippers peeked from under the drapery.

What is the woman doing, hiding behind the curtains? he wondered.

"Val!"

Swearing under his breath, Val turned from the alcove, which he'd meant to investigate. "Bertie," he said in terse greeting.

"Saw you earlier this evening," said the man, leering.

"I missed you," responded Val, and refrained from adding, "deliberately."

"Nice little armful you had in tow," said the man suggestively.

"Was it?"

"Not that I could see much of her. Had her bundled up against all eyes, didn't you? Found a new little bird of Paradise and didn't want anyone else cutting you out?"

"Such a bright fellow you are," murmured Val.

"Ha! Thought so. Also thought you swore you were done with the Cyprian's Ball. Come to think of it, *haven't* seen you there. Not for years."

"Half a dozen, I'd think. Perhaps more."

"That long? We miss you," said the man and there was something of a wistful note in his tone. "Seems like you always made things more exciting, Val." He continued thoughtfully. "You added . . . I don't know . . . a . . . a . . . what's that Frenchified word? Fill-up?"

"*Fillip*?"

"That's it. Fill-ip. Didn't stay long enough this year to add any fillips," he added accusingly.

"I'd not have been there at all except . . ." Val realized he didn't wish to complete that thought and could think of no way of smoothing over what he'd almost allowed out of his mouth.

"Except you wanted to collect that little lady bird," said the man and laughed. "Glad to see it," he added, his tone obviously sincere. "*Very* glad. Thought you'd reformed entirely, you see, and was sorry for it. Happy to find you are still one of us."

Val winced. *One of them*? Was he ever "one of them"? He hoped not.

"Ah! There's that youngest Thomilson chit. Think I'll just go see if she's a dance left." He slapped Val on the shoulder and walked away.

"Did you hear enough?" asked Val, stepping nearer the curtains, his back to them. "Or do you wish an explanation for anything overheard? I want no misunderstandings or false interpretations. The sweet little armful, for instance, was our mutual friend."

"I knew that," he heard the folds of heavy damask muffling the words. The curtain moved and Althea appeared. "How did you know I was there?"

"Your shoes. The pansies embroidered on the toes gave you away."

She looked down but, of course, her skirts hid her toes. She glanced at the curtain. "I suppose it pressed my gown against me so the toes peeked out?"

"I suppose it did. Why did you hide?"

She sighed. "Embarrassment."

"Does that make sense?"

"Probably not," she admitted. "Except to me."

He chuckled softly but soon sobered. "That fiasco was not your fault. I have yet to check on the man I sent to Bow Street," he added pensively, "and I have a dress of Clair's to deliver to an acquaintance of mine. There is still much to do tonight, so I cannot stay but a moment."

"Val, Mr. Andover is sporting a black eye. I don't believe I've ever seen more glorious color."

"I rather wonder if he didn't get a trifle more *color* than he requested."

"You suggest he hired someone to . . . to darken his day-lights? Is that correct?"

"Quite correct. On both counts," he finished dryly.

"I cannot believe he'd actually pay someone to hit him."

"Even if it convinced everyone he was innocent of plotting to ruin Clair—and, of course, you, just in case I was *not* hanging around to rescue *you*, while allowing *Clair* to fend for herself?"

"You suggest he expected you to go after me rather than Clair?" Althea cast Val a shocked look.

A muscle jumped in his jaw. "What bothers you the most? That he is aware of my feelings for you or that he used you to assure his plot would not fail?"

"But it did fail," she said, sidestepping his question.

"Yes. But Loth and both men, blast them, lost track of Clair when she escaped her captor. Fortunately, I am tall and managed to catch a glimpse of her. We were lucky."

Althea sighed. "This cannot go on, Val."

"No. I wish I could magically waft my agent across the Atlantic and back with the information we need."

"Will you inform Lord Lambert of this latest debacle?"

"I mean to send a messenger to him despite Clair's demand that I not bother him. She insists that it is all over and not to be thought of again. Is there anything we can do to make that woman understand that she is in serious danger?"

Althea sighed. "I don't think so."

"I feared it."

"It is up to us to keep her safe, is it not?"

"It is. And I believe—" He straightened, staring over the heads of the young women standing between them and the dance floor. "—we must go into action again." He scowled.

"Drat it," she said, staring down the floor at the couple whirling away from them.

"She *promised* . . ."

"Be reasonable, Val. How could she turn him down if he asked for a dance where others could overhear him? What excuse would she use?"

"That she had given away all her dances? That she didn't mean to dance this evening? That she had to go to the ladies' retiring room? I don't know. Althea, go to the doors into the garden and if he tempts her out, join them. I'll guard the main exit."

CHAPTER 9

Val left Althea on the words and moved gracefully among the guests. He disappeared and Althea, silently chiding Clair for a credulous little fool, headed for the French doors into their hosts' garden.

Then, standing near the only exit onto the terrace, Althea berated herself instead. Why had she ducked behind those drapes? What if someone besides Sir Valerian had noticed her toes sticking out? How would she have explained herself?

Horror filled her as she realized she could *not* have explained. Had she even given Val—Sir Valerian!—an explanation? She could not recall. Why could she not put aside her irrational feelings for that rake? The ambivalence! Why could she not discipline her mind and heart?

Why could she not put him from her mind for good and all? Turn to a man she could trust to treat her properly, one who would respect her and, if he did not truly love her, would, at the very least, never embarrass her.

But then, *was* Val such a very bad man? That Bertie . . . he had sounded . . . wistful?

Althea's father had occasionally had her mother in tears.

Even her mild and generous father had taken a mistress once or twice or thrice. Val was neither mild nor—oh yes, he was. *No one* could say he was not generous.

But he was a *rake*. There'd be no changing him . . . Or was he?

While disparaging herself as a dreamer, Althea scanned the dancers. It was, she realized, some time since she'd last seen Clair. Quickly, she searched as much of the room as she could see, then moved nearer the doors. In case the couple had somehow slipped by her guard, she visually searched the terrace, but saw no one. Nary a soul. No one was taking the air, let alone an illicit pair hiding from hawkeyed parents— or another sort of couple avoiding spouses or the tongues of the *ton*'s gossips.

Once again Althea scanned the dancers in hopes she'd missed the bright yellow flowers adorning Clair's Grecian knot. Nowhere. Not a petal to be seen. She sighed, wondering what she should do now.

"They have gone into the garden?" asked Val urgently.

Althea turned. "I missed them if they did and I don't think I could have. I don't believe anyone has gone in or out. And why would they? When they can enjoy a waltz?" Her brow arched.

He grinned, but the smile faded instantly. "Then where?" As he spoke, he turned on his heel, checking from his greater height. "I walked by Lady Sarah. Clair isn't there."

Althea bit her lip. She had hoped that Clair was at the elder Lady Lambert's side when it appeared the couple had left the floor,.

"Ah!" said Val. "Come."

"What is it?" she asked, trailing his broad back through the crush.

"I think . . . yes! Blast." Sir Valerian continued with a touch of vitriol. "Someone should put that man out of his misery."

He stopped near a closed door where their hostess, one of the *ton*'s most vicious-tongued gossips, wrung her hands in seeming agitation—agitation belied by eyes that flashed with excitement.

"Lady Morningside," purred Sir Valerian, "What appears to be the trouble?"

"That poor young lady! Locked in there! *Alone,* one must hope!"

Not what you hope, thought Althea.

"The key has disappeared," continued their hostess breathlessly.

"Have you sent for another?"

"Sent for . . . ?" Her eyes widened.

Val sighed, a sound that was very nearly a breath of prayer pleading for patience.

Althea noticed that Mr. Andover's eyes glittered in an odd fashion. "Perhaps," she said gently, "you might ask this footman—" She stopped the servant by the simple procedure of touching his arm lightly. "—to find your butler or your housekeeper and ask someone to bring keys?"

Sir Valerian smiled at Althea, turned back to their hostess, and with a brow arched, asked, "Well?"

"Oh! Oh, of *course!*" Lady Morningside gave the order and waited rather breathlessly to discover all—whatever the "all" might be.

It was very nearly another quarter hour before the housekeeper arrived and the correct key found on her jangling key ring. The door opened and Val, taller than the rest, looked over Lady Morningside's head. He relaxed. Demure and without a hair out of place, his cousin sat on a *tête-à-tête* on the far side of the room.

Lady Clair set aside the ladies' magazine she perused and rose gracefully to her feet. "Excellent. I feared I might be forced to raise a row in order to free myself." She strolled toward the small crowd that blocked the doorway. "I cannot understand how it happened," she said softly—but Althea saw that her friend was sober behind her social smile. "Did you notice I was lost, Val? I am very glad to be rescued.

Lady Morningside? It has been a delightful party, but I shall call for my carriage and take myself home. I fear I was weak enough to feel just a wee bit of panic when I could not open the door. Althea? You will call in the morning I hope?"

"Of course I will."

"I will escort . . ."

"I will escort my cousin," said Val overriding Andover's offer. "I was about to depart in any case. Come, child. Miss Althea, will you inform Lady Sarah that Clair has returned home?"

"I will."

"You will not forget to call?" asked Clair with just a touch of anxiety. She refused to meet Andover's attempts to catch her eye.

"Of course I will." Althea also kept her eyes from Andover as she turned away and moved into the crowd, glad to escape his cold reptilian gaze.

They had made an enemy tonight. Before this, the villain had merely wondered if Sir Valerian and she were doing their best to play spoilsport. Earlier that evening they had escaped his most vicious plot yet and now, far too quickly, they appeared on a scene where he pretended, for Lady Morningside's benefit, to be worried about Clair. He *must* know they had twigged his game.

Except, wondered Althea, confused by the innocent situation in which they'd found Clair, *just what* is *his game*?

Althea arrived at the Lambert townhouse at an unconscionably early hour the next morning. Even so, Clair was anxiously looking out for her. The young matron took her to the sewing room and, once she saw her guest comfortable, ordered tea.

The tray came and the tea steeped. Clair leaned forward to serve it, the amber-colored liquid streaming into a delicate cup. She passed cup and saucer to Althea and, finally, met her friend's worried gaze.

"Yes," she said, apropos of nothing, her tone morose. "I admit it."

Althea frowned and Clair sighed.

"You were correct," she added, "and I wrong." She drew in a deep breath, let it out, and bit her lip. Then she added, "We will wait for Val before I tell my tale, since I've no desire to tell it twice. Now," she brightened, but her smile was *too* bright and her eyes glittered in a fashion quite unlike her, "do tell me if anything of interest occurred after I departed."

Althea sighed. "Do not come over the great lady with me, my dear. It will not wash. You are upset and, I think, worried."

Clair bit a lip that looked red, as if she'd been gnawing at it. "I do wish Jason were home. I do not like it when he must be gone for days and days."

"He returns by the end of the week at the latest and very likely sooner," said Althea soothingly. "In the meantime you have me and, more important, Sir Valerian to keep you safe."

"I thought," said Clair rather wonderingly, "that you did not like Val."

Althea felt her jaw tighten and forced herself to relax. She sipped tea before answering. "My dear, I cannot like a great deal of the sort of behavior it is well known that he indulges—"

She recalled that Bertie Horner had hinted that Val—Sir Valerian!—no longer indulged, but put that insidious and possibly misleading memory aside for later consideration.

"—so, it is impossible to consider him someone I can esteem," she said firmly, "but, however that may be, I believe him truly concerned for your welfare—" To Althea's surprise she *did* believe it. "—and capable of seeing to your safety." She had never doubted the last.

Clair tipped her head studying her old friend. "You speak in such a careful way that I wonder what you are hiding."

Sir Valerian, reprehensibly listening from behind the partially open door, wondered the same thing but was not so lost to honor he dare stay to discover it.

Or perhaps, he thought, his cynical side to the fore, *it is that I fear what I'll discover?*

He returned to the hall where Jimson, his nose out of joint, was pretending to sort cards announcing new arrivals in Town. Sending footmen around to friends to drop off the cards in order to announce their arrival was proper form and, the Season now firmly underway, there were many new cards each day.

"I forgot Lady Sarah's demand that I allow you to announce me, Jimson," said Val with an easy smile. "Will you do so, please, or are you too angry with me to oblige me in this?"

Val spoke in a particularly coaxing fashion that could melt even the coldest heart—except perhaps Althea's. The butler, at least, was no exception and hiding his approval that Val admitted his error, turned to "oblige."

Clair rose the instant she heard Val's name and swept across the room, putting her arm through his and drawing him toward the tea table. "I had begun to think you'd forgotten us," she said, casting a teasing look up at him.

He looked down at her and smiled his sleepy smile, which instantly roused jealousy in Althea. She told herself not to be a fool and then forced a smile of her own for Clair's benefit. "You have, as is usual with you, a more than adequate excuse for your lateness, have you not?" she pretended to scold.

"Actually, I do," said Sir Valerian. Seating his cousin behind the tea tray, he took a chair nearer Althea's for himself. "I have been to Bow Street where I sent one of last night's villains. He had an interesting tale to tell."

"Well?" asked the two women in concert when he didn't continue.

"The man we know as Jason's cousin and heir appears to be unwilling to wait patiently for his chance at the title. That is, he doesn't wish to rely on the course of events in the normal way. Andover revealed to my captive, inadvertently I believe, that you, Clair, are a stumbling block but *at the same time* you are his greatest asset."

"Which means?" asked Althea as Clair asked, "What could he possibly mean?"

"I have been searching for a logical answer to that myself. Frankly, I don't know. The stumbling block is, of course, obvious. You might present your husband with a much to be desired token of your affection—as the saying goes. A *male* token. That, of course, is undesirable from Andover's point of view." Val frowned. "But we knew that. What I do not understand is how you are an asset . . ."

The three drank off their tea in silence, each puzzling over any and every possible meaning. Finally Althea shook her head. "It is beyond me. Or perhaps it is merely that it is early in the day and I am never at my best at this hour. Clair, why do you not tell us what happened last night? I do not believe you were locked into an empty room."

Clair seemed to withdraw slightly. "This time Mr. Andover revealed himself for the devil you have said he is." She sighed softly, sadly. "I so dislike believing evil of anyone . . ."

"What particular evil did he have in mind this time?" asked Val, drawing Clair from her thoughts.

She sighed again. "The room was *not* empty. That young devil, Marsham's youngest, was waiting for me. He instantly drew me into his arms and attempted to kiss me. When I objected, he frowned at me. When I continued to object, he drew me to the *tête-à-tête* and seated me and then asked if it were not true that I told Andover that I was secretly enamored of him."

She sighed again.

"So! This time Andover's name is prominent in the plot."

"Yes."

"So . . ."

"Shush," scolded Althea. "Let her tell the story her own way."

Clair grimaced. "First off, the Marsham owes Andover a great deal of money. Money he cannot pay."

"Ah yes. Much easier to cajole someone into agreeing to do wrong if you've a hold over them," said Val, nodding.

Althea and Clair glared at him and he rolled his eyes. "Continue," he said. "I promise I will be good." This time only Althea cast him a *look*. He chuckled. "I *can* be good," he said softly. "When I *want* to be good."

She glowered before turning back to a much-subdued Clair. "Tell us the whole story, Clair. Unless it is too painful?"

The young woman's eyes had a puzzled look to them—and then widened in understanding. "Oh no. Nothing like *that* happened. I told him I loved Jason with all my heart and that I had never ever suggested to Andover I . . . I . . ."

"Yearned?"

Clair nodded. "Yearned for anyone's attentions other than Jason's."

"That cannot be the end of the tale," insisted Val. "*You were alone when that door opened.*"

His words were almost an accusation and Clair's eyes actually twinkled. "Well of course there is more. The Marsham hit his one palm with his other fist—" She demonstrated with her own little hands. "—and said that did it for him. He looked very unhappy but only for a moment and then he shrugged and gave me a jaunty smile and said that if he must leave London ahead of the bailiffs, he'd better be getting on with it and then he walked to the window, opened it, and stepped out onto the sill. He stuck his head back in to suggest I close and lock the window after him and—" She shrugged the pretty Frenchified shrug she'd learned during her recent travels. "—that is all."

"He climbed down the side of the house?" asked Althea, a trifle shocked.

"He must have done. He was gone by the time I managed to overcome my surprise and moved to do his bidding. I looked out before I locked the window and he was nowhere in sight."

Val frowned. "If he owes Andover, it is highly probable he was cheated. That cub has the devil's own luck at cards and there has never been a hint that *he* cheats. He is simply very good, a sensible man who never drinks when he plays, and one who can figure the odds in his head."

"So there is still another thing of which you will accuse Emerson?" asked Clair, her tone sharp. "You will say my husband's cousin not only tells fibs but is a *cardsharp*?"

Althea and Val looked at each other. They both felt astonishment that their friend called Andover's lies to young Marsham concerning her feelings mere fibs.

"Clair," said Althea soothingly, "surely if he is the one thing, you cannot think it improbable he is the other?"

Clair looked exceedingly unhappy. "Why must people do such things?" she asked in almost wailing tones.

Althea pressed her lips together, an understanding look in her eye. "I doubt anyone has the answer to that."

"But what are we to *do*?"

"Do about what?" asked Jason, walking into the room unexpectedly.

Clair once again rose and ran toward the door. Very nearly she could be accused of casting herself onto her husband's chest and, although he looked gratified, he also looked a trifle bemused. When she burst into tears, bemusement veered toward worry.

"What is it?" he asked, looking toward Sir Valerian for the answer.

Briefly Val explained what had occurred the preceding evening, both the attempt to ruin *both* Clair and Althea at the Cyprian's Ball and then, when that failed, the later scheme at the Morningsides' ball. "We were lucky in both cases, but we cannot continue to depend on luck."

Jason looked stern and held Clair still more closely. "No.

It must not be allowed to continue. I will remove Clair from London. If she is gone away, he cannot harm her."

"Gone? I am to go away?" Clair wailed. She pressed far enough away from him she could look up into his face. "But *where* am I to go?"

"*We* are going to the Continent, my dear, and we leave almost immediately." A muscle jumped in his jaw. "Napoleon has arrived in France."

"Oh no! Oh, but surely the French will not welcome him."

"Ney has vowed to bring him to the king in a cage—but I doubt it. Ney was too enamored of his little colonel, as the Emperor was once called. I suspect the French court will be running for its very lives in the not too distant future."

"You foresee more war?"

"Yes. The French army is dissatisfied. Too many half-pay officers gnash at the bit to get back into harness—back to full pay and, of course, the sort of glory they knew in the past."

"So," said Val, "the Commission leaves for the Dutch court. Where will you be housed?"

Jason, still clutching his wife, although he had settled her under one arm, frowned. "Does it matter? Once we've left England?"

Val rolled his eyes in a give-me-patience sort of look. "Yes, Jason. It matters," he said as if speaking to a child. "Surely you do not believe your cousin incapable of following you."

Clair, who had relaxed, tensed up again. "No, no. He must not. I cannot bear it."

"Why not?" asked Val whose patience was nearly at an end. "You have borne it very well for weeks and weeks."

"Val," said Althea, soothingly. "Of course things are different now. Before this, she did not believe us that Andover was a danger to her. Now she knows he is. That makes it different."

Val grimaced, pressing his lips tightly together, a glitter in his eyes that boded no good for someone. "Luckily, we've a means of pulling Andover's fangs. My prisoner at Bow Street. Once he gives evidence before the beak—the *judge*, Althea—" Val inserted the explanation when she seemed about to ask. "—and swears Andover hired him and the others to do that job at the Cyprian's Ball then Andover will be arrested. Jailed. *That* will put him where he can do no more harm."

At the mention of Bow Street, Jason raised his head from where he was pouring soothing words into his wife's ear. "Bow Street? I forgot. This message came just as I arrived." Jason let go of Clair long enough to remove a sealed note from a pocket and hand it over. Then he took his wife back into his clutches almost as if he was afraid to let her go.

Val opened the note and when Althea moved nearer, held it for her to read as well. When he swore, softly but fluently, Jason once again looked up.

"What is it Val?" he asked.

"My prisoner got into a fight with another prisoner. He is dead. Unfortunately it was *before* he'd officially given his evidence against Andover."

Althea was not surprised at Sir Valerian's language. She had an urge to use a few of those words herself.

"Poor man," said Clair.

"Poor man indeed. Andover meant for that man to—" Just in time Val recalled himself and to whom he spoke. He changed a far too blunt word to the less specific. "—to *ruin* Althea. You *cannot* pity him."

"I can't," agreed Althea. "I will never forget the fear I felt—" She caught and held Val's gaze. "—or the faith I had within my heart that you would rescue me."

"Your screams frightened me," he said. A half smile tipped one side of his mouth. "They also surprised me."

"*Of course* I screamed. So you would know where to find me. But I knew that even if I did not you would keep your promise to me."

Val's ears turned bright red. "Well, yes, there was no question but that I'd rescue you if I could. But Althea, did it not occur to you that I might *not*? That I might fail?"

"No."

He closed his eyes, his features a perfect blank. "Thank you," he said softly. "Your faith means a great deal to me—even though I fear it misplaced. No man is infallible."

Then, hearing the door open, they turned toward it.

"Ah. There you are, my son. This came as I was coming down the stairs just this moment." The dowager held out a missive to Lord Lambert. "That is a *very* interesting crest," she said in a coy tone unlike her normal voice.

"Studied it, did you?" asked Jason absently, already reading the floridly written message covering thick laid paper embossed with the royal crest in gold. "My dear—" He looked at his wife. "—can you trust Mother to pack for you and send your trunks on after us?"

"Of course."

"Then go upstairs instantly. I can give you a mere half an hour to put together what you will need until your wardrobe catches us up."

"What can you mean?" demanded the elder Lady Lambert.

"I mean that a carriage drawn by *eight* horses is to collect me and a number of others in half an hour. It will take us to the Royal Yacht for transport across the channel. Our Regent wants us on our way. If you read between the lines," he added more lightly, "I think you will find his majesty is afraid of Napoleon." Jason had removed to the door as he spoke and opened it. "Come Clair. We must pack what we can."

"The royal carriage may be overcrowded," said Val, going with them. "I'll order your travel coach around immediately. You'll need it for your valet and Clair's maid, in any case. If Clair cannot be fitted into the royal carriage, I will attend her to where you take ship and then return to London to see to my own packing," said Val.

"Very good. I had not thought of that."

"I will help you pack," said Althea to Clair, also leaving the room.

Val soon returned from giving orders to Jimson. "Lady Lambert, we must lay plans as soon as we know they are safely on their way. Andover has finally shown his hand. It is barely possible he will give up plotting now he's unmasked, but it is more probable he will simply disappear and carry on in secret, reappearing once his plot is complete."

"I had hoped their leaving would mean it was over," said her ladyship.

"We dare not take that for granted."

She sighed and nodded. "I will order my packing begun. Clair's may commence once she is out of the house. There is no sense of having maids and a room full of trunks getting in her way when she must hurriedly throw together enough to be getting on with!"

"You are an excellent woman, Lady Lambert. I commend you on your good sense."

He closed the door on her "bah" but thought he heard a pleased note in it nevertheless.

The half hour turned into something nearer to a full hour, others on his royal highness' list not managing so quickly as the royal decree demanded. When the carriage set off with Jason and several other men, he and his wife were not *quite* so ill prepared as they might have been—although there was no question but that they would be in dire straits if their luggage did not catch them up in a few days.

Val managed, in the extra time given him, to hire outriders. He himself rode in the carriage with Clair and the servants, alert and on the watch all the way there and while the yacht loaded. Then he and the outriders returned to London where he found that not only Lady Lambert scrambled to pack far more quickly than one could like; so too were Lady Bronsen and Althea.

"You will escort us, will you not?" asked Althea a trifle hesitantly.

"I will happily escort you to the moon if that is your desire. *As you know*. It is all too soon, but is it possible you can be prepared to leave day after tomorrow?"

"It will not be easy, but we will manage somehow. I've two new gowns nearly finished that I'd like to take if my mantuamaker can manage it. I've sent round a note that I will pay extra to have them finished at once . . ."

"We'll not leave without them." He pursed his lips. "Did not Clair, too, order three or four costumes . . . ?"

"So she did. I will dash off a note to Lady Lambert and perhaps their woman can contrive to finish in time as well."

Val nodded. "My dear, you are aware that you may be going into more than one danger?"

She stilled. "You mean there may be war?"

"It needs thinking on."

"If it comes to that, will there not be warning of the French army approaching?"

"One would hope our scouts are up to the job of noticing the approach of a whole enemy army," said Val, grinning.

"Then I will worry only about our own personal villain. Someone else can deal with the French Ogre. Speaking of our villain, do you know where he is or what he is doing?"

Val sobered. "Andover has disappeared. *Not* a good sign."

Althea swallowed. "No. Not good." She straightened her shoulders. "Very well. It merely means that we must take still greater care. I will not leave the house without a footman in attendance and will not allow Mother to do so. Andover is capable of taking his revenge by harming someone close to anyone close to Clair."

"I always knew you were an intelligent woman, Althea. Allow me to say you are more than I ever expected and I expected a great deal. If this danger has done nothing else that is good, my dear, it has revealed your courage and your ability to think and to act. I not only love you to distraction, I admire you beyond any other woman of my acquaintance."

"Any other?"

"Oh well," said Val, feeling he had become perhaps a trifle too intense, "there is always Elf, of course. But she stands in a category all her own, does she not?"

Althea, who had been both flattered and a little upset by his encomium, chuckled. "Oh yes. She is very much her own woman, unique and outrageous, and it is always a question of deciding whether she is a prize without peer or, on the contrary, so irritating there is no putting up with her."

Val grinned. "You have hit the nail on the head." He sobered. "I hope you do not dislike her, because I count her among my few friends. I would not like to give her up."

Althea felt herself withdrawing. "I see no reason—" She spoke as coolly as she could manage, but feared her voice wobbled more than she could like. "—that you should ever be required to give her up, as you call it."

"Ah. Then I will put aside that particular concern," he said lightly.

Val berated himself for not controlling his tongue, for pushing his beloved more than she could bear. It seemed that every time they edged a trifle closer, he said something more and Althea would withdraw behind that icy shield that protected her from him. He sighed but not quite so softly as he'd have wished.

"What is it?" she asked, her tone a trifle sharp.

He caught her gaze and held it steady. "Nothing new. Merely that I sometimes despair of convincing you of my sincere regard and that I would never do anything to harm a hair of your head. But," he added, changing the subject that, once again, he feared might lead to her telling him to depart from her presence forever, "perhaps I should *not* escort you to the Continent, but should take you and your mother home to the country and then go on to do what I can to see to Clair's safety when Jason cannot."

Althea pretended to glare. "You will not be rid of us so easily, Sir Valerian. We have been promised the treat of traveling on the Continent and travel we will."

"Ah well—" He felt a as if a coiled spring within him un-
wound. "—if you will travel, then you will. Day after tomorrow. Early."

With that he made his adieus and departed, already thinking of all that must be done before he could leave the country for an indefinite period of time.

CHAPTER 10

"But Jason, this is Brussels. I was certain we were to join the Dutch court." Lady Lambert's bewilderment induced chuckles in the men.

"Mother, accommodation will be arranged in the palace for the commission, but not for wives and children. And certainly not for mere mothers."

The dowager, appeased by the fact that Clair was not to enjoy royal hospitality, hid a grin behind her hand.

"Not only I leave my family here in Brussels. It appears all London is flocking here. You'll not be bored as would be true if you must maintain court etiquette hour after hour, day after day."

That all London was moving to the Continent was an exaggeration, but it *was* true that several friends were known to have set up residences in Brussels—people who had sons or husbands in the military, were already arriving in great numbers.

"This house," continued Lord Lambert to his mother, "should prove adequate for the needs of you, Clair, and the Bronsens, but is not so large as to allow anyone, Emerson Andover in particular—if he were so stupid as to request a bed—to join you in it. Val has rooms across the street. He'll not be far off if needed."

"But does that mean you will be gone *all* the time?" asked Clair, her eyes widening and her mouth turning down in a pout.

Jason crossed the room and put his hands on her shoulders. "I fear I must be elsewhere more than I would like, but I promise that, whenever I can, I will return here to you."

He squeezed gently and then walked her to the far end of the salon that provided the privacy he felt he needed. Once there he spoke softly, all those things a lover wished to say to his beloved—although, given it was Jason, they included words like "my duty" and "responsibility."

"My dear?" he finished.

Clair hung her head for a moment and then looked up, biting her lip. "I am sorry I didn't understand. It is just that . . ."

"That you are afraid of Andover?" he asked after a moment.

She fiddled with a button on his vest and nodded. Once. "But that is not the important thing. I remember those days here when you crossed the channel to take your mother and me home. It was so . . . pleasant. I guess I thought it would be the same again, which was nonsense, was it not? You must do your work."

"It *will* be the same. Soon. As for Andover . . . All his attempts have been to ruin you rather than to hurt you. I trust Val to prevent anything happening that you would dislike, but . . . my dear—" He lifted her chin and made her look into his eyes. "—can you not believe that even if something *did* happen to you that gave the *ton* a disgust of you, I would love you still? I will *not* allow that man to come between us, whatever he might manage to do to you. *I will not.*" It sounded like a vow.

Clair's eyes widened. "You love me?" she asked in a very small voice.

"Deeply and forever," he said.

She smiled a glorious smile that, to her husband, seemed to light her up from the inside out. "Then I will be good. I have *hoped* oh, quite desperately that you loved me as I love you—but you never said . . . Oh, Jason, I am so happy!"

"Then I must be happy, too."

At the other end of the salon, the dowager and Lady Bronsen came to an agreement concerning their housekeeping responsibilities. Lady Bronsen, it was decided, would manage the maids and see that the cleaning and polishing was done to everyone's satisfaction, while Lady Lambert saw to the menus and that the cooking was up to snuff.

Althea, hearing them divide up the work, sighed ever so softly. She feared she was in for a period of great boredom. Their acquaintance in Brussels was limited and, with war on the horizon, there would be little entertaining even among those who did visit the city at this particular time. Everyone would be concerned for loved ones: young officers and aides de camp, and so on, and would not wish to spend time at play.

For all of two minutes Althea considered returning to London but then she shook her head. It was going to be difficult finding occupation that held her interest . . . but it must be endured for Clair's sake.

Of course Althea was wrong in her expectations and was, with everyone else, soon caught up in a hectic round of pleasure seeking that appeared to have no end. Whenever she managed to find a moment or two alone, it occurred to her to wonder if everyone wasn't doing their best to forget every danger, forget that black cloud lurking on the horizon. France, after all, was not all that many miles to the south and everyone, she thought, feared for the men, who would fight a horrendous battle when the colossi, Wellington and Napoleon, faced each other for the first time.

There was a ball somewhere nearly every evening. There were riding parties and picnics and excursions to nearby places of interest. There were parades and military reviews and walks through parks full of bivouacking soldiers, men arriving daily from every country and in every sort of uniform, ranging from the stark black of the Brunswickers to the bright tartans of Scots regiments.

And, when there was nothing else to do, there were visits back and forth among friends who had, only recently, met daily in London. It was, in fact, as exhausting as a London Season. Perhaps more so, because the underlying fears surrounding the approaching battle were a constant tension that wore on one.

"A book, Althea?" asked Clair, one afternoon in mock horror. "I do not believe I have seen you reading since we arrived. Not once."

"You have not. And, such a bookish creature as I am, I have missed it. Sir Valerian found this in a little shop outside the walls. He thought I might enjoy it."

"What is it?"

"*Fables de la Fontaine* in two volumes," said Althea, looking up.

"French? Is it very difficult?" Clair chuckled at Althea's wry look. "Perhaps when you finish I could try?"

Althea sobered. "I do not think it the sort of work you would enjoy, but I will lend it to you when I finish and you may judge for yourself. You are dressed for riding." Althea bethought herself of her duty to help guard Clair. "Did you join a party? Would I intrude if I joined you?"

"Of course not. You are always welcome. But Val means to come, so you need not unless you wish to do so."

They had seen no sign of Emerson Andover, but they had not let down their guard. It was *possible* that he had cut his losses and disappeared. No one quite believed it—even the dowager—and there was no predicting from what quarter the attack would come next.

Althea closed her book on her finger. She debated. She needn't go if Sir Valerian were there. But . . . *Sir Valerian would be there*. Laying the book aside, she rose to her feet.

"I *will* come," she said as she made for the door, "if you can wait until I change?"

Since it was Althea, Clair knew the wait would not be long. Her friend was not one to primp and pose before the mirror and change her mind half a dozen times before considering herself ready for an outing. Instead of fretting, Clair asked a footman to run to the stables and order Althea's mare brought around as well as her own.

Sir Valerian joined his young cousin in the drawing room and nodded when informed Althea meant to join them. His features gave nothing away, of course, but inside, he felt his heart race and knew that whatever else might change, he would never anticipate his love's presence without that little rush of emotion. He only wished he had the right to her presence on a continuing basis—that he could go to bed at night and hold her in his arms, rise and sit across from her at the breakfast table, watch her dress for an evening's entertainment—and perhaps interfere and make it necessary that she begin dressing all over again!

"Val!"

"Hmm?" He blinked and then smiled. "Did you speak to me, Clair?"

"I did. I have had a message from Jason. He arrives this evening in time to join us for dinner before Lady Winter's ball."

"Excellent news. And not just excellent for you, my child! I, too, will enjoy his company while he is here."

"Only if I do not manage to occupy his every moment, and I assure you I will try." Clair adopted a thoughtful expression. "You know, Val, I fretted that I spent so little time with him in London when he had so much work to do, but at least he did a great deal of it at home in his study. I knew he was near. And he ate his meals with us quite often. And, oh, all sorts of things. Now he is simply not there. I didn't—" She grimaced. "—realize how well off I was, did I? Perhaps this is my punishment for fussing and wishing things were different?"

Val chuckled. "Nonsense. Besides, if current rumors have any basis in fact, I believe you will soon see more of him. You might," he teased, "actually begin to wonder if you are not seeing too much of him."

Clair came to him and clutched his arm. "Val. Tell me! What is it that you have heard?"

He grinned, his white teeth flashing. "Merely that the various countries involved appear to have reached agreement on most of the problems facing them in a war of this nature."

Althea, entering just then, felt her heart thud at the sight of Val's smile. She wondered if it would ever be any different for her or if that particular teasing grin would always make her insides turn to water and her head feel hollow. She found it difficult to find the necessary will power not to go to him and demand he hold her. She sighed a silent sort of sigh. Very likely it would always be a problem. It was true, certainly, that, as time passed, the urge got harder to control.

But even as such thoughts flitted through her head, he sobered and was again speaking. "The commission's most important task was to convince the Prussians and Russians that Wellington be made commander-in-chief. There was even one idiotic proposal that the Prince of Orange be commissioned to that role."

"Silly Billy?" asked Althea. "Surely not!"

Val turned and, for a moment, his eyes burned her to her very core. When she stiffened, his gaze dropped and—

She could see the effort he made.

—he brought himself under control. He even managed to relax, which was more than she could do.

"You, my love, had best watch that biting tongue of yours. You are not in England where one has the freedom to say pretty much what one wishes. There are those here who would not appreciate that particular sobriquet for their crown prince."

Althea chuckled. "I know. But you startled me by suggesting that even those most loyal to him would think him capable of facing Napoleon on the battlefield."

"There are sycophants in any royal entourage. Think of those who surround our own prince."

Althea nodded. "Yes. I should have recalled that. Are we ready? I have delayed us unconscionably and we will have delayed the others. Tell me, whom do we join on this jaunt?"

Val and Clair told her as they left the house, and then Val helped the women to mount up. He threw his leg over his gelding and they moved off, the grooms coming along behind. When they reached the city gate where the party had planned to meet, they found it had left.

"I should have sent a message asking them to wait. Do you know where they meant to go?" Clair asked Sir Valerian.

"It is my fault," fretted Althea. "I should not have decided to join you at the last minute. I am so sorry, Clair."

"There is a military review south of here near a village called Waterloo," said Sir Valerian. "I think that is where they went. Shall we ride that way and see?"

They joined a fair sprinkling of riders and carriages headed south toward the review. When they arrived, Althea and Clair saw friends standing and sitting on a rise of ground not far from where troops were drawn up. "Shall we join them?" asked Althea, pointing. The three rode in that direction and, coming from behind, were not seen until almost upon the group.

Althea tipped her head. Surely that was not the sudden sort of silence one heard when a group realized that the subject of their conversation had appeared unexpectedly. What, after all, could they have been saying? Twice more that afternoon she noticed an oddly embarrassed look following a pause before conversation rushed off in a new direction.

"Sir Valerian," she said, softly, after the third such occasion, "is there gossip circulating concerning our party?"

"What have you seen?" he asked.

She told him and he frowned. "I have heard no tittle-tattle, but then I would not, would I? Not if we are the subject of the latest *on-dit*." He looked around, saw a friend, and strolled over to him.

Althea watched. It seemed to her that Sir Valerian's friend was embarrassed and reluctant to divulge his knowledge. She saw Val put a hand on the man's shoulder, saw the fellow look away, saw his mouth moving quickly as if in a rush to get the words out . . . and saw Val sigh. The two spoke for a bit longer and then parted.

"You were right," said Val, his tone bland and his gaze drifting around the groups of gaily dressed ladies and soberly dressed men. "I suspect we've discovered Andover's latest ploy, although it is possible, of course, that some other malicious tongue has been busy."

"What is it?"

"I am said to be more than Clair's cousin and friend," he said, bitingly.

Althea swore softly.

Val chuckled. "I was unaware you knew such words."

"Most women know at least a few," she retorted. "There are times when it is necessary that we relieve our feelings with such language and this is definitely one of them. What do we do now?"

"I must get word to Jason before he hears the gossip from some earnest friend determined to warn him that he's wearing horns."

"Lord Lambert returns this evening, or so Clair told me earlier."

"Hmm."

"What?"

"I wonder if I should ride out and meet him."

A premonition raced through Althea. "*Don't.*"

Val blinked. "Why?"

She sorted through her suspicions. "Because," she said slowly, "if the two of you happen to meet on a deserted road, if you are *alone* when you meet, then if Andover has followed you, there is no telling what might happen."

Val frowned. "I don't understand."

Althea felt herself turning bright red and she could not

keep her eyes from drifting toward his left hand and the scar marring it. She bit her lip.

"Ah." Very gently, he said, "I did not acquire it in an illicit duel, my dear. That is what you've heard, is it not?"

She nodded and turned away.

"Loth—my man—and I were set up on. It was," he mused in a reminiscent manner, "quite a fight."

"Then why have you allowed the nasty tale of a duel fought under suspicious circumstances to circulate without contradiction?" she asked, half bewildered and half angry.

His eyes widened. "But surely you know?"

She frowned and shook her head.

"My dear, I *never* explain myself. I don't know why I'm explaining myself to you!" He drew in a deep breath. "Yes I do. I cannot bear that you believe ill where there is no ill. There were enough goings-on in my callow youth that you must swallow without adding those that did *not* happen."

Althea felt herself trembling. His words utterly disarmed her and she wished they were alone. "You are a devil, Valerian Underwood."

"Perhaps," he said absently, obviously thinking of something else. "You have a point," he continued. "That particular rumor is believed by all too many and *could* be used against us. I must stay away from all of you until *you*, my dear, explain to Jason what we suspect. It rarely shows itself, but he has a temper. He *might*, if he has heard the rumors, fly off the handle at the sight of me."

"I will talk to him. You come to dinner, do you not?"

"Perhaps," he said with a rueful look, "but I'll wait until you send a footman telling me all is well."

If Sir Valerian had not informed Althea that Jason had a temper, she would not have guessed that he was holding himself carefully in check when he entered the salon just before dinner. "Ah!" she said brightly. "I see some kind soul told you of the vicious rumors circulating among our putative friends," she said.

He turned a cold gaze on her. "Rumors?" he said.

"Of course. I'd guess they were started by Andover, but that, of course, is a mere guess."

"What rumors?" demanded Lady Lambert, her voice sharp.

Althea made a tale of it and managed to bring forth Clair's trilling laugh.

"What nonsense," said Clair. "As if Val would. Not only is he my cousin, but he is Jason's friend. How could *anyone* think such a thing?"

"I presume because he has been seen in our company on each and every occasion we leave this house," said Althea.

"Yes, and there are far too many who are happy to believe the worst of anyone," said the dowager in biting tones.

Althea had been watching Jason. "Have you come down out of the boughs?" she asked, her tone innocent.

He grimaced and relaxed another notch. "You would say I am a fool to have believed anything bad of Clair."

"I note," said Althea, her voice dry as dust, "you do not say you'd be a fool to believe the worst of Sir Valerian."

That brought a laugh to Jason's lips. "There was a time when that was true, but I should have remembered what a reformed soul he has been for years now. I—" He sobered again. "—should also have recalled that there is a very good reason why he would *not* be interested in seducing my wife!"

His gaze held Althea's and, for the second time that day, she felt a rush of blood up her shoulders and into her face. "I will," she said, marching toward the door, "send a footman across the street to ask Sir Valerian to join us. He's been awaiting word it is safe to come."

"Safe?" asked Jason to her back.

"He didn't wish to subject you to the temptation of issuing a challenge if you were foolish enough to believe the nonsense being said of us."

"But how," asked a bewildered Clair, "could anyone possibly . . . a duel? Jason, you wouldn't! Would you?" she finished, her voice small and scared.

"I will admit I was livid when I entered this house. Frankly," he admitted, "I don't know what foolish thing I might have done."

"But I told you I loved you," whispered Clair, her hand clutching his lapel.

He covered her hand. "You might have lied, Clair. To throw dust in my eyes."

"I wouldn't," she said, outraged by the very notion.

"Now I'm rational, I know that," he said, pacifically.

Never one to hold a grudge, she relaxed and flirted a look at him. "I suppose I should be flattered that you thought I am the sort to catch Val's eye!"

He chuckled and, his arm around her, drew her on to where his mother and Lady Bronsen stood near the chairs in which they'd been seated.

"Will someone," asked Lady Bronsen rather plaintively, "please tell me what is going on?"

Althea did, describing what had happened at the review and the decision to explain to Lord Lambert before Sir Valerian appeared on the scene.

"And you think," demanded the dowager Lady Lambert, "that this is a new plan made by that scoundrel in order to ruin Clair and interfere in my son's marriage?"

"I fear it may have been more," said Sir Valerian, entering just then. "Knowing the two of us fairly well, I think he hoped that I would rush off to meet Jason on the road—and when I did, he meant to kill Jason and put it around I had indulged in another duel without seconds."

"What? *Another*?"

Val grimaced. "There was never a first, but the story made the rounds to explain how I hurt my hand."

"I have done my best to scotch that rumor, but it persists," said Jason, scowling.

Val waved it away. "Rumors to my detriment have never before bothered me. The notion one might have been used against us, does."

"You had no business allowing such scurrilous gossip currency," said the elder Lady Lambert. "You should have denied it."

"And who would have believed me?" asked Val politely.

Spots of color appeared on her ladyship's cheeks. There was, of course, no answer to that. "It is your fault," she scolded. "You should not have forbidden me to tell the world how you saved Jason's life from those Mohawks or whatever they are called these days. If you had not allowed your reputation to become so tarnished, then no one would have believed these new rumors."

Val bowed. "I agree, but my reputation has been tarnished and by my own behavior. It has interested no one that I reformed my way of life. That wasn't worth a gossip's time, was it? And, besides, it is far more entertaining to believe the worst, is it not?"

He looked at Althea as he said that. For the third time she blushed. "It was never *entertaining*," she said, her voice low.

"No of course not. I apologize." He continued to stare at her, a pensive look about him. "My dear, just how far are you willing to go in order to scotch these particular rumors?"

Althea felt herself stiffening. "No . . ."

"Ah. Then I will say no more."

Althea thought about it. "But it would be just the thing, would it not?" At his hopeful look, she hurried on. "And then, once this is all settled and that awful man's fangs pulled, then . . . ?"

Val sighed. "Then of course you would tell the world it was a hum and we would go our separate ways."

Lady Bronsen had never been one to follow a quickly paced conversation in which much was left unsaid. She looked more than slightly confused—but the dowager sat straighter in her seat and looked from one to the other. "Yes, yes, it is an excellent notion," she said. "We will hold a dinner party to announce it."

"Announce *what*?" asked Lady Bronsen very nearly wailing the words in her need to understand.

"Yes, and perhaps a *soirée* afterwards to which we could invite others," enthused Clair, her eyes shining. She clapped her hands. "Oh yes. It would be perfect and would solve all our problems."

Althea's grim expression faded. She blinked. "All our problems?" she asked.

Clair chuckled. "Oh yes, I think so. It is the perfect solution of why Sir Val has been in our company on every possible occasion. *And* it will allow him to woo you as he wishes to do with no one thinking it is other than the proper thing for a prospective bridegroom to do."

"Bridegroom!" Lady Bronsen grasped the word as a lifeline. "Sir Valerian? And my Althea?" Suddenly she beamed. "Oh yes. *Delightful!*" She rose to her feet and came to Sir Valerian. Taking his hand she turned the smile up at him. "Let me be the first to congratulate you," she said and, standing on tiptoe, reached up to kiss his cheek.

Faintly bemused, Val studied Lady Bronsen's plump features. "So now I know where Althea gets that wonderful smile," he said softly and chuckled to see her ladyship blush rosily.

He looked over her ladyship's head at Althea, his brows raised. Althea closed her eyes, drew in a deep breath and let it out in a whoosh. Her mother did not understand it was merely a pretense. She thought they were really engaged. It worried Althea that her mother was so very pleased by the notion her daughter would wed—and then she understood.

My mother has only been waiting for me to marry before she agrees to marry Sir Robert, thought Althea. She was horrified by the notion it was her spinsterhood that stood in the way of her mother's happiness. *What,* she thought, a trifle frantically, *am I to do now*?

CHAPTER 11

London Interlude

Jared Emerson Andover stood on the pavement before the office of his only contact in London and frowned. The letter of introduction he had handed to Mac's London agent had had the man looking up with rounded eyes and a whistle on his lips.

Jared tipped his head slightly, thinking over what he had learned. Most important, his aristocratic cousin was on the Continent and not in London at all. That was, it seemed, common knowledge.

So thought Jared, *should I follow on or should I attempt to learn more here before doing so*?

A carriage stopped at the edge of the pavement and Jared absently stepped out of the way when a footman hopped off the back and came to open the door. He was deep in cogitation when he heard a soft gasp. He looked up.

"Young man, since I do not believe in ghosts, I presume you are an Andover of the current generation. Very likely, from the clothes you wear, an offspring of the scoundrel the Lord Lambert of *my* generation sent off with a flea in his ear."

Jared blinked. "Er, ma'am—"

An outraged whisper from the footman informed him, "It's *My Lady*, booberkin!"

"—my lady," he corrected without looking at the footman standing behind him. "I am his son."

"His only son?" asked Lady Elf, her eyes narrowed.

"No ma'am—my lady." Jared's lids lowered slightly. "Am I to understand you have met my half brother, Baron Maker?"

"I have met," said Lady Elf slowly, "a man calling himself Emerson Andover who also has the look of the Andovers. A different Andover, but still very much an Andover."

Jerod stiffened. His eyes narrowed. "My lady, *I* am Jared Emerson Andover."

Her ladyship pursed her lips. "Hmm. Yes, your grandfather to the life!" She grimaced. "One of you is lying, of course, but until we know which, I believe we should keep you out of sight of the gossips. Climb in and I will take you home where we will discuss the next act in this charade."

CHAPTER 12

"Well, Althea?" asked Val. He had gently released himself from Lady Bronsen's clutching hands and moved to stand before her. He studied her pale features and sighed. "Very well, then," he said, for her ears alone. There was a touch of despair in that which brought Althea's eyes to his face. He had turned an ashen color but when he spoke it was with firm resolve. "When this is done, I'll go away. When the time comes to dissolve the engagement, I promise to give you good reason—if, that is, you will allow it to be announced."

Althea bit her lip. "You would, would you not?"

"What I promise, I do."

Althea felt as if her insides were roiling and boiling and she felt both hot and cold at the same time. "I . . . don't know what to say."

Clair rose. "You will do it, will you not, Althea? I mean, what can it mean to you?"

"To be labeled a jilt?" she asked softly so that only Val heard. She turned.

"It is too much to ask," said Val, turning. "We will find another solution."

Althea, given the opportunity to say no, perversely decided to say she would. ". . . I am not, however, a very good actress," she finished. "I don't know if I can . . . can pretend to be happily affianced."

Val suffered both elation that, for some little time, he could call her his own, and a creeping depression that, once it was over, he had lost her forever. "I will try not to do anything to embarrass you, Althea, but it will be necessary, if we are to convince anyone of the truth of it, that I behave as I would toward the woman I . . . desire to marry." At the last moment he could not admit before the others that he loved her. "No one will believe we are engaged if I never touch you in any way."

Althea felt her head swim. Did he mean he might once again kiss her? As he had, that never-to-be-forgotten afternoon in the vicarage garden?

"You must accept my arm whenever it is offered. You must dance only with me. You must, at the very least, allow me to hold your hand."

"But only when there is someone to note that you do," she said quickly, with some confused conviction that she must protect herself.

He nodded but she saw the return of the bleak look to his eyes that made her wonder.

"What is it?" she asked softly.

"My dear, have you no notion how difficult it will be for me to restrain myself as I must since you do not truly accept me but agree to only the pretense of accepting me?"

"Difficult . . . ?"

"When I have longed all these years to take all of you back into my arms," he said too softly for the others to hear, "how can I bear to merely hold your hand?"

Althea blushed and, quickly, looked from one to another, but everyone was, with exquisite politeness, pretending to ignore them while they discussed their new relationship. Except, of course, Lady Bronsen. Althea smiled weakly at her mother who nodded brightly, happily, and, once again, Althea wondered what would happen to her mother's happiness when she and Val staged the *dénouement,* and the fake engagement was broken.

It occurred to her that perhaps her mother and Sir Robert might have come to an understanding before that happened, in which case surely her mother would go ahead with her own wedding . . . ?

"Enough dalliance, Sir Val," said the dowager, her voice raised a trifle to reach where they stood apart. "We must discuss the dinner at which we announce that you've come to an agreement. Do tell me who in particular you wish placed on the guest list."

"You are aware of the paucity of relatives available in my family tree," said Val. "Except for Clair's family, all are distant and none, to my knowledge, visit in Brussels. Unfortunately the vicar will be unable to leave his parish. I can think of no friend that Jason would not also wish included at his table. I have," he added, pensively, unable to sustain his *amour-propre* another instant, "an errand or two I must run. I know I can safely leave all such plans in your capable hands. Althea, will you walk me to the door?"

The two exited and, once in the hall, Val sent the footman off to order his horse brought round from the stables they all shared. He checked that they were alone.

"My dear, I know you are unhappy. I will do my best to make it easy for you, but some things must be done. An announcement in the London papers, for instance." He touched her pale cheek. "I know. It makes it so very official, does it not? But we will not draw up settlement documents and we will not have the banns called. *We* know it is not real whatever the world must believe."

Althea nodded, her heart thudding a dirge-like message. She couldn't think why . . .

"Also we must be seen together occasionally without the company of the others. Tomorrow, about four, I will pick up you and your maid and we will make ourselves the talk of the town by driving out to one of the little *cafés* beyond the wall and enjoying a coffee there." He touched her again. "It will not be thought so very *outré* so long as your maid is with us and it is the sort of thing that would be expected of me. Can you bear it?"

She nodded.

He sighed. "You are awfully silent, my dear. Have you nothing to say?"

She shook her head.

"Ah well. At some point I must find a nicely secluded spot so that you are free to rant and rave at fate, at Emerson Andover, at Clair who is too enthusiastic and, of course, most of all at me for my very existence."

His light tone brought a weak smile to her lips.

"That is better. I very much dislike seeing you unhappy. I will discover reasons so you can find your wonderful smile and I must think very hard to find things at which you can laugh."

He touched her cheek once again, softly holding his finger there a moment longer than might have been considered necessary, and then turned, moving swiftly across the hall and out the door which the returning footman just then opened.

Althea, her hand lifted to cover the spot on her cheek he'd touched, stared after him for so long that the footman, clearing his throat nervously, asked if there was something she wanted.

There was, of course, but true love from a rake was not something the footman could supply.

Oh, if I could only make myself believe him. If only I believed he truly loved and wanted me. It occurred to her that she did believe he wanted her and she amended that thought. *Wanted me and only me. Forever.*

* * *

The dinner party announcing their engagement was more of a strain than Althea had expected and she had not stinted in her concern for her poor worn out nerves. Accepting congratulations from their friends—any number of whom pointed out in a seemingly jocular fashion that she'd need to watch Val like a hawk and keep him on a proper leash—did not ease her.

"He is a man's man, dear," said one of the more kindly disposed. "He will not mean to hurt you and indeed I believe he will take great care not to do so, but are you certain you understand what you are taking on?"

"I believe so," said Althea, and for once could speak firmly and with assurance. After all, what she had *taken on* was nothing more than a sham engagement that would end when the danger to Clair disappeared.

And why, she wondered, *do I always feel this awful* sinking *when I think of its ending? When it is what I should want more than anything?*

"You will reach heights you have not dreamed," continued the woman. And then muttered as if to herself. "And depths one should never plumb."

Althea recalled bits of gossip about the lady who spoke to her and wondered if, once again, someone knew Sir Val's reputation but not the man himself. Because, almost against her will—since such knowledge weakened her resolve—she was seeing strengths in him she had not dreamed existed.

A few months previously she would not have believed the lengths to which he'd go to protect those for whom he cared. At another level of caring, she had noticed an odd kindness in him toward the dowager Lady Lambert, whom he understood as she never had, an attitude combining a sort of jocular manner with a firm determination not to be governed, which the old lady appeared to find highly entertaining. Or, when speaking to Lady Bronsen, he was gentle, his conversation cloaked in something approaching an old-fashioned courtliness. It was behavior which would have appeared nonsensical on a modern man's shoulders, but which he wore with ease and seeming comfort.

And then there was his attitude toward the servants. He demanded service from them, yes, but never of an irrational sort. He knew the names of those with whom he regularly dealt and something of their lives and families. Althea had watched with a sense of horror the ease with which he received slavish devotion . . . until she realized he was sincere in his interest in those around him—even the lowliest knife boy or a dirty crossing sweep—drawing loyalty by deserving it.

The things she observed, compared to what she'd believed for so long, confused her. How did one make logical sense of the contradictions?

There was one way, of course. One could *believe* him when he claimed his reputation had been acquired in his first years on the *ton*, that it was based on perhaps half a decade of wildness. Anyone knew that, once gained, a reputation was nearly impossible to live down. Her dinner partner demanded her attention just then and, realizing how rude it was of her to sink into her thoughts, she forced herself to pay proper attention.

Once dinner ended and more guests arrived for the following *soirée*, she watched Val circulate among them, heard chuckles here, saw admiration there, coy flirting from the bolder women, and a bonhomie he didn't appear to appreciate from men of a jovial nature. She watched as he devoted time to wallflowers and elderly women sitting in the little gilt chairs placed here and there around edges of the room, and once, when an older man well known as a bore grabbed hold of his arm and would not let go, she watched him listen attentively until he saw a legitimate excuse to slip away.

This was not the care-for-nobody man she had thought him to be. Had he ever been that man? Or were her fears based on something other than who and what *he* might or might not be?

Was it possible that it was herself she feared? Was she so fearful of her reaction to that one kiss that she had had to blame him? Had she not *dared* believe him more than a seducer and user of women? The unexpected notion left Althea so aghast she didn't know where to look. She turned to leave the salon—only to find her way barred by Emerson Andover.

"Sir!"

"It is true then?" he asked, a sneer drawing lines around his nose and mouth.

"That Sir Valerian and I are engaged? Of course. He first asked me a year or more ago." It had been nearly three, but who counted? "This season he convinced me we should wed. What do you find surprising in that?"

"When he has laid court to my cousin's wife day in and day out? Are you certain he does not use you in order to remain near to dear little Clair?" said Andover.

Althea's eyes widened and her mouth parted. Her lips tightened and spread. And then she laughed. She had not realized how tense she had grown, how uncertain, until Andover's words registered.

"Mr. Andover, I had not realized you possessed such an entertaining sense of humor. I would never have thought it of you." She nodded. "You will have to excuse me. I was to run an errand for my mother," she said mendaciously, "and have postponed it far too long." She nodded again and slipped out the door and into the hall and climbed the stairs to her room.

Once there she closed her door and stood stock-still. Emerson's unexpected presence slipped from a mind occupied with her need to understand her own emotions.

Was that it? Had her hot uncontrolled reaction to Val's kiss frightened her to the point she had recoiled from any thought that his feelings might be as he said? Had she assumed that only *evil intentions* on his part could bring forth such . . . such *passion* in a chaste woman? Had she assumed that he *must* be a devil to make her feel so . . . so *aban-*

doned? So ready to throw her bonnet over the windmill? Right that moment? Right there in the garden behind the vicarage?

Granny, she thought, *would tell me I was a goose for feeling frightened*.

For the first time she thought about the words she'd used when telling Clair how to behave with her brand new husband. Althea wondered how she'd learned the *sense* of the thing but no *understanding* of it. She stared blindly into her dressing table mirror.

Was I, she wondered, *such a silly goose*?

She recalled the years since that kiss, recalled Val's loyalty, his constant pursuit, his tenaciousness, and was forced to a conclusion.

I was.

Her mouth drooped. Another long moment and she squared her shoulders and glared at her reflection. *Goose I was, but no longer. I am not afraid.*

Sir Val had proposed a temporary engagement, one he promised she would dissolve when no longer needed. Could she find the courage to show him she didn't want to jilt him? That she wanted a *real* engagement? To wed him, live with him, and achieve those heights someone mentioned?

But then, once again, she felt her shoulders slump under the weight of old fears. Would she endure the lows as well? She nodded, but this time less firmly.

Nevertheless, she wished to wed him. Somehow she must convince Sir Valerian Underwood that she meant to have him even though, at long last, he had given up and had determined to be free of her. A touch of panic filled her. He meant to go away! To leave her.

Alone.

That was why I felt low every time I thought of our ending this.

Her shoulders straightened and her spine stiffened. *If he*

loves me, all will be well. And if he has stopped loving me?
Well, he loved me once, so he can just fall in love with me all
over again.

Althea returned to the lower floor and scanned the crowd
until she saw Sir Val's tall form. She moved gracefully to his
side and took his arm, smiling at the red-haired woman flirting with her Val.

"Are you acquainted with Lady Barbara Childe?" asked
Val, smiling down at her and squeezing her arm gently with
his free hand.

Althea nodded. "I have had that pleasure, but perhaps
Lady Barbara has forgotten. It was some years ago."

"Of course I remember you. But call me Babs. Everyone
does," said her ladyship. "You must stop by one afternoon. I
have the greatest curiosity to learn how you snatched one of
the *ton*'s most interesting men from under our very noses."

Althea felt the warmth of a blush. She glanced up at Val
who chuckled.

"You embarrass me, Babs," he said. "Besides, it was quite
the other way around. You might ask me to tell how I caught
the most interesting woman in the *ton*."

Althea's skin felt as if it was scalded.

Babs' throaty laugh was no help. "I will believe, since I've
never known you to lie, that she is interesting, but I must also
assume she is one of the more modest—if her color does not
lie." Her ladyship sobered. "I will be good," she added, turning to Althea. "I meant it, you know. Do come. If you are to
join yourself to Val, then you must become better acquainted
with his true friends—and discover who among the *ton* it is
best to ignore, those who are *not* his friends. And," she added
thoughtfully, "have not been for some years now."

"You, too."

Bab's darkened brows arched. She half laughed as if she
were not quite certain of Althea's meaning.

"I only mean that you are not the first to attempt to convince me Val is a reformed character."

"Oh, he is. He is." Lady Barbara chuckled, a husky sound that was quite contagious. "I myself have done my best to seduce him and he absolutely refuses to be seduced. Goodbye Miss Bronsen. I see someone with whom I wish to speak." Babs moved off, her graceful walk a delight to watch.

"What a strange woman she is," said Althea.

"True gold, although there are not many who agree. She is another who earned a reputation and has been unable to live it down—not that she has tried so very hard. I think we are friends in part because we both suffer from characters that are only in part deserved. And," he said more softly, "very likely for the same reasons. We cannot be bothered to worry about every word we say and all too often, when merely jesting, are taken seriously. Then too, we both suffer unrequited love so we understand that in each other." Almost as an afterthought, he added, "She has *not* attempted to seduce me, by the way."

"I know."

"You do?"

Althea smiled, her brows arching. "My dear Val, if she *had* I do not think she'd have *failed*."

He frowned. "You do not trust me to control my baser urges?"

"There are temptations that are beyond the control of any man," said Althea. She stared across the room at Lady Babs' flaming red hair. "I think she may be one of them."

"I hope you will learn to like her," said Val hesitantly. "I would dislike giving up her entertaining company."

"I will try to get to know her. She is rather brittle and I think it may be difficult unless she willingly cooperates in that endeavor, but I *will* try." Althea realized they were talking as if the engagement were real. Which, she remembered, she wished it to be. Drawing in a deep breath, she glanced around the room. "Thank Heaven."

"What?"

"I believe the crowd has begun to thin." She frowned.

"And what else?" he asked, seeing there was more.

"Andover."

Val's head came up and he stared across the room to where their nemesis talked with a rather plump man, bringing forth chuckles and the occasional quick startled look toward one person or another.

"Frankly," she continued, "I forgot I'd seen him earlier. Perhaps I thought—*hoped* would be a better word—he'd left."

"What is he up to now? That is Creevey with whom he speaks. The man is the biggest gossip in all England."

"Let us assume he is merely entertaining the gentleman and forget him. I am so tired of Emerson Andover and his tricks."

"Then, since you refuse to worry your head about him, shall we see if anyone has left some trifling thing on the supper table? Perhaps there will be a lobster patty to delight your palate."

They moved into the dining room where servants stood behind a long table that appeared to have been raided by locusts. Althea made a quick survey, ordered several depleted platters removed, and others rearranged before she took up a plate and chose a few morsels for her supper.

"You will note that there are no lobster patties," she said, pretending to a moroseness she was not truly feeling.

"When we are wed," he said in teasing tones, "I will order our cook to prepare them twice a week without fail."

She laughed. "Once a week will be sufficient. What you might order up more often is that fruit cup with the lemon sauce to top it. I have become quite addicted to it since arriving in Brussels."

"I will see those responsible for my succession houses are primed to deliver all the fruit you desire the whole of the year round."

Althea glanced at him, saw the glint in his eye, and wondered if their banter might be more serious than she'd thought, that he might *not* be jesting.

"Do you *have* succession houses?" she asked.

"Oh yes," he said, surprising her. "At first it was something of a minor hobby. Gradually I grew fascinated. Half a dozen sea captains bring me new varieties of plants from the strange places at which they touch shore. My latest acquisition is inedible, but quite beautiful. Have you seen any orchids? This orchid has very small and pale pink blossoms but is highly scented which many of them are not."

"I like scented flowers. Have you lilacs? I find them especially delightful."

"I do. Also something called a mock orange. It has the scent of the ripe fruit which is where it got its sobriquet."

They discussed gardening for a time and discovered similar tastes. Neither liked the formality of a certain type of English garden, but *did* like the quite different and equally rigid form of the Italian water garden.

"I mean to put one in at Underwood Manor," he said. "There is a good spring in a hillside not too far from the house. A ride must be cut through the woods that stand between in order to have a view of it, but I believe something quite exceptional could be achieved with only a trifling effort."

Silently, Althea swore to have a part in that effort. But before that could happen she had to show Val that she didn't wish to break their engagement. That she wished for a real engagement.

If only it were possible to simply tell him. She might dare to do it if she were certain it was *love* that had led to his long pursuit, but perhaps it had not been *love* but *the chase*. Perhaps once he realized she had yielded and the pursuit ended he would no longer be interested.

Althea's insecurities had found a new dragon with which to plague her.

CHAPTER 13

The last guest left and the evening ended. The household gathered around a small but cheery fire in the small back parlor where Val watched Althea as she discussed the evening with Clair.

She looks happy, even contented, he thought. *It is that I have agreed to cease my pursuit of her once this charade of an engagement is ended. Perhaps that I told her I'll go away? She knows that soon she will be able to relax her defenses.*

Abruptly depressed, he covered a faked yawn with his palm. "I fear I will fall asleep here on the sofa if I do not take myself home. Will you ride with me tomorrow, Althea?" he asked, wanting every moment with her that he could manage.

"Of course. Not too early," she added, glancing at the clock.

"No, of course not." Then, forced by convention, he turned to Jason. "Will you and Clair ride with us?"

"We will," said Jason with satisfaction.

Val was saddened further by his friend's insensitivity.

Jason continued. "I cannot tell you how pleasant it is to

have the work ended so that I have time to pay proper attention to my wife." He smiled at Clair. "Why do you not join
us for breakfast afterwards?" he asked, turning back to his
friend.

Val forced a grin. "It is obvious that you have been away
or you would know that I dine here with great regularity and
without an invitation. Breakfast will be much appreciated.
As usual." He then forced another yawn. "I'll just be off,
then," he said—and was pleased when Althea rose to accompany him into the hall. Unfortunately, she left the door open,
which did *not* please him. He wanted desperately to steal another kiss, but dared not break the rules of their sham engagement. But, especially, he dared not when those in the
room beyond might see it.

He compromised by putting an arm around her shoulders
as they left and, as they approached the door, gave her a gentle squeeze. "You did very well tonight, Althea. I was proud
of you. No one would ever guess our plot."

"Then we have succeeded, have we not? In dealing with
the rumors concerning Clair?"

"Hmm. We have certainly gone a long way on the road to
scotching them. We must continue our efforts tomorrow," he
said—and unable to resist, dropped a kiss on the side of her
forehead. "Sleep well," he said rather gruffly and, opening
the door, quickly departed before he did still more to upset
her.

Althea watched him cross the street and sighed. Softly. It
would not do to allow him to hear her. She wished it were
possible for a woman to simply tell a man she fancied him
and would he please kiss her. Properly, that is, and not a little peck on the forehead. She wondered if the world would
ever change so that women had such freedom and concluded
that it was unlikely. She sighed again as she closed the door,
wishing she were not quite so well trained, quite so restrained by convention . . .

Val, for his part, entered his rooms and, knowing he'd not

sleep for a time, paced the floor in his overcrowded sitting room. When he'd bumped into the same small table for the third time, he picked up his hat and gloves and stormed out—walking the nearly empty streets for well over an hour before, having yawned a true yawn, he returned to his rooms.

Forbearing to wake Loth, he prepared himself for bed. But then, having tucked himself in, he stared at the ceiling, one arm curled up under his head.

She is so very special, he thought sadly. *I must not upset her more than is necessary for our plot.*

He mused about that for a bit and a rather sardonic grin crossed his features. He knew himself too well, knew he'd take every advantage he could, with propriety. Perhaps a step or two beyond propriety?

But only when in company. When we are alone I must not, he thought. *I must not touch her, caress her, kiss her—even the sort of kiss I gave her tonight is wrong.*

He sighed and closed his eyes—and was immediately assailed by the memory of the single kiss they'd shared, the sweet untutored passion she'd revealed. How joyful he'd been to discover it! How he yearned to rouse it again, yearned to teach her to enjoy it . . . and how lucky the man who eventually did so.

A frown creased his brow. A gentleman was taught he shouldn't expect passion from the woman he married. One was expected to find passion in one's adventures among the muslin company—not in the marriage bed.

A gently bred female was trained to fear her passions, to think them wrong. Ah! What a mistake it was that a woman did not enjoy marital love. Althea would not fear ardor, he told himself. She would glory in it. He knew she would and had held himself in check for three long years waiting for the right to take her to his bed, the right to teach her and enjoy her discovery of the pleasures they'd share.

But that hope was ended. Another man would teach her,

another would enjoy her passion, her loving, the love—assuming the lucky one was sensitive and loving and knew how to go about rousing it.

Despair filled him. How could he bear it? He could—but only because he must.

Tomorrow he must begin dividing his emotions, revealing for the *ton* his love for her, restraining any hint of it when they were alone. It would not be easy. He stared into the dark, his eyes painfully wide open. It would be, he knew, a very long night.

And knowing it, he rose, lighted his bedside lamp, and found the book he was currently reading. Plumping up his pillows, he settled himself under the comforter and read until the first dim light of morning found its way between his badly closed drapes.

He was roused only three hours later when Loth entered the bedroom, shaving water in one hand and coals rattling in a brass coal scuttle in the other.

"Beautiful day," said his man of all work.

"You didn't tell me Andover had arrived in town," said Val, sleepily.

Loth swung around, water sloshing over the lip of the ewer. "He can't have done."

"He has. He had the gall to attend the party last night."

"How could he and I not hear it?" asked Loth, bemused.

He had had his ears cocked for any hint of the man's arrival—servants usually knowing the news far in advance of their masters and word most often circulating among the belowstairs staff before it reached the ears of those dwelling abovestairs.

"I haven't a notion how he did it, but he did. I suppose it is possible he arrived only in time to come to the *soirée*. After all, he didn't attempt to join us for the dinner preceding it, which, as Lord Lambert's heir presumptive, he had a right to expect . . . except of course, he knew he'd never be invited after his last attempt to ruin Clair." Val frowned. "I wish I could understand his purpose in ruining her. One would think his effort would be bent toward assuring that Jason suffered a fatal accident."

"He's a deep one, all right and tight," said Loth. He gave Val's razor a couple of more swipes along the strop and set it down beside the bowl, the blade running north to south, which was said to keep it sharp. The mirror was not quite straight and, reaching to set it to rights, noticed his master's reflection. "You look like you been pulled through a knot hole backward," he groused.

Val grimaced. "Thanks. Just what a man needs. His valet telling him he looks like death warmed over." He yawned.

"Late night?" Loth's eyes fell on the book. "Oh ho! Up to old tricks, are you?"

Val, stretching, slowly relaxed his arms. "What do you mean, old tricks?"

"Reading all night and wasting lamp oil, that's what. Do you know how hard it is to clean a chimney that's all sooted up like that?" Loth pointed an accusing finger toward the lamp beside Val's bed.

"I apologize if my bad habits cause you work," said Val, a touch coolly. "I ride with Miss Bronsen this morning. I'll want the old coat, please."

Loth shook his head. "No you don't."

"I do not? And why not?" Val's tone was still crisper, a touch of frost stinging it.

Loth ignored the danger signal. "Because it ain't up to the knocker to look like a coal heaver!"

"My coat is that dirty?" asked Val with studied politeness.

"Your old riding coat," said Loth, disgusted, "is loose enough you could put it on without my help. I can't have you out looking like you dressed by guess, can I?"

"Lothario Bitterhouse, I believe I am about to lose my temper. I am too tired to argue. I want to be comfortable and Althea will not care. No one else matters."

"I don't matter?" asked Loth—but he pulled the desired garment from the armoire and began brushing it. "Won't be able to hold up my head with m'peers. Everyone'll be laughing at me."

"You can tell them I'm starting a new style."

"Oh yes, of course. A new style. And what are you calling this here new style?"

"The coal-heavers' comfort style."

Loth's eyes widened and the concern for Val, which the discovery of his reading all night had roused, disappeared. A sharp laugh burst from him. "Oh no. No, no. I'll call it a coal-heaver's Sunday best!"

Val eyed him. "You'll do it too, won't you?"

"And why not? You wait. You'll see half a dozen would-be dandies sporting loose fitting coats within a week! Here now," he finished, "you mean to gab all morning or do you mean to shave while your water's still hot?"

Val was soon ready for his ride and sent Loth to order his horse and then to hang about outside until he saw the others were ready to leave. "Then come get me," he said and yawned.

Val lay on his newly made bed and closed his eyes. Long ago he'd learned to catnap during the odd available moment and he put that ability to use now, waking easily when Loth came to inform him Jason wished words with him.

At once.

In London, Lady Elf looked her *protégé* up and down. "You'll do," she said, her tone satisfied.

"I do not see why we had to order me a whole new wardrobe," complained Jared Andover who had chaffed at the delay—to say nothing of the unwanted expense.

"Because I'll not be seen with you dressed as you were when we met," explained Elf with assumed patience. "No one would believe you were the heir. Not in that rough coat and those ridiculously baggy trousers. Your brother—"

"Half brother," corrected Jared.

"—knew the importance of dressing well. He didn't show his face until he'd a proper wardrobe."

"Very well. I have the clothes," said Jared impatiently. "When can we leave? I am concerned for the Marquis. You do realize his very life is at stake, do you not?"

"Yes, well, your half brother has had nearly a year to do Lord Lambert to death and has not bothered. I doubt he'll take it into his head to kill him in the next week or ten days."

"But you cannot know that. Baron is not to be trusted an inch. I fear for my cousin."

Lady Elf nodded. "Very proper attitude. You may be as concerned as you please, but I know better. Jason Andover, Lord Lambert, is well able to care for himself and—what is more important—Sir Valerian Underwood is awake to the time of day."

"Which will do nobody any good if Baron decides to shoot from ambush."

"I think," said Lady Elf frowning, "he has a far more complicated plot in mind. Besides, from what I hear from correspondents, we need not worry, for the simple reason he has yet to show his face in Brussels. I suppose," she continued, "we cannot put it off forever. If only Lord Lambert had sent off an agent the moment Baron—what a ridiculous name your father gave him—showed his face . . ."

"His *mother*."

". . . here in London, he would have had the truth long ago and I would not be forced to stir my stumps in order to take you to Brussels."

Humor put dancing lights in his eyes. "Oh now, that's doing it up far too brown! I am on to you, you know. You have been seeking an excuse to cross the channel and you should thank me for supplying it instead of complaining about it."

She hid a smile behind her hand. "Perhaps I have thought of joining friends in Brussels," she admitted, "but it was no part of my plans to do so in a hole-in-the-corner sort of fashion which you would have had me do. Another thing was accomplished by the delay you find so irksome. My agent has found us a suitable property in which to reside, hired servants, and prepared it for our arrival. How quickly can you be ready to depart?"

"Fifteen minutes?" he asked innocently.

She scowled at him. "And have everything packed as it *should* be?"

"Yes. I ordered that man you found me to leave things folded as they came from the tailors and the shops and have worn only those few things necessary to turn you up sweet, my lady, and—"

Elf hid another smile at that impertinence.

"—whether you believe it or not, I can be ready in approximately a quarter of an hour."

"Very well," she said, her features perfectly blank. "A quarter of an hour it shall be. Ring for my butler and order him to have the traveling carriage, the two post chaises hired for servants and luggage, and that courier I hired outside immediately."

Jared had no knowledge of how long it took a lady to pack for a journey and was unaware Elf had, for days, had her maids working at it diligently. He frowned. "Was a courier necessary? Could I not have seen to the business of travel?"

"You could if you were a courier, but you are not," she said, bitingly. "Now ring."

Lady Elf and Jared Emerson Andover crossed the Thames on their way to Dover not more than an hour and a half later.

"I do hope there are rooms available at the inn," fretted her ladyship.

"The inn?" asked Jared, startled. "Will we miss the evening packet?"

"Cross at night and arrive at who knows what hour?" She stared at Jared. "Nonsense. We travel in the light of day like godly creatures and, if we must drown, at least we will see what is happening to us. And besides," she added as an afterthought, "the good Lord will not have so much difficulty finding our souls with the sun to light them up." With that she huddled into her corner and brooded, muttering about all the things that could go wrong when one traveled.

It occurred to Jared, who listened in amazement, that it was a very good thing they'd a courier. He would not care to give her his head for washing every time her ladyship decided something was not exactly to her liking. He made a bet with himself concerning the number of times the courier would bear the brunt of her rage before they reached their destination and hoped the man's pay would compensate for the number of scolds he must endure.

CHAPTER 14

Val, wondering what had happened that Jason had asked for his immediate presence, was quickly admitted. Jimson led him to the room at the back of the house where Jason stared out into a small badly-kept garden, his back to the door. He turned as Val was announced.

"Something new has happened," said Val.

Jason nodded. He extended his hand from which a sheet of paper dangled. "This is unsigned, but I've no doubt it is from my putative heir."

Val took the page, tipping it toward the light. The insinuations concerning Clair and Val were vile and were followed by suggestions that Jason's honor required revenge if he were ever again to hold up his head in society.

Val sighed. "I hope you don't believe this farrago of non-sense."

Jason laughed harshly. "Even if I could believe it of Clair, which is impossible, I'd not believe it of you. You were never one to have petticoat dealings with married women. I'm sorry I was so irrational as to ever allow such a suspicion into my mind."

His eyes on the vicious words, Val said, "I could never get

it out of my head how *I* would feel if some dishonorable creature attempted to seduce *my* wife. I could not do that to another."

Althea, standing in the doorway, blinked. His words shattered still another rumor attached to his name, one that suggested that when his rakish tendencies were roused he'd no conscience at all concerning the woman. She sighed softly, but not so softly she was not heard.

"Good morning," said Val, his features lighting up as he took several steps toward her . . . and stopped. His eyes strayed from her unshod feet to her hair, which was only half pinned up. "Althea," he said, frowning, "what has happened?"

Silently she held out a folded sheet of paper.

He approached near enough to take it and once again tilted a page to the light in order to read the words. He closed his eyes, drew in a long breath, and let it out slowly. Even more slowly he turned to her. "You did not believe this, did you, my dear?"

"No, of course not." She waved a hand dismissively. "But it is so terribly nasty. It frightens me. I think our enemy is losing patience."

"Jason received a similar piece of twaddle. His suggested he should call me out."

"A duel?" Althea seemed to become still more pale, if that were possible.

"You must not think we are so foolish," said Jason sharply. "Val has been my friend forever. I know him very nearly as well as I know myself. He would never play me such a trick."

"But I am correct, am I not?" She looked from one man to the other. "Emerson Andover is losing patience."

"And all sense," said Val bitingly. "Jason, you will never ever again allow your outrageously strict sense of duty to our nation to interfere with personal work that should be done immediately and not put off. Not even if Napoleon is knocking at our doors."

Val sounded more exasperated than Althea ever recalled hearing him.

Jason grimaced. "You refer to the fact I did not instantly send an agent to our colonies to check on Andover's *bona fides* and what sort of man he was reputed to be."

"Exactly."

"Your man will discover what we need to know. He'll not be more than another couple of months returning to us."

Althea clenched her hands into fists. "Two more months of this . . . this . . ."

Val grinned. "How unlike you, Althea, that you are unable to come up with an appropriate *bon mot*!"

"This is too serious for jesting. Val, what are we going to do?"

"We are," he said, "going for our morning ride and coming back here for breakfast. I suggest you return to your room and finish preparing for it."

Unable to resist, he reached out and lifted a long tress from where it lay on her shoulder. He curled it around his finger and tugged ever so gently and then, his rakish grin appearing, smiled his sleepy-eyed smile at her expression, which was one of horror that she had appeared before them in such a state of dishabille.

"My dear, we'll not let anything happen to you."

That changed her chagrin to anger. "You cannot promise such a thing. Do not treat me like a child or a simple goose of a woman who is foolish enough to believe your every assurance, however wild and unfounded it may be."

His lips pressed together, half a repressed smile, half a self-deriding sneer. "I apologize," he said quietly. "You are correct and that was exactly what I attempted. I should know you better. I *do* know. You would not wish me to pretend there is no danger. Instead I will promise that we will take every care. Can you accept that?"

She nodded and reached up to pull her hair from his fingers. He released her although with obvious reluctance and then watched her move swiftly from the room.

"She would not be so concerned for you if she had no feelings for you," said Jason from behind him.

"I think she would feel the same concern for anyone in danger." Val swung around. "We need to think about this, Jason."

"This. You mean my cousin."

"I've set Loth to finding where he has put up. That is the first step. Once we know where he is, I can hire several good men to divide up the day and follow him, watch what he does."

"I'll do the hiring, Val. It is my skin he's after."

A gasp turned their heads to the doorway.

"Clair . . ."

"What is it? What has happened?" she asked, finding both her voice and her feet. She rushed across the room and into Jason's arms. "What has that man done now?"

"You are certain it has to do with Andover?"

"Is there someone else who wishes holes in your skin?"

"You have guessed it, then. Both Althea and I received anonymous letters of a particularly nasty sort. Val and I will see that no new plot takes us by surprise so we can assure ourselves of your safety. And our own," he added when she opened her mouth. She shut it. "Is that a new riding habit?" he asked, holding her away from him so he could look it up and down.

"Do not change the subject. I would know what is in those letters."

"You might as well tell her," said Val. "She will persist until she knows all."

"Yes, I have learned she can be surprisingly stubborn at times," said Jason, teasing lights in his eyes.

"How can the two of you jest?" she asked, bewildered. "I am so very much *afraid*."

"Perhaps, cousin, because right this moment, we know

there is nothing to fear. Why waste energy when there is no need?"

"*Do* men think that way?" she asked, tipping her head. "How strange. I wish I could turn my emotions on and off in such a fashion."

Althea returned just then. "Turn emotions on and off? How does one do that?" she asked.

The four discussed the subject as they exited the house and mounted up. The conversation concerning the differences between a woman's way and a man's progressed slowly and with some difficulty, as they threaded their way through streets crowded with uniformed men and wagons full of military gear.

The roads beyond the walls were not much freer of traffic. The combined armies of the allies were bivouacked for miles around and, as the time had not yet come when they were needed, the men were allowed far more liberty than might ordinarily have been expected.

"It might be less congested to the north," suggested Val. "There is a street just ahead that leads east and out of the city. Once beyond the town we may choose a lane going north."

They turned and, not too much later, found themselves in open country where they rode and talked, cantered for the exercise, and eventually headed back to the city and breakfast. They entered Brussels by a different gate and Val, finding it necessary to back his gelding away from an over laden cart, happened to turn slightly toward the rear. His mouth tightened when he caught a glimpse of Andover trailing them.

And I promised Althea we'd be on the watch, he thought, scathingly. *We'll have to do better than this.*

When they'd returned to the house and the women went up to their rooms to change, he told Jason what he'd seen.

"The animal was following us?"

"It would seem so."

"Why?"

"Perhaps Althea was correct. Perhaps he has lost patience and looks for a moment in which he may safely shoot you."

"Thank you for your soothing words," said Jason, biting the words off sharply.

Val put his hand on his friend's shoulder. "We must come up with a plan," he said. "Join me in my rooms once breakfast is over, all right?"

Jason nodded and, hearing his wife and mother approaching, moved to the sideboard where he lifted the lid off a serving salver to discover what had been supplied for their morning pleasure.

Well after dark that evening, Lady Elf looked around the salon of her rented house. She sniffed. "Oh well. It will do."

Jared raised a brow in disbelief. Her ladyship had complained vociferously on each and every occasion she had an excuse and occasionally when she'd none at all. They had, as a result, been delayed for any number of inane reasons and had only just reached Brussels. In a deliberately dry tone, Jared expressed his surprise at her mild response to their mediocre surroundings.

"Yes, well, we have arrived, have we not?" Lady Elf grinned. "And just as I meant to do. Best of all, we'll not have raised suspicions in the mind of that totally incompetent courier."

"Suspicion? Of what?"

"Why, that we meant to *sneak* into town with no one knowing of our arrival, of course. *Your* arrival, that is," she said, giving him a look of surprise that he'd not understood her intent. "Which I managed very well. My timing could not have been better."

Jared thought of the crowds of soldiers thronging the streets even so late in the evening, but, of course, mere soldiers were not considered of any importance.

But they are of significance, he thought. "Are you certain you wish to stay here, my lady? It appears war is imminent."

"Pooh." She waved a hand dismissively. "The Duke will see to Nappy fast enough. Wellington is well up to Napoleon's weight. He'll have the French running for their lives in no time at all. You'll see."

"I hope you have that correctly," said Jared a trifle grimly. His republican tendencies set him, to a degree, on the side of the French but he'd no desire to find himself in a besieged city or under French control if they were to win the coming battle.

"Besides, we'll have seen to our business and be long gone while war still looms on the horizon. See if there is something resembling ink and paper in that secretary, will you?" she said, waving her cane at the closed desk against the far wall.

There was a surprisingly good quality of paper, decent ink, and, once Elf was assured the pen was properly sharpened, she heaved herself from her chair and, stiffly, moved to the desk chair Jared held for her.

"Now." She touched the top of the pen to her chin. "How best to manage . . ."

"Surely all you mean to do is tell my cousin I am here."

"No, no. Where is the fun in that?" Elf nibbled on the end of the pen and then grinned one of her nearly evil grins. "*That* is what I will do. *Just* the thing . . . but who?" She pursed her lips. "Lady Lambert, of course. She is *most* necessary. Lambert and his wife, of course. Now, should I invite anyone else . . . or is your immediate family sufficient to begin?"

"Invite my family? To what? Why?"

"Dinner. Here. And so they may get to know you, of course." But she didn't look at him and Jared, who had come to know her, wondered what her ladyship was up to.

* * *

The next morning Val joined the others in the Lamberts' breakfast room as usual. "You will never guess," said his cousin as he entered. "Mother Sarah has received an invitation for the three of us from Lady Elf. She invites us to dinner tomorrow night."

"Elf is in Brussels? She crossed the channel? But she hasn't left London for years. I have heard her say that if she must need to ever travel again it will be in the hearse that takes her into the country to a final resting place in her husband's family crypt."

"Great goodness, Sir Valerian," exclaimed the elder Lady Lambert, her eyes bulging. Ice coated her voice when she continued. "Is it strictly necessary to quote the lady on *such* a subject?"

"Sorry, my lady," said Val, bowing towards the dowager.

"So you should be . . . but," she added slowly, "there *is* a mystery. What can have got her away from London to Brussels?"

"There is a solution," said Althea, looking up from her shirred eggs and hot roll. The others turned to her, a questioning look on each face. She shrugged, slightly embarrassed at the simplicity of what she had to say. "All you need do is accept the invitation."

"I do not care to wait so long," mused Val. "Althea, finish your breakfast, put on your bonnet, and collect your maid. We will pay dear Elf a call. Merely to welcome her to Brussels, of course."

"An excellent notion. And then you can report to us," said Lady Lambert, who settled more firmly into her chair before reaching for another of the truly excellent rolls.

Val made shooing motions at Althea who sipped the last of her morning chocolate. She set her cup aside and went to do his bidding.

Althea and Val arrived in Lady Elf's drawing room only to find themselves twiddling their thumbs. Voices, arguing, could be heard in the room beyond. The tone was clear. Unfortunately, *words* were indistinguishable.

"Well-well-well." Elf came through the doors dividing the rooms and closed them firmly behind her. "Didn't know you were here," she said. "In Brussels I mean."

"Where else would we be?" asked Val absently, his thoughts on the voice he'd heard speaking to his hostess. It had sounded very much like Emerson Andover. And yet there had been a lack of arrogance in the tone that left him uncertain.

"I think very nearly half the *ton* must be here, Lady Elf," said Althea. "We are never still, it seems."

"Hmm. Well, cancel whatever you have planned for tomorrow night and join me for dinner."

"We will be pleased to do so," said Val promptly and then was surprised when Lady Elf rose to her feet and held out her hand.

"Very good of you to stop by, but the truth of it is, it isn't quite convenient. Tomorrow. For dinner." She nodded firmly. Once.

Val, caught off guard by her sudden rudeness, didn't think to rise to his feet as he should have done when a lady was on hers. When Elf stared down her nose at him, he blinked and, hurriedly, corrected the situation. "Should I wait until then to reveal our news, Lady Elf?" he asked, adopting a teasing note in the hopes of lengthening their visit.

"Hmm?" Her thin brows arched. She looked from one to the other. "*Ha.* She said yes, did she? Well, I told you she would," said Elf with satisfaction.

Val cast a quick look at Althea. Her brows were arched high.

"You did?" asked Althea sweetly.

"Oh yes. Knew you would eventually. Can't love a man as you love our Val and keep on saying no, can you? Wouldn't be reasonable."

On more than one occasion Val had wondered if Althea loved him. Unfortunately, he'd been unable to *believe* it—except intermittently and then only briefly.

When her ladyship continued to suggest by her manner that their absence was much to be desired, they departed.

"What do you think that was all about?" asked Val. "Elf can be abrupt, but I have never known her to be outright *rude*."

"Why do you think something was the matter? Was it not our own fault that she felt harassed? After all, she *has* only arrived."

"Do you think that was it?"

"What else might it be?"

"That argument in the other room," he responded promptly. "When we first arrived. Did you listen? She was quarrelling with someone before coming in to us, do you not agree?"

"I tried very hard *not* to listen," said Althea dryly.

"I, to the contrary, did my best to overhear. Unfortunately the voices were muffled. The *tone*, however . . ." He trailed off, thinking.

"Tone?"

"Althea, I would swear there was something in the man's voice very like Andover's."

"Andover! What would Lady Elf have to do with that man?"

"*Like*," repeated Val. "It wasn't quite the same."

"*Another* man from the provinces?"

"That is my guess. Think Althea. Did you hear nothing that would make you wonder . . .?"

She searched her mind. "Val, I fear I was thinking of . . . something else. I'm sorry."

He mimicked her pause, curious about what had held her thoughts. "Something . . . else?"

Althea felt her skin heat at the faintly teasing note in his voice. "Why do you think Lady Elf—" She, when his arching eyebrows made it clear he saw through her ploy, grew rosier. "—is playing some sort of game with us?"

"Elf gave up all travel some years ago." He touched one finger and then the next. "We heard a voice from across the Atlantic." And a third. "We have an invitation to dinner when she will barely have had time to settle herself. That is three oddities. Believe me, Althea, the lady is up to something."

"You know her better than I," said Althea.

"I thought I did, but I wonder," he retorted. "Well," he added after a moment, "let us report our failure."

Another anonymous message arrived before anyone else got around to leaving the house. This one, to the dowager, informed her that the *ton* was aware of the breach between Jason and his wife—due to Val's interference in the marriage.

A muscle jumped in Val's jaw. "The man is foolish beyond permission. No one has any reason to suggest the two of you are at odds or that you and I have had a falling out."

Jason sighed. "When do the foolish need a *reason* to believe what they *wish* to believe? What are we to do?"

Val shrugged. "Go on as we always have? If we are seen to be on the best of terms, belief will fade. Or, if someone mentions something, we will laugh it off. If there are hints, we will merely look blank and lacking in understanding."

"I do not like it," said Jason. "I do not think it will suffice."

Looking thoughtful, Val admitted that, given the *ton*'s willful liking to believe the worst, he was forced to agree. He turned to Althea who stood nearby, her hands clenched together at her waist. "My dear," he asked, "are you willing to become something of a byword?"

"How so?" she asked, a wary expression and a hint of withdrawal in her face and manner.

"No." He shook his head and stared off into the far corner at nothing at all. "I cannot ask it."

"Ask *what*?" she insisted.

He turned to her and shrugged. "That we be caught in a

mildly amorous situation by someone we know. Someone who will pass the word on to every gossip in Brussels—in strictest confidence, of course," he finished with harsh sarcasm. "It is a bad idea and I withdraw it."

"It would suggest," she said slowly, "that any hint that you have been romancing Clair is nonsense, would it not?" Her mind raced. He would kiss her again. Kiss her as she wanted him to do . . . *and in a good cause so that I need not feel guilty.*

"That was my notion, but it will not do. I did not think of how it would tarnish your reputation."

The bleak look Althea had noticed before, returned to his features. Val had intimated he was playing with the notion of leaving England forever. She did not know it, but the thought of his losing her forever and still seeing her on occasion was harrowing in the extreme. At that particular moment when he looked so sad, he was considering whether to travel in Europe or to go farther afield—South America, for instance.

Althea touched his arm and drew him from his reverie. "I think it a good notion, Val," she said, her eyes downcast.

"A very *bad* notion. Forget it."

"No. We must lay our plans carefully, however." She frowned. "We are invited to a picnic, are we not? Where is it to be held?"

"Out near Quartre Bras," said Jason who made no pretense he was not listening to them argue. "Val, if Althea is willing, I agree that it is a good plan. Everyone knows you never shower attentions on more than one woman at a time. If you are known to . . . to . . ."

"Be making love to Althea?" suggested Val, his voice hard.

"Well, yes . . ."

"And then, when she tells the world we are no longer engaged and I deny I've ever touched her, so as to leave her with her reputation intact—what then?" If anything, his tone was still more harsh.

"Val," said Althea, hesitantly, "it is known we are engaged. It would be thought *more* strange, would it not, if we did *not* indulge ourselves in a trifle of dalliance now and again?"

Val looked harassed. "I would think you'd realize it is in your best interests to refuse. I should never have mentioned the notion."

"It is my decision to make," said Althea quietly. "I believe we should allow ourselves to be caught while—" She felt herself blushing hotly. "—embracing."

He touched her cheek. "My dear, even the thought embarrasses you. Can you not see how difficult you would find it to face the sly looks, the jests—perhaps some idiot concluding you are fast and attempting something of the same nature with you?"

"I *have* considered all that."

"Did you? Really?"

"Of course."

"I think not."

"Val . . ."

He shook his head, laying a finger across her lips. "We won't mention it again. Instead, let us put our minds to finding another means of confounding Andover."

"I could be caught kissing my wife," suggested Jason.

"That could not hurt our efforts," agreed Val.

"Then I'll do it."

"I will find Clair and warn her," said Althea.

"No!" Both men spoke together. Jason continued. "I think it best if she not be warned. Clair is a loving and wonderful woman, but she cannot dissemble worth a groat and it would be necessary that she do so. Instead, I will catch her unawares—and you or Val can be responsible for assuring someone suitable to our purposes happens upon us while we are so occupied."

Althea frowned. "Is it any different? Do you wish to subject *Clair* to the sort of teasing you mentioned?"

"Everyone knows Clair. No one will say anything vicious to her."

"As they might to me?" Althea choked on half a laugh and half an angry sound. "What is there in my character that makes me different?"

The men looked at each other. "You are older," said Val.

"You have been on the town much longer," agreed Jason.

"You are, frankly, more intelligent," added Val and waved his hand at Jason's mild outrage. "Intelligence is, for reasons I've never understood, associated with a certain sort of style. A . . . a freer way of life?"

"Ah! I would merely be doing what is expected of me, whereas it will be thought Clair was drawn down the garden path by her lascivious husband?"

"That sounds about right." Val nodded. "In addition, given my unfortunate reputation, they would say you walked into my arms knowingly." His dark features hardened at the speculative look in her eyes. "Althea, do not think to trick me into misbehaving. It will not do."

She chuckled and spoke to her fingers, which she studied with great interest. "Is it not a trifle odd that the rake is warning off the innocent?"

Val growled but Jason chuckled. "She has you there," said Jason. "So, are we agreed? I am to be caught seducing my wife and that will surely put paid to any rumors that we are estranged."

CHAPTER 15

A goodly number attended the picnic party. There were three open carriages filled with young ladies and their mothers. Still other women rode with the gentlemen. Lady Babs, for instance, sat the back of a magnificent animal that Althea envied her—until the creature acted up and Babs was forced to struggle with it.

"She is enjoying herself," murmured a shocked Althea to Val when her ladyship's ringing laugh sparkled on the air.

In fact, when an officer approached, obviously meaning to help, Althea was still more shocked that Lady Babs used her crop on him—and astonished when her ladyship, having brought her mount under control, told the officer in no uncertain terms he was never ever to do such a thing again. Babs followed that rudeness by putting spurs to the horse's sides and riding off in a pet.

"What a terrible temper," said Althea softly so that only Val could hear.

"A family trait, I fear. Her grandfather ran off with her grandmother to France, as perhaps you know."

Althea hadn't known.

"That was temper as well, according to the story Elf once

told me. It seems the Devil's Cub, as he was known, meant to take the sister, but the woman who is his wife wanted to save the other one from a life of degradation and secretly took her place. She intended, according to the story, to return to her home before anyone was aware she'd left it—but *not* until she taught the Cub a lesson."

"And he abducted her?"

"I think at some level she must have been willing," mused Val. "After all, they are married and it has, from all anyone has ever said, been an exceedingly happy marriage."

Althea shook her head, bemused by such behavior. In her nursery, tantrums were not tolerated for a moment and, later, when she was older, any show of excessive emotion was firmly repressed by her governess. Eventually she was capable of taking her emotions in hand under any and all situations.

Well, almost any situation. There was that kiss . . .

"I always thought," she said, quickly repressing those memories, "that it is a distinguishing characteristic of gentility that one did not reveal oneself in such a manner."

"Certainly that is true for *us*," said Val and chuckled. "I suppose," he added, explaining his laughter, "that at Lady Babs' level of society, one lives by a different standard." He changed the subject. "We are a large group today. Will we, do you think, have a opportunity for Jason to enact our little plot?"

"How can we not?" She answered her own question. "Or perhaps not if our destination is destitute of bowers and copses or other means of achieving privacy. I do not see Clair, however smitten she is with her husband, allowing him liberties where all can watch."

"You will notice he has been flirting with her madly ever since we set off."

"I noticed. Did you notice Clair's blushes?" She frowned slightly. "If he is not to anger her, I think he should, perhaps, ease off a bit?"

"I'll tell him," said Val, and prepared to ride forward and join his friend.

"No."

He settled back into his saddle. "No?"

"I will. We are, after all, attempting to rid the *ton* of the notion you are particularly taken with your cousin, remember?"

Val chuckled. "Very well. Aha! Babs has forgotten she is in a temper and has rejoined her officer. Assuming I am not making a third in a conversation meant for two, I will join them. When you've smoothed things over with Clair, come to me, will you?"

There was a wistful note in his tone that startled her and she turned a surprised look his way.

"You did say that not revealing oneself was a sign of gentility, did you not?" he asked, a harsh note replacing the other. "I find that where you are concerned, my love, that I am not at all civilized. Not if I must hide from you how I feel about you."

He rode off and Althea stared after him, her mind awhirl. It had begun to sneak through her defenses that just possibly Valerian Underwood believed himself in love with her. The question remained, was he right to do so?

She forced the notion well back into the deepest closet of her mind and, putting her heel to her mount, joined those surrounding the carriage in which Clair rode. By indulging in a trifling rudeness, she managed to get between Clair and Jason—who cast her a surprised look.

"Clair," said Althea, ignoring his lordship, "I have just recalled something you must hear."

Clair glared at her, revealing the stony expression she'd worn as Althea rode up. Then she appeared to relax. "Yes, Althea? What is it?"

Althea laughed gaily. "Do you remember a wager you made with my Val?"

"A wager . . . ?" Clair frowned and then her features lightened. "About a certain bonnet?" she asked.

"Yes. You will not be pleased to hear that Val has won the bet."

Clair pouted. "You actually saw . . . ?"

"I did. I remembered it when he told me about your wager. I told him he'd won but he forgot to tell you, did he not?"

"Yes, but it makes no difference. If I did not win, he keeps the sixpence."

A dandy riding near and listening avidly, laughed. "A sixpence? The wager was for nothing more than a sixpence?"

"Yes, but a very special sixpence. It has an odd nick along one edge and is a lucky coin. I have been trying to win it back from him for ever so long," said Clair soulfully.

"But if it is already his, then do you not lose . . . something valuable to you?" he asked in a suggestive tone.

Clair looked blank.

Althea sighed. "You are suggesting something nasty, are you not?" she asked in a bored tone.

Clair, to whom such at thing would never occur, gasped and turned accusing eyes on the dandy who actually blushed, and stammered excuses and apologies.

"I—"Althea continued to sound bored, adding to the man's embarrassment. "—have known Lady Lambert and Sir Valerian for ages and have seen them trade the sixpence back and forth on previous occasions when one or the other has lost it."

"That is true," said Clair, nodding. Althea's comment allowed her time to recover herself. "Val seems to win far more often than I. I guess he is more knowing than I will ever be." Clair sighed. "It is not fair, but then life is not always fair, is it?"

The dandy, completely cowed, made some sort of inarticulate response and, bowing to the two women and then to the others riding in the carriage, seemed, even on horseback, to slink away from their particular group.

"Life is unfair." Althea watched the fop look for other prey. "And *that* was unfair of you, Clair."

"What was unfair?" asked Lady Lambert who, up to that moment, had been uncharacteristically silent.

"She became overly serious and philosophical, which frightened poor Mr. Sawyer out of what poor wits he has."

Those in the carriage chuckled and Althea noted that Jason, unable to get close to his wife, had fallen back to join some friends. He was involved in what she hoped was an all-absorbing conversation that would keep him occupied for some time so that she could safely leave Clair to shift for herself. She saw that Val *had* joined Lady Babs and her officer, and, excusing herself, rode forward.

"All well again?" asked Val when she reached his side. He slowed and gradually let the others go on ahead.

Althea matched his pace. "All is well for now," she said, "but I have no notion for how long."

They reached a wide path beside a canal and those leading the party turned in to it. About a mile farther along beside the slowly flowing water they came to a very pleasant park-like area where servants were busily setting up tables and putting out refreshments, including a keg a liveried man was tapping and, nearby, large pitchers of lemonade.

Val collected two glasses of the lemonade and strolled with Althea to where they could walk farther along the water's edge. They returned soon, and were there to watch as Jason plucked Clair from her carriage, swinging her around so that her petticoats revealed deep ruffles of gossamer lace. Once again Clair looked embarrassed.

"Val, I guess you will have to say something to Jason before he goes too far and sets up Clair's back. She is quite capable of cutting off her own nose to spite her face if she becomes too irritated."

"I know," he said, speaking a trifle grimly.

Val took Jason aside, but it did no good. Jason was in a rollicking mood and had, as well, been nipping at a flat-sided flask. He pooh-poohed Val's warning and—not much later—said something to Clair that made her look as if she would burst into tears and had her turning on her heel and stalking off.

Val restrained Jason from going after her while Althea followed her friend along the water until they were quite alone.

"He is a beast to treat me so," exclaimed Clair. "As if . . . as if I were a . . . draggle-tail!"

Althea looked at Clair's gown of expensive voile, trimmed with still more expensive lace and fought to restrain chuckles. "I was unaware you knew that word, my dear. Perhaps someone had better point out to you a true draggle-tail so that, never again, will you apply such a term to yourself. But I think you misjudge Jason. He has had exceedingly heavy responsibilities for months and months. Perhaps for years? Suddenly he is free of them. I suspect his freedom has gone to his head and now that he has time with you he is overly amorous and . . ."

Clair gradually relaxed as Althea spoke, but then Althea went too far, reminding her of Jason's behavior. Clair pouted. "He is making a byword of me by the outrageousness of his conduct. I do not like it, Althea. I have never liked being the center of attention, as you very well know. But he is teasing me and teasing me and saying such *shocking* things!"

"I doubt anyone cares, my dear. *Everyone* is engaged in teasing each other in similar fashion. Perhaps you have been preoccupied with your own feelings and have not noticed that everyone is a trifle wild today. Perhaps it is concern about the approaching battle? That we wish to kick up our heels just a trifle because we cannot know what will happen next, how soon many of these young men must face horror and death?" She gestured toward the many officers gracing the party with high spirits.

Clair sobered. "Althea, I fear I am more my father's daughter than I'd thought. They should be thinking of their souls and preparing themselves for the worst while praying it will not happen. They should not revel and jest, dance all night, and play frivolous games all the day."

Althea sighed. "Perhaps you are right, but I think even your father would understand that seeking an excess of pleasure in the face of danger is natural."

Clair sighed in turn. "I wish . . ."

"What do you wish?"

In a small voice, Clair said, "I wish we could return to England and go to Jason's estate. I want it to be like it was when he found us here at my *belle-mère's* friend's chalet, when we had that handful of wonderful days together."

"Soon you will do just that. But you forget that first we must make it safe for the two of you. We have not yet managed that—"

Clair looked suddenly stricken, her eyes flying toward her beloved husband, her lips caught between her teeth.

"—but," Althea continued, musing over a conclusion she'd reached, "I do not think it will be long now."

Althea had thought long and hard about Lady Elf's behavior and about the other voice Val had heard. Elf, she knew, loved surprises and Althea was almost certain that when they went to dinner with the lady, her ladyship had a plan in hand that would neutralize Andover forever. She prayed she was correct.

"Come, Clair. We will return to the party and you will be as gay and frivolous as everyone else, will you not?"

Obviously rather doubtful that she was capable of obeying, Clair nodded. They reached the others just in time to see Sarah, Lady Lambert, collapse.

Jason was not so up in his altitudes that shock could not

bring him down and, instantly, he moved to his mother's side. Clair gave a tiny gasp and picked up her skirts. She rushed to the dowager's aid as well.

Kneeling, she looked across the prone woman into her husband's face and saw the fear there. She placed her fingers to her mother-in-law's neck, felt the pulse, which seemed strong enough although it fluttered slightly. She nodded and, again, met her husband's worried gaze.

"I do not believe her in immediate danger, my love," she said softly, "but perhaps you should order our carriage harnessed so we can take her home." She picked up Lady Lambert's gloved hand. "I will wait with your mother, Jason, while you do so."

The carriage pulled near and there was no shortage of helping hands to lift the elderly woman into it. Althea stepped up to cover her ladyship with a blanket someone handed her. She tucked it around the woman and murmured words of encouragement she was unsure her ladyship would hear.

Therefore, she was more than a trifle shocked when Lady Lambert opened one eye, winked at her, and then closed it again. More briskly, Althea pushed the blanket into place and allowed Val to help her down.

"Should we go with them?" he asked, concerned.

"I think they will do better without us," said Althea, her tone neutral. "Clair, do not worry so. You yourself said her pulse was strong. I haven't a notion what happened," she lied, "but I doubt very much it will be any more than a tempest in a teapot."

Clair cast her friend a shocked look from her place in the carriage and Jason looked unhappy with her. Lady Bronsen actually sniffed. "My dear child, how can you be so unfeeling?" said Althea's mother, as she climbed into the carriage.

The driver, driving slowly so as to not jar his mistress, set off for Brussels where her ladyship could be made comfortable and a doctor called.

Val knew his Althea and when, gradually, the party resumed its natural rhythm, walked her away from the others. "What, my dear, was that all about?"

"I think her ladyship felt her son was about to overset Clair and needed curbing. Does she know we'd formed a plot for today?"

"I don't know. I don't think she was there when we made our plans but Jason might have told her." He sighed. "However that may be, their leaving puts paid to it."

Althea bit her lip. *Do I dare? Have I the courage?* She decided she did and squared her shoulders. "The original plan was a trifle different," she said with uncharacteristic diffidence."

He turned a quick sharp look on her. "You are suggesting . . . ?"

She nodded.

He drew in a deep breath. "My dear . . ."

"Val, we must scotch any rumor there is a breech between you and Jason, that there is any sort of liaison between you and Clair."

He nodded but continued to stroll, his hands behind his back, his fingers intertwined, opening and closing them in an agitated manner. "My dear, there is a problem."

"Yes?"

"I don't believe I can *pretend* to kiss you. Once I have you in my arms—" He cast her a burning look. "—I fear I will . . ."

When his words stopped, she nodded. "You will truly kiss me." She swallowed, knowing it was what she wanted more than anything, knowing that, as a well brought up young woman she should *not* want it. "I will . . . not struggle or do anything to make anyone think I do not like it," she said.

"I will think about it, Althea. I am so afraid I will give you still more of a disgust of me."

"I . . . think I may have overreacted when you kissed me that day in the vicarage garden. I had, at that time, had no experience of such things—"

He cast her a sharp questioning look.

"—and was . . . surprised?"

"Althea . . ."

"I will not be surprised this time. I will know how a kiss makes me feel and it will not shock me as it did then."

"Althea . . ."

"So I do not think," she said earnestly, "you need concern yourself that you will give me a disgust of you. It is not that."

"Althea . . ."

She tipped her head, looking straight ahead, a frown creating a vertical line between her brows. "In fact, I don't think it was ever *disgust* . . ." Startled, she looked over his fingers that were pressed against her lips. He released her. "Yes? You've a question?" she asked.

"Althea, did you imply that you have, since then, experienced the kisses of other men?"

She blinked. Then, understanding him, she frowned. "Now *that* suggestion *may* give me a disgust of you! Surely you know me better."

Relieved, he laughed. "Oh, my love, you are a delight. *My dear delight.*"

"Val . . ."

He shook his head. "We are where we may be overheard so I think we will continue this another time. Althea, I have not decided . . ."

Again he could not find the words and she nodded. "I will trust you to do what you think best," she said—and continued to hope that, finally, she would have an opportunity to experience again those very strange sensations that had, at the time, frightened her half to death by their strength, the oddity of them.

They found that food was set out and that the guests were filling plates, some already seated at small tables or on blankets, continuing the laughter and the teasing as they ate. Val gestured and Althea nodded and, soon, they joined a hilariously giddy group that centered about Lady Barbara. They were welcomed.

"Miss Bronson," said Babs, "do you know Colonel Audley?"

Introductions were made and Althea found herself laughing just as much as anyone else at the droll stories and very slightly bawdy songs produced by the revelers around them.

She had forgotten there was a plot. She had, in fact, forgotten that Andover existed. It was a shock, then, to see him strolling around seemingly in search of someone. He stopped by their group.

"Pardon," he said, his sneer well in place. "I was told my cousin meant to join this party . . . ?"

"The dowager," said someone, "fell down in a fit of some sort and Lord and Lady Lambert took her home."

"Hmm," said Andover and, for just an instant, looked irritated. The frown faded so quickly that Althea was uncertain she'd seen it. "Do you think our host will object if I help myself from that exceedingly tempting array of food?" he continued, smiling his most charming smile.

Althea noticed his eyes did not smile and felt, inside, as if she cringed away from the man.

He was assured that he was welcome and wandered off. It was an assurance Althea and Val wished they dared contradict. Val rose to his feet, pulled Althea to hers, and, after telling the group he needed exercise after eating far too much, put her hand on his arm and strolled away in quite the opposite direction from that taken by Andover.

They were not alone in their wanderings. Twice they stopped to chat with others exploring the lovely sun-warmed glades and paths shaded by tall trees. Here and there were comfortable bowers with seats in them and elsewhere patches of grass starred by low growing flowers. They had wandered rather far from the picnic party when, Val looking all around, pulled Althea behind the fat bole of a large tree, the branches of which hung down in a rather protective fashion.

Althea looked up at him trustingly and he groaned. "I

love you," he said softly and, just a trifle roughly, pulled her close, enclosing her in encircling arms that held her both protectively and possessively. When she didn't look away, his head lowered—and their lips met.

Althea felt her heart race, felt a strange but welcome warmth surge through her body. She lifted her arms and pushed them up his chest, up around his neck, and for long moments, reveled in the feel of his hair in her fingers, the taste of him, and the joy of being close to him.

She hadn't a notion how long it was before she heard a giggle. Her eyes opened and she blinked. Val felt her withdraw from him and lifted his mouth from hers, looked at her—and smiled. "I love you," he repeated softly, unaware they had an audience.

"By golly, who would have guessed? It is a love match!" said a rather slurred voice.

Val's head lifted sharply and turned. "Sawyer. Go away."

Althea pushed gently against his chest. "We are finely caught, Val, and perhaps it is as well." Feigning humor she added. "We are not married. *Yet*," she added.

He stared down at her, bemused. "No. Not yet. When?" he asked softly.

"It cannot be instantly, of course," she said, teasingly, "since my mother will insist on all the conventions."

"Conventions?" he asked, still more than a trifle preoccupied by emotions that had grown beyond his expectations.

"Things like bride clothes and invitations and wedding breakfast," she said and, surreptitiously, pinched him.

He jumped, looked around and was reminded that there was an audience. He was not pleased, but hid it. "Ah. Yes," he said, realizing that Althea was carrying them through their little plot with no help from him. "You do not think it better if we simply elope and forget all that?" he asked, his voice lightly teasing, as it was not before.

Althea noted the change but could not decide to what it should be attributed. *If only*, she thought, *it were that he for-*

got, until just now, that we were scheming to overset Andover's latest nastiness.

But she could not believe it. Not quite.

"We'd best return to the others before I ravish you and we are forced to the altar at once," he growled and glanced again at Mr. Sawyer who, eyes wide, had taken in every word. "Do you not know when you are *de trop*?" asked Val, something of his old self-deriding manner about him that was half a sneer at mankind in general and half at himself in particular.

"De trop?" Sawyer blinked. "Oh! *De trop*." He looked ever so slightly confused. "That means I'm not wanted?"

"It means you are very much in the way, Mr. Sawyer," said Althea, smiling. "But since we mean to return to the picnic, perhaps we should all go together." She looked beyond Mr. Sawyer to a small mixed group of girls and officers who were either blushing, looking very knowing, or pretending nothing at all out of the ordinary was happening. "Val?"

"Hmm. Yes, I suppose the mood is broken and we may as well return." But he put her hand on his arm and held it there with his other hand, a warm and comforting touch that also insisted she not move apart from him. Since Althea had no desire to move away from his side, she made no objection. None at all.

And poor Sir Valerian was convinced his Althea was a far better actress than he had had reason to believe.

But surely they had succeeded. Word would spread that they had been caught in a rather compromising situation and even if it were not exaggerated beyond recognition to far more than the kiss it was, Althea's reputation would be in the mud if she did not wed him.

Is there no way I can convince her to do so?

CHAPTER 16

Val struggled to think of a means of convincing Althea she should wed him, but despaired of doing so. How could she, after all, when it meant disregarding the whole of her training as a proper lady?

Althea spent still more time wondering how a proper lady told a man she loved him and wished to marry him. To do so in so many words would mean going against who and what she was. In fact, it was impossible to convince Val that marriage to a rake was exactly what she wanted.

Even if he did not love her to distraction—which notion was not such an impossible thought as it had once been— she loved him so much she could not bear to lose him. So what if she was forced to suffer the lows that marriage to such as he must entail, would she not also enjoy the greatest joy and pleasure given to a woman? Assuming that kiss earlier today was anything by which to judge, far *more* pleasure than she'd known existed?

And there would be children. Val was good with children. On occasions when both attended the same house party, she had watched him secretly. The first time she'd seen him entertain a nursery party with invented games it had amazed her. At another he'd taken older children in hand, teaching a spindly-legged, all arms, lad to fish, and archery to a brother and sister.

And, most important, was his patient tenderness to a little girl who feared horses. Althea had come upon them when he'd sat beside the child on a bench in the sun. Despising herself for an eavesdropper, Althea had nevertheless listened as they gravely discussed just why it was a good thing if one did *not* fear horses. Once agreed there *were* good reasons, they discussed how one could rid one's self of such fear. After that, each day, he had spent time with the child and, before the party ended, had, with the girl's reluctant cooperation, introduced her to the gentlest of mares and overseen her first lessons.

Althea had asked him about it. He'd shrugged. "The house party is a bore," he'd said. "That child is far more interesting than anyone else attending—except you, of course. Now if *you* were to offer entertainment, my dear . . .?" And his eyes smoldered at her and she'd found herself retreating from what had become far too intimate a moment.

But his liking for children was another reason to wed him, was it not? Somehow I must find a way to wed him.

Althea went to bed that night and dreamed of marriage, dreamed she walked down the aisle toward Val who waited before the altar. His dark eyes seared her, but the strength of his hand holding hers was a comfort, a strength on which she could rely. The wonder of it warmed her and comforted her and somewhere deep inside there was the relief that, finally, all was settled and she need not stew and fret and worry about him ever again . . .

Ah dreams! What a sham and deceit they were! It was a great shock to hear the curtains rattling along the rod as they were pulled back, a shock to feel cold sheets on either side of her. She was not pleased to open her eyes to lowering skies and rumor of an approaching storm. She hoped it was not prophetic of her future.

Because they could not ride or walk in such weather, because the streets were too full of military men and wagons loaded with the accoutrements of war to take out the carriage, they did not go visiting. The same reasons kept others from coming to them. Val was, for some reason, in a teasing mood, so Althea spent a great portion of the afternoon in her room where the washing and drying of her long hair gave her an excuse for absence from the group gathered in the salon.

Not that they missed me, she thought ruefully as, later, she looked around the room.

Gowned for their dinner with Elf, she had finally descended to discover the others enjoying a rollicking game of crambo—a game more often relegated to country house parties where finding rhymes to witty lines of poetry could lead to much hilarity—and could, occasionally, become a trifle wicked. Val was posed in the posture of an orator, speaking his line when something caught his attention and he turned to see her framed in the doorway. His mouth snapped shut in midword and, his eyes never leaving hers, he prowled toward her. A small occasional table stopped him and he put his hands flat against it, leaning toward her.

"You are," he said, his voice deep and full of emotion, "more beautiful every time I see you."

Althea saw the dowager's brows arch in surprise or was it distaste? She blushed and looked down. "You spout nonsense, Val. I have never been beautiful."

"You are."

"You," said the dowager, acid in her tone, "forget yourself, Sir Valerian!"

He didn't even glance at her. "No. I have found myself." He stepped around the table and stalked—it was the only word that fit—nearer. Althea looked both ways, wondering what to do. And then, before she could decide, his hands pressed against her upper arms and he backed her into the hall and beyond sight of the others.

His kiss was something neither of them would ever forget. "You do love me," he said softly. "I know you do."

And then, before she could gather her dignity around her—or even before she could find her voice—he turned on his heel and returned to the salon where, seemingly unperturbed by what had passed between them, he finished his contribution to the game.

But then, having done so, he went to stare into the smoldering fire in the fireplace as if no one else existed.

Lady Bronsen, a tiny frown of worry between her brows, went to where her daughter stood, rigid, just within the doorway. "My dear . . . ?"

Slowly Althea relaxed. She forced a chuckle. "The day will come when he embarrasses me once too often!"

"He loves you so much, my dear, and he is a man. Men do not have our . . . our ability to . . . to wait patiently for . . . for . . ." Tangled in embarrassing thoughts she could not put into words—especially not to her unmarried daughter—Lady Bronsen waved one hand in a weak and undecided fashion. "My dear, it is simply something you need to . . . to accept. Men are . . . they are just that way."

Althea's temper drained away and when she chuckled again it was with true humor. Val, hearing it, turned. Their eyes met. He grimaced. She twitched one corner of her mouth. He drew in a deep breath. She closed her eyes for a moment.

And, somehow, without either of them saying a word, his apology was made and accepted. Both moved into the center of the room and joined the others as if nothing at all had happened. The dowager Lady Lambert, looking from one to the other, threw up her hands in disgust. "The sooner," she said, bitingly, "we get the two of you wed, the better it will be for all of us. Such emotions should *not* be revealed where just anyone can be singed by them."

She then left the room, a minor whirlwind of temper, and, calling back, suggested that perhaps Lady Bronsen and Clair might wish to think of going up to dress for their evening at Lady Elf's.

Jason, after a few words to Val, also left the room and, reprehensibly—or, more generously—*absentmindedly* closed the door behind him. Val instantly moved to the fireplace. More slowly, Althea followed.

"I should not stay here," he said. "Not alone with you."

"We need to talk."

"Yes, well, perhaps. But not now. Tomorrow. Preferably—" His brow quirked in that self-deriding way he had. "—when we are on horseback."

A startled burst of laughter escaped her. "While riding?"

"When we are riding, my dear, I can refrain from putting my hands on you," he said, and even more clearly heard was the derision she had learned meant that he mocked himself.

She nodded and turned slightly. "I think I have begun to understand your difficulty," she murmured.

Unsure he'd heard her correctly, he moved nearer. "Althea . . ."

She turned and looked, steadily, into his eyes. "Val, I wish I knew how to say this . . ." She broke off when he abruptly turned away.

"Say no more." His voice was as harsh as she'd ever heard it. "I will do better. I promise you."

"Val, you do not underst—"

"Hush," he said, turning back. "I have promised. You need say no more."

She felt a growl rise up her chest and actually made some sort of odd sound—but he had moved to the far side of the room and, just when the jumble of thoughts in her head worked themselves into some sort of order, the door opened and a footman announced, "Mr. Andover."

"Good evening," said their unexpected guest.

Althea felt Val stiffen.

Andover peered ostentatiously around the room. "Is it, then," he asked, "correct for an engaged couple—" His sneer as he spoke those words was exaggerated. "—to be alone behind closed doors?"

"For brief intervals," said Val, his self-control firmly back in place. "Did you wish something?"

"Only to speak for a moment with Clair. Lady Clair," he corrected himself when Althea cast him a shocked look. "I have hopes she will join a party I've gotten up. There is a delightful little coffee shop just beyond the walls to which I wish to introduce her."

"I do not think she is down from dressing," said Althea. "We are dining out this evening, so it should not, I think be long before she comes."

The door opened as she spoke, but it was Jason who entered. "Val, I was told . . . Oh. Emerson."

Andover's ears reddened slightly. "Good evening, cousin," he said, bowing. "I was just telling these good people that I hope to have the joy of your good wife's company on a small excursion I have arranged for tomorrow."

Val and Jason exchanged a look. Jason cleared his throat. "We would be happy to join your party. Only tell me when and where . . . ?"

A muscle jerked in the side of Andover's jaw and, for a moment, he lost the urbane expression he'd adopted. His features hardened into a cold mask—but then it softened and he bowed. "Excellent," he said and suggested he come by so they could go together. "We drive out into the suburbs, dine, and, when ready, return to town as a group," he said. "Miss Bronsen tells me you are dining out, so I will remain no longer. Good night," he added, bowed to Althea, halfway between Val and Jason, and, turning on his heel, moved quickly toward the door. As he opened it, they heard a slight gasp. "Lady Lambert," he said. He held the door for her, again said good night, again bowed, and finally, he left them standing still as statues and as silent.

"What did he want?" asked Clair, moving toward her husband, her eyes huge in her pale face.

Jason explained. "But you need not concern yourself, Clair, my love. Val will be somewhere near and he and I will see that you come to no harm."

"He is planning something. Something nasty."

"Very likely. He was not happy when I accepted his invitation as if it had been given to the both of us."

"But . . ."

"Clair, love, trust us?"

"We will not let that villain harm you," said Val.

"Should I join the party?" asked Althea. "Would you be more comfortable if I pretend I believed it was an invitation to all of us? Perhaps Lady Lambert and my mother should come as well?"

Val chuckled and even Jason smiled. But then Val tipped his head, thoughtfully. "And why not? We will all go. With all of us there he will find it very difficult to do anything. Whatever modification he makes to his plot to take *your* presence into account, Jason, will surely be nullified if he has *five* extra guests."

Jason chuckled. "You are devious to think of such a thing, Val. We will ask the ladies if they will join us."

In the carriage taking them all to Lady Elf's, they discussed it. "Of course we will all go," said Lady Bronsen firmly. "I never liked that young man and he has made himself something of a nuisance. I think you should tell him he may be your heir, Lord Lambert, but that does not make him welcome in your house."

Althea rolled her eyes at her mother's naivety. Val patted her ladyship's hand, and said, "It's a trifle more difficult than that, Lady Bronsen, but soon now, with any luck at all, he will go off with a flea in his ear."

They arrived and, as they exited the carriage, a drunken soldier fell against Lady Lambert, grasping her skirt to save himself, and not only did he dirty it, but his grasp ripped a bit of the seam where the skirt was attached to the bodice. The dowager, upset by the damage, demanded that a maid make repairs before she was announced to Lady Elf. Elf's lady's maid was called and led Lady Lambert upstairs as the others were shown into the drawing room.

Elf limped toward them, her ivory-handled cane firmly in her hand. "Ha. You have come."

"We have come."

Elf frowned. "But where is Sarah? We need Sarah."

"We?"

They looked across the room toward the fireplace where a stranger stood, his back to them. Very slowly, the man turned.

Jason paled. "Father . . ." He blinked and shook his head. "But that is nonsense, of course." He marched across the room. "Another cousin, I dare swear," he said, his voice harsh. "Who, exactly, are you?"

But the door opened before a response could be made and Lady Lambert entered. She too looked across the room. Her eyes widened. She mouthed a name and, her lids fluttering, slowly sank to the floor.

"Mama," said Jason and rushed to her side but the women, who were nearer, reached her first.

Althea had the dowager's wrist in her hand. "Her pulse is a trifle fluttery, but it is strong."

"Oh dear, oh dear," said a worried Elf. "I did not mean this to happen! It was supposed to be a *good* surprise."

Sarah, Lady Lambert, groaned. Then she struggled to sit up. "What . . . ?"

"You had a shock, Mother, as had I. It seems I've another cousin arrived from the colonies." He glanced over his shoulder to where, his arms hanging at his side, and a frown marring his young brow, the stranger still stood by the fire. "Lady Elf, you've some explaining to do!"

Jason helped his mother rise and, soon, everyone was seated. "Now Elf?" asked Val, a touch of humor in his tone. "Do you think you could do something about the suspense we feel?"

Lady Elf grimaced. "I meant it for a surprise, yes, but I

didn't think it would be so much of a one. This is Jared Emerson Andover, legitimate son of your uncle, my lord, unlike that blackguard, Baron Maker, who has been masquerading as your heir."

"Masquerading . . . ?"

For the first time, the young man spoke. "Perhaps you will allow me to explain?" he said, looking from one face to the next. He spoke firmly, with only a trace of an accent. "I only discovered Baron had fled when I finally made it back to my summer home," he continued. "A friend, who deals in furs, saw him here in London when he made his annual journey to sell the winter's take of furs. He saw that Baron wore my ring."

"Your ring," said Jason. He was not about to be taken in still again.

Jared nodded. "We'd had a fight the previous spring. He decided that his share of that winter's catch was inadequate for his needs and wanted it all. He's always been stronger than I and, as usual, he won. When I came to—" The provincial looked embarrassed. "—I was up to my chin in fast running water and had a bump on my head the size of a beaver lodge. I'd been pushed by the current against a log that had jammed against a rock outcropping and I was barely high enough out of the water to breathe. Indians rescued me." A grim look dimmed his eyes. "They were not the most friendly of Indians," he said.

"You were enslaved?" asked Althea who had read of such things.

Jared nodded. "Yes, but I was lucky. I rescued the chief's youngest son from a wildcat attack and, as a reward, was given my freedom. So I made my way back to town where I learned Baron had sold our furs and fled."

"And?"

"That was also when the trader told me my cousin was here, masquerading as me."

"Why," asked Jason, "should I believe you over the other one? Over . . . Baron?"

"Because I don't want anything—except the return of my ing. It is the only thing I have that belonged to my father." A muscle jumped in the man's jaw. "Baron stole it after knocking me out and before dropping me into that river. The—" His eyes flicked to the women. "—scoundrel," he finished rather lamely.

It was not, Althea assumed, what he'd meant to say.

"If what you say is true, *you* are my heir," said Jason.

"Yes but—" Jared flicked a quick, almost mischievous glance toward Lady Elf. "—if what I am told is true, *that* problem should disappear within the year or so." He bowed toward Clair, who blushed.

"You consider it a problem?" asked Val, idly playing with a curl that had escaped Althea's coiffure when she knelt to help Lady Lambert.

Jared nodded. "I am a republican. I find it reprehensible to be in the position of possibly inheriting a title I find abhorrent."

"I would not admit to such beliefs anywhere less private," said Val, grinning. "You might find yourself denounced and sent to the Tower to await beheading—which would, of course, also solve your, er, *problem*."

The stranger barked a laugh and Althea found herself liking him. "I will take your advice," he said. "All I want is to return to my life—preferably without concerning myself about my half brother's continued existence." Once again there was a hard look to the man that revealed that life for those living and working in the wilds of the new world was not easy.

"You would accuse him of attempted murder?" asked Val.

"Not here. Back home I would do so—which he knows. Assuming he's got the guts to show his face ever again. Which I doubt."

"Please tell me the relationships involved. I know you are both sons of my uncle, but the other Emerson is obviously the elder. Why is he not my heir?"

Jared looked as if that should be obvious. When they expectantly awaited his response, he shrugged. "He's illegitimate, of course."

Val and Jason nodded, and the women, given their various temperaments either grimaced or blushed.

"My father," continued Jared, "had a relationship with Baron's mother, Mavis Maker, when he first arrived in Canada. I suspect he abandoned her not too long after Baron's birth. He had met my mother, you see. Mother was—" His eyes grew soft and memories could almost be seen flashing through his mind. "—special. She, she once told me, did not fall into his arms as did most women of whom he became enamored. Her father was an itinerant preacher and had reared her to value herself above such behavior—" He shrugged. "—so Father married her."

At that he stood and went to the mantel from which he plucked some official-looking documents. "You will," he said to Val, "wish to see these. They include their marriage lines and my father's will which states in so many words that Baron is a bastard. I don't know if you need more, but I've an affidavit from the trader who saw Baron here in England if that will help. Not much, I suppose, since it could be sworn by anyone willing to lie for me."

Jason quickly scanned the various papers and handed them on to Val who allowed Althea to read them over his shoulder.

"I will admit," said Jason after he'd read everything a second time and more carefully, "that I hope these can be validated. I do not like your brother."

"Half brother."

"If your father abandoned his mother," said Lady Lambert, "then how did this brother—"

"Half brother," said Jared a trifle more loudly and a lot more insistently.

"—manage to come into *your* life?"

"His mother died when he was thirteen. He knew Father. Not well, but *mon père* had, on occasion, visited them. Baron came to Father and insisted it was his responsibility to finish rearing him since there was no one else."

"It is more common for a boy that age and in his situation be put to work," said Lady Elf.

Jared nodded. "My father was amused by Baron's arrogance in making the demand."

"Baron."

Jared chuckled. "His mother knew father came from a titled family but not exactly what rank. She named the boy Baron as way of getting back at my father for refusing to wed her."

"I cannot simply accept your word for all this," said Jason, slowly.

"I understand that. I know you'll have to send a man to determine the truth, but my fear was that you'd find yourself —er— difficulties before you accomplished that."

"Difficulties?"

"I can think of nothing that Baron would find beyond him," said Jared quietly. "He . . . hasn't got a heart, I think."

"That is certainly a kind way of putting it," snapped Lady Lambert who had been uncharacteristically quiet, staring at the stranger as if she could not get enough of him. "You know," she said harshly, "that you've the look of your uncle, do you not?"

"My uncle . . . ?"

"My father," said Jason. "There is a portrait of him painted when he was about your age that you might have stood for. Frankly, it is uncanny how alike you are to it."

"Lady Lambert," said Jared softly, "I cannot change how I look, but I apologize if my form and face caused you to swoon when you first saw me."

Lady Lambert frowned mightily, the only way she could hide her emotions. "So like Mathers. When I first knew him . . . oh, yes. So *very* like him."

Val stood. He turned his back to the fire and studied everyone. "This is all very well, but we've decisions to make, have we not?"

"Yes," said Elf, also rising, "But not on empty stomachs. We will dine."

On the words, the doors to the salon were thrust open an
her butler cleared his throat. Haughtily, he announced th
dinner was served—and was offended when everyone laughe
at his speaking so exactly to Lady Elf's cue.

During the excellent meal no one discussed anything tha
could not be overheard by the servants. Finished, they a
journed to a cozy little parlor at the back of the house. One
the butler had set down the tea tray and overseen the pourin
of brandy for the men, Lady Elf spoke to him. "I do not wis
to be disturbed," she ordered. "I am not at home to anyor
who might find their way to my door this night."

The butler nodded, trod out in stately manner and, quietl
closed the door. Everyone relaxed when the man's footstep
could no longer be heard going down the hall toward th
front of the house.

Val looked around the room and grinned. "We are a
such sobersides. If no one has a better notion, I have a plan

"Tell it and we will discuss it," said Lady Elf, noddin

"It is quite simple. I assume that your half brother think
you dead?" asked Val, turning a questioning look on Jare

"He left when the first ships went east last spring," sai
Jared. "I didn't return until late in the summer and foun
he'd given out a story about sickness and my not survivin
it."

"Then why was your fur trader surprised to see him wea
ing your ring?" asked Val, quickly.

"Because he also said that when he returned from check
ing our traps, our camp had been ransacked, our best skin
taken along with everything else of value—which was though
to include the ring, of course."

"He'd gone off and left you, sick and helpless, just t
check your traps?" asked Clair, shocked.

Jared grinned. "You forget. I was not sick. It was a tale—
but yes, the traps must be checked regularly or the pelts de
teriorate. Then they lose value. If I *had* been ill I would hav
encouraged him to go."

Althea shook her head. "It is a harsh life, is it not?"

"Yes, but also a life full of wonders. Someday you must visit me in my own place. You will see a world that is new, that is real, where nature rules with both an iron fist and a softness and beauty that one absorbs through one's skin—air like wine to which one becomes addicted, the smell of pine and good earth, of fresh rains of spring and the clean icy cold of winter, wildflowers and singing birds, flocks of geese beyond belief and . . ." He broke off, looking rather embarrassed and cleared his throat.

"I rather hope that was a true invitation, because if it was not, you will be surprised when we turn up on your doorstep," said Val, humor riding his voice. "I, at least, am intrigued to the point of desiring to see it."

"I didn't mean to give a speech," said Jared, his ears red. "But we were speaking of a plan?" He glanced around.

Val nodded. "Yes. I wonder if perhaps Baron might not give himself away if he were, unexpectedly, confronted by you."

Everyone gazed at Val.

"Someone say something!" He frowned when no one spoke. "Will it not work?"

"I'm awestruck."

"The simplicity of it!"

"How could it fail?"

"And," said Val, slowly, "even if it *does*, we have our villain hobbled. With Jared added to the equation, he will be forced to see that enquiries must be made and that he can no longer automatically be assumed to be the heir. In fact, the mere fact that enquiries are to be made may convince him to give up his plotting, since, even if he succeeded, he would not inherit in the end."

"Why not?" asked Lady Bronsen. She had followed the conversation with difficulty.

"He is illegitimate and cannot inherit. That would be proved."

"There is still revenge," said Elf. "A man as bitter as he must be to have tried what he has tried would not be happy at finding he's unmasked."

"Wait just one little minute," said Jared, looking from one to the other. "Does this mean you believe me? Before you've checked? I have reason to hate him, so how do you know I've not made up my tale in order to harm him? *I want him dead.*"

Val chuckled. "Frankly, even if you lie, we like you far better than we do your bro—*half* brother," said Val, correcting his slip of the tongue. "Don't bristle. I'll remember. If the man truly tried to kill you," he went on, "and you suffered months of slavery, which can be *worse* than death, then you've reason to hate him. *But*, however you feel about him, however *we* feel about him—" A certain grimness was evident in both face and voice. "—there is the law." He caught and held Jared's smoky gaze. "We will not take it into our own hands."

"Bah!"

"Hothead," said Jason. "Val is correct. If you've any notion of taking revenge, then you should set it aside. At least," he added when, once again, his cousin looked ready to insert a hot comment, "until we do what we can within the civilized canons of society. If we were in the forests that you love, we would need to learn your ways, would we not? It works both ways."

Jared sighed. "I have dreamed of the day I would confront him, face him down, make him pay . . ."

"Of course you have," said Lady Elf. "Any man would. Still, I think there is a better way than killing him. That is much too fast for the snake he is. Sir Valerian's plan may very well lead him to reveal himself. If he does, then he will be arrested and tried . . . and hanged from the neck until dead. As does any murderer. I don't think he'd like that," she said thoughtfully.

Everyone laughed. "No," said Jason in a tone very like Val's dry humor, "I, too, doubt he'd like it."

"I meant," said Elf, very much on her dignity, "that the humiliation would be worse for him than facing a gun and knowing his time had come. That he could understand. It would be the sort of thing he'd do. But a trial! Having crowds watch him die ignominiously . . . no, he'd not like that."

Althea sobered. She swallowed. "It is all so horrible."

"He is horrible," said Lady Lambert, looking down her nose. "And if he is horrible, then he deserves whatever horror comes to him!"

"I am still astounded that you have accepted me so easily," said Jared, wonderingly.

"You are either by far the best actor I've ever met or you are transparently honest. I would prefer to think the latter," said Val with just a hint of a bite.

"I haven't been acting," said Jared. He flared up. "The notion I'd act a part is insulting!"

"That," said Val, "is why I prefer to think you honest. Or is it also an insult to be thought honest?"

"No." Recalling the rest of Val's first comment, Jared grinned, his volatile emotions swinging toward humor. "Only that I am transparent. How lowering to one's self-esteem!"

Plans were made and, everyone emotionally exhausted by the revelations and planning, the evening ended. Althea climbed into her bed that night wondering what the next day would bring. Would the man they now called Baron reveal his guilt? Would he see that further attempts to harm Clair and Jason were fruitless? Or would he seek revenge? *Or* would he be under arrest and unable to take revenge?

Would their fears, in short, be ended in one short confrontation between the half brothers? Fervently, Althea prayed it would be so—but she feared that Baron Maker was the sort who would not be satisfied that all was lost but would seek revenge one way or another.

CHAPTER 17

Althea was unable to settle to anything before the hour at which she intended to dress for their outing as guests of the imposter. They had decided to pretend that nothing had changed those plans, since he must come and remain unsuspecting while the plan went into effect. She envied Clair who sat setting stitches, working diligently on one of the chair seats. Finding it nearly impossible to resist twitting her friend, she excused herself and went into the main salon.

She was delighted to find that Lady Babs and her friend had been shown into it while Jimson went in search of the ladies to see if they were at home to guests.

"Lady Barbara, Colonel Audley! I am so happy you came by," said Althea with enthusiasm.

Bab's chuckle warmed the air. "Why have I this odd suspicion you were bored to tears and in need of any sort of distraction at all?"

Althea sobered instantly. "Not bored. A bundle of nerves. You do not know."

"But you," said Val, standing in the doorway, "are about to reveal all. Do you think you should?" he asked, his voice touched with just a hint of frost.

Babs eyed him. "On your high horse, are you?" When Val turned hard eyes in her direction, she tipped her head. "You are excessively rude today, are you not? Do you mean to say hello to Charles or should he call you out for cutting him?"

Val nodded a curt greeting to Colonel Audley, but without saying anything, turned back to Althea. "My dear," he said more calmly, "I believe you must not."

"Ah! But now you have gone too far and you surely *must*," insisted her ladyship. "Do remember whom you would deny," she added, her impatience revealed in a wave of her long slender hand. "You know we are to be trusted if it is something of which we must not speak."

Val sighed. "Althea, indiscretion is so unlike you," he complained.

She too sighed. "I know. I should be angry with you for scolding me, but I am much too . . . too *twitty* to care." She frowned when Val barked a laugh. "You men do not understand how it is with we poor females. The *waiting*. How do you bear it?"

Lady Barbara and the colonel looked from Val to Althea and back again as each spoke.

"What is there to do but wait?" he asked Althea softly. "Why waste energy and emotion before it is needed?" he continued, obviously bemused by her attitude. "We've discussed this before, have we not?"

"But what if . . ."

He cut her off. " 'What ifs' are a still greater waste of time. We have done all we can to assure that all happens as it should. There is nothing more to do." He turned to their company, each of whom wore a speculative look.

"It has to do with that arrogant fool calling himself Lambert's heir, does it not?" asked Babs.

Val's lips compressed into a hard line. "You'll not be happy until we explain, will you?"

"No." Babs smiled. "So, old friend," she urged when he looked stubborn, "get on with it."

Val remained silent and she tossed her head impatiently. He grinned suddenly, his ill humor fading. "*Just* like a feisty mare I once owned," he said. When Lady Barbara frowned and Colonel Audley chuckled, Val explained *that* comment instead of revealing what Babs *wanted* to know.

"Charles, call him out," ordered Babs.

"On what grounds?" he asked mildly.

"I don't know." Then she brightened. "Because he called me a mare?"

"I cannot hand him a challenge when I agree with him," said the officer, putting on a plaintive air. "That little head toss in which you occasionally indulge, is just like a horse that wants its own way and has taken the bit between its teeth."

Lady Barbara growled, her eyes narrowing.

"Do not lose your temper with me, Babs," said Charles softly. "We have discussed your temper on other occasions, have we not?"

Althea watched as strong emotion appeared to ooze out of the red-haired woman. Babs shrugged and smiled in the self-deriding manner that was Val's habit.

"On the other hand," continued Charles, looking at his fingernails. "I too would like information concerning that Andover creature. He is far too lucky at cards for my liking." He looked up and caught Val's gaze, held it. "If you know something to his discredit, then I will thank you for sharing it. I've several young fools under my command who need a good reason to cease sitting at whatever table that man gives his attentions. You will note I do not say *honors* with his attentions. I've no proof, merely a strong suspicion, but think it far more likely that he *dishonors* it."

Val shrugged. "I suppose explaining makes no difference at this point. With luck, all will be at an end—assuming our scheme works—and you will have no need to concern yourself. The man will be unmasked as a fraud." He paused and grimaced. "If it does *not* proceed as planned, then I guess we have no choice but to wait for word from the agent who sailed west to check on him."

"I see." Charles' hand closed over Babs' when she'd have demanded more. "Is it permitted that we know when and where your plot is likely to unroll?"

"Our first thought was to arrange it publicly when we were out together this afternoon. Second thoughts led to the decision to get it over and done with in a more private setting. We disliked the notion of hanging out dirty family linen in public, you see. Andover, as we still call him, is to arrive here about three to collect us. We are invited to a party he arranged at a little *café* he discovered in the suburbs. Our plan is that he enter the house as if there were some delay and, while here, he'll be confronted by someone he knows. Someone who knows him well. Someone he will not expect to see. His reaction should tell us everything we want to know."

Charles' eyes narrowed. Again, much to Althea's surprise, he silenced Babs when she tried to say something. His easy management of the difficult and strong-minded woman was unexpected. Lady Barbara had a reputation of being ruled by no one.

"Have you," asked Charles, "arranged for men of known honor to overhear what goes forward?"

"Blast! We cannot keep it within the family as we'd hoped, can we? You are correct that such a man is needed." Val's lips pulled in tightly as he thought. "There is so little time . . ."

"Nearly one," interrupted Charles as he glanced at the ormolu clock on the mantel. "I know where the Duke of Richmond is to be found. He would oblige you, I think. And we might track down Creevey, assuming you want word to get around of what happens? Which—think about it—you should want. I can't think whom else . . . Babs? Have you a suggestion?"

"Wellington," she said promptly. "He is in town today, is

he not? If you need a man of honor to attest to what happens, there is no one who will be believed so quickly as he."

"Wellington—but he is completely inundated with his work as commander in chief, is he not? With plans for the coming battle?" asked Althea, rather horrified to think of asking such a favor of the great man.

"Not to the point he never does anything else," said Charles, grinning. "I'll see what I can do. Three o'clock, you say?" They nodded and Charles rose to his feet drawing Babs with him. "I will have two or three men here at two thirty. We can come as if to see Lambert, which can also be your reason for the delay. You can have your butler show Andover to whatever room you will use for your *dénouê-ment.*"

"Babs has changed so much," mused Val when the two had gone.

"Changed? Do you mean she used to be more . . . ?" Althea could not think of a word that was not derogatory. "Volatile?"

The suggestion was as good as any. Althea nodded.

"She has a temper that can shoot more sparks than one of Whinyates' rockets. Charles seems to have the happy knack of defusing it without raising her hackles. I wonder," he mused, "if, in the end, they will make a match of it."

"Are they not already thought to be a couple . . . ?"

Val grimaced. "Babs is likely to test his temper beyond what it will bear or he might expect more of her than she can manage." He shrugged. "He would be good for her. I hope it works out for them."

"You do not say you think she would be good for him?"

He grinned. "That point, my dear, is more debatable."

Jason entered then, Clair on his arm, and Val explained the change in plan. Jason nodded. "We should have realized witnesses were necessary, whatever occurs. Even if it turns out negative, from our point of view, and we know no more than now. But if we do prove Emerson a fraud, someone outside our circle must attest to it." He looked around, thoughtfully. "They'll need to be hidden," he said, speaking slowly.

Jason ordered Jimson and the footmen to rearrange the salon in such a way that there was a screen along the back. The large room was thereby divided into two unequal portions. The smaller part became a sitting area hidden behind potted plants and an unusually tall and wide escritoire that faced into the rest of the room. The larger portion retained its more formal arrangement.

Once finished, the room looked natural to them, but they tested it in several ways, ascertaining that anyone seated in the chairs facing the windows could not be seen from the main room.

"Do you think he'll be suspicious?" asked Clair.

"Why?" asked Althea. "We have simply replaced a rather boring sort of *décor* with one that is a trifle out of the common way."

"Perhaps he will wish to explore . . ." suggested Clair.

"It is still cloudy and it is damp," said Althea. "Perhaps if there is a fire in the fireplace, that will draw him. At least long enough so that we can set in motion the entrance of our, er, umm, *ghost?*"

"Perhaps he too should be hidden in the room. Rather than come through the doors which will have been shut behind Andover?"

They discussed the notion and discarded it. If Jared was seen by Baron to come from around the screen, then Baron might suspect others were there as well.

"You have it worked out logically," said Lady Lambert from the doorway. She went to explore the new arrangement and returned to where the others stood awaiting her decision. "This should do. I will be *very* glad to have it over and done," she finished, made cross as crabs by her concern that all go well.

"Not so very long now," said Jason, soothingly. "Jimson is laying a luncheon in the back parlor. Shall we adjourn there?"

"Not until Lady Elf and Jared arrive," objected Lady Lambert.

"You have invited them to join us?" asked Jason.

"You are not the only one capable of foreseeing problems. I do not want that creature arriving early just as *they* arrive and seeing his brother—half brother—before time," she corrected herself even though Jared was not there to object.

Lady Elf and Jared were announced and they adjourned to the parlor where they enjoyed a very good luncheon indeed. Or some of them did. The others *would* have done if they'd had any appetite.

Val touched Althea's cheek. "It will be all right. You will see," he said softly.

"Yes, but then if he does not reveal himself we must worry that he will ambush any or all of us merely for the sake of revenge," she muttered so softly only he could hear.

"Cassandra," he teased.

"I am not a character in a Greek tragedy. And I am not predicting disaster. I am only worrying about what might happen."

"Once again wasting energy on what you can do nothing about," he said. She smiled weakly and his finger tapped the corner of her mouth. "Ah. The hint of a smile. More?" he asked, cajolingly. She pressed her lips together, the lower pushing the upper into a downward curve. "Please?" he coaxed—and traced the ups and downs of her mouth, the warmth of his finger reaching her and the sensitivity of her lips raised by his touch.

Althea reached up and grasped his fingers, holding them tightly. "I promise I will find reason to smile once this is over. Do not make me pretend all is well when it is not."

He nodded. "Very well. Do you think you would be distracted by a game? Or by one of us reading aloud? I see Clair has returned to her everlasting sewing, but that is not your way . . . Perhaps a walk in the garden?" he finally suggested when nothing else appealed.

He looked out into the ill-kept grounds when she cast him a look of disbelief.

"No, perhaps not," he agreed. His eyes smiled at her and, at that rather rueful look, she managed a weak smile. He nodded and, giving her fingers a squeeze, moved to talk to Jason who was discussing the government's colonial policies with Jared who, they discovered, was scathing to the point of treason in his views.

They were arguing about tariffs when Babs and Charles arrived with the Duke of Richmond, Mr. Creevey, and, much to everyone's surprise, the Duke of Wellington.

"Your Grace. We are honored," said Lord Lambert, welcoming the great man.

"How could I not come once I heard the tale? Not to be missed, your little scheme!" Wellington's braying laugh filled the room. "Need a bit of entertainment these days," he added more quietly. "Too much of everything is made dark with worry."

"You've had news?" asked Val softly.

Wellington glanced toward Mr. Creevey who was all ears. "No, no," he said briskly. "Nothing new. The Emperor, so far as we know, remains in Paris. Now, tell me what you mean to do and how we are to help."

The plan was once again explained and the witnesses shown the chairs, complete with small tables to hold a glass and the most recent journals which Jason had brought over regularly from England.

"Not that we'll dare drink or read once the man comes," said Wellington. "He'd likely hear us swallow or the rustle of a page."

"It would be best to lay things aside when Jimson taps on the door," agreed Val who had wondered how to give that warning tactfully.

"Is it time then, that we hide ourselves?" asked Mr. Creevey.

"Not just yet. I've my valet lurking near Andover's chambers. He's to bring word when our quarry leaves them." He looked at Jason, silently suggesting he fill the waiting time somehow.

"I've just purchased what I think is a very good wine," said Lord Lambert, after a nod of understanding. "I wonder if I could beg your opinions of it." He bowed toward the visitors and gestured toward his butler who left the room.

Jimson soon returned carefully carrying a dusty bottle. Reverently, he opened it. Soon the men sipped thoughtfully.

The women departed as soon as they saw that they were not wanted. They joined Lady Elf and Jared in the dining room, a room that, even if the villain would not allow himself to be put into the main salon was not one he was likely to enter.

"You will pace a path in the carpet if you do not settle down," scolded Elf.

"I wish this over. Done. I dislike playing the Judas."

"Mr. Andover, if it is repugnant to you, then you should not do it," said Clair softly. "We will understand."

Jared shook his head. "The bastard—pardon my language, ladies—must be stopped. I doubt there is any way we can manage it except that he condemn himself from his own mouth."

"Is that the style of clothes you'd have worn the last time he saw you?" asked Althea, interested in the open necked shirt of soft leather, the sleeves fringed, and the loose-fitting leather trousers. "Is that deer skin?" she asked.

Jared looked down and a rueful look twitched his features. "You have guessed it. I am unsure why I brought such things with me. They are my working gear." He laughed softly. "But, even when new, I don't believe they looked as they do now. I've no notion what the man Lady Elfreda hired for me did to them, but they are not only softer, but a far lighter color."

"Since we suspect Baron thinks you dead," said Lady Elf, a chuckle in her tone, "then likely he'll merely think the paler tone a ghostly tint!"

Everyone laughed, but, with the mention of the enemy, their thoughts returned to the seriousness of their plot and, almost immediately, they sobered. Althea had asked the only question she could think of to pass the time in a sociable manner and could manufacture no other means of lightening the atmosphere. She glanced at Clair and wondered how her friend could sit setting stitches. She herself felt as if she could chew her nails down to the quick and, obviously, Jared felt much the same.

"Fiddle," grumbled the dowager, displaying her taut nerves. "This waiting is a nuisance. How much longer?"

They heard the front door knocker and stiffened. The door opened and Althea, disappointed, grimaced. "It is Bitterhouse, Sir Valerian's man."

"Shush," said Lady Lambert crossly. The elderly woman had crossed the room and was, shamelessly, listening at the door. "Your brother—"

"*Half*," said Jared under his breath.

"—has left his rooms. He is strolling this way. It will not be long."

"Thank heaven," said Clair softly, glancing up and then back down at her work.

Althea realized her friend was not so relaxed as she appeared. Of those in the room, only Lady Elf was her normal self. She looked up and saw what Jared did. "Idiot! Come away from that window. We do not want him seeing you."

Jared moved, but only to the side where he'd be less visible. "I must check that it is Baron."

Elf fumed, glaring at him, but then, after several minutes, Jared backed still farther into the shadows and she relaxed. "Well?" she demanded.

"It is he." A muscle jumped in his jaw and his eyes narrowed. "That sneer. He hid it pretty well before Father died.

Father was not one to put up with nonsense from either of us. Since then it has become very much a part of him . . ."

Althea, watching, could almost see Jared growing angry. "He is an evil man," she said softly, "but perhaps to be pitied. Reared by his father, but knowing he could never be acknowledged in the same way you were. It must have grated on his soul, exacerbating an already weak nature."

"Baron is not weak."

"Evil comes from weakness, Mr. Andover," said Clair. "I understand what you meant, Althea, but I disagree. I have known men born on the wrong side of the blanket who are perfectly decent men who have made something of themselves despite their poor start in life." When she was looked at in surprise, her brows arched. "Should I not have mentioned the blanket bit? But I grew up in a vicarage. I suspect I know all sorts of things I should not and it is not possible to remember, always, which I should pretend to forget."

"I see no reason why you should forget and you are right," said Elf. "But I am afraid that Althea has a point as well. I have lived a very long time and have seen about all there is to see in the way of mankind. A bastard-born man may be honorable and upright and it is equally true that a *gentleman*, born to the purple, may turn out as wicked as can be. I have come to the conclusion that birth has nothing to do with character."

"You are a republican, then?" asked Jared, interested.

"Now where," asked Lady Elf, her nose elevated to an arrogant angle, "did you get a ridiculous notion like that?"

That comment, made in the huffiest of tones, induced laughter—but it was choked off when the door knocker once again brought the sound of Jimson's steps crossing to the door. They waited, tensely silent, until they heard Andover's demand to see Lord Lambert.

" . . . *instantly*, my good man!"

"Not only the sneer but insolence as well," muttered the brother waiting in the dining room.

"A delegation arrived to speak with his lordship and he asked that you join him in the salon," said Jimson. They heard Jimson's soft rap at the salon door, heard him open it and heard the butler announce Andover's arrival. But then they heard a muttered 'botheration.' "Sir," continued Jimson, "Lord Lambert and the others have left the room. If you will be so good . . . ? Ah, yes. Very good of you. I will find him. *Instantly*, of course."

Althea felt a chuckle at Jimson's wry mimicry and sternly repressed it. The doors across the hall closed with a touch of a snap and Jimson's footsteps were heard crossing to their door. He opened it and nodded to Jared. Then he stood aside with a querying look as if to ask: "for what are you waiting?"

Jared drew in a deep breath. He swallowed. Then he strode through the door without a look at the other occupants. When Jimson would have closed it, Althea, who was nearest, prevented him from doing so. He looked disapproving—after all this was not *women's* business—but he did not insist.

Jared did not close the salon door, either. The listening women heard, "Hello, Baron."

There was a strangled sound. Then a loudly spoken, "No." That was followed by a brief silence and then. "No, stay away. You're dead. You must be dead!"

Althea thought, *It is not going to work. He is not going to admit he attempted to murder Jared.*

"Oh you managed that, did you not?" asked Jared. "You knocked me out and threw me in the river where, unconscious, I could not help but drown. Yes?"

"Don't come a step closer. I'm warning you!"

"But, Baron," said Jared softly, "if I am already dead, that pistol will not harm me."

The women froze.

"You are *not* dead," was the cold response. "I don't know how you survived, how you got here, but this time I'll make certain. A . . . a *housebreaker*." The false brother spoke wildly. "That's what you are. You attacked me. It'll be believed that I had no choice . . ."

There was a sudden flurry of sound and motion. A shot. Another. A chunk of the dining room wall exploded outward, showering Clair, who was nearest, with plaster.

All that happened in moments and, intermingled with the other sounds, Althea heard a body hit the floor and roll, and a scream and a second body fall. She could stand it no longer and rushed to the salon door—but retained enough sense to peer into the room before entering.

Jared Andover was, cautiously, rising to his feet. Slumped near the fireplace, Baron Andover stared in astonishment at his bloody hand. As Althea watched, Jared moved nearer. Baron looked up. "I hate you," he said distinctly and, with those words, he died.

Althea looked further around the room. Colonel Audley stood near the potted plants, a pistol in his hand and his face rather white. Beyond was Mr. Creevey, also staring, his eyes starting from his head and the Duke of Richmond, his lips pursed in a thoughtful manner.

And coming around the other end of the screening greenery was Wellington. "My boy, you cut that rather fine, did you not, dropping down like that?" he asked Jared in a friendly manner. "Don't suppose you'd care to join my army? I could use another cool head or two or three. No? Didn't think you would." Wellington sighed and then brightened. "Ah well, this has ended better than it might have done." He toed the body. "Might have had to stand his trial, you know. And suffer a public execution. No, no. Much better this way although I'm sure you do not think so just yet." He turned to the Colonel Audley who had shot Baron Maker. "I'll write up my testimony, Colonel. There will be no problem. Good shooting, by the way. One of Manton's, is it not?" he asked gesturing at the pistol. "Well, well, must return to business. Never enough hours in the day and here I've wasted time on

his business. Glad it worked out so well," he said, shook
hands all around and, taking the colonel and the duke off
with him, he was, quite suddenly, gone.

Creevey remained. "High drama," he said to Lord Lambert
who approached to thank him for standing witness. "Must
admit I didn't expect anything so out of the ordinary when I
agreed to tag along with the others."

"Perhaps you would care to know more before you depart. You must be wondering what this is about. First of all,
may I introduce my true heir presumptive?" He beckoned
and Jared approached.

While Jason spoke to Creevey, telling him what they wished
him to know, so that the story, when retold—as Creevey was
sure to do—would be what the world should know, Val talked
the women into adjourning to the small parlor at the back.

"It is all over," he said. "We've a bit of a mess to clear up
with the authorities, but with Wellington's testimony that
will be no problem. I am glad, frankly, that Charles fired the
actual shot. It would not have looked good for family or me
to have killed Andover. Go on, now. It is over. Truly. We will
join you as soon as we can," he added when Althea, with her
questioning gaze, asked a question.

Despite his assurances, Clair was not convinced. "It is
truly over?" she asked. "I no longer need worry that Jason is
in danger?"

"Believe me, child. *He is safe.*"

Clair nodded, allowing herself to be reassured.

"*Have* you worried?" asked Althea, curious.

"Terribly. You will never know how awful it has been hiding it from everyone. Oh, what a relief that Jason is safe!"

"I wonder why I have worried more about *you*, Clair, than
about him," said Althea.

"Because you are so very conventional, of course," said
Clair. "You feel *he* can care for himself but that *I* cannot."

Althea, remembering what happened before Clair would

admit the villain was a villain, did not argue, but her frien
was wrong. In this particular case *both* Clair and Jason ha
needed someone to look after them and Althea's thoughts i
stantly turned to Val. The pair were indeed lucky to have ha
that someone, someone as able as he, to take on that rol

CHAPTER 18

The next few days were not easy. There was the official enquiry, but thanks to Wellington's statement that was soon over. Practical problems were less easily solved. Finding a British curate who would officiate at Andover's funeral was difficult. The women's presence was not required at the brief service held at the graveside, but the curious flocked to watch, which made the whole exceedingly distasteful for the men.

Most difficult of all was the gossip, the questions, the speculation, that followed them everywhere. Clair became fine-drawn and *more* rather than *less* unhappy. Finally, deciding something must be done, Althea searched for and found her friend alone in the back parlor.

"What is it?" she asked. "What is upsetting you now? I'd have thought that all would be well and that you could relax and enjoy life."

"I hate it."

"Hate *it*?" repeated Althea.

"Everyone talking about us. Everyone wanting to hear all about it. It *isn't* over, Althea. It is *worse*. Living it again and again and having to pretend we are sorry, unable to tell people how terrible a man he really was, merely that, when confronted with Jared, he admitted trying to kill him once before and was killed when he attempted to shoot him, right there in our salon."

"I'd think that enough."

"But it is lying, Althea. Lying by omission, of course, but still a lie."

"No. It is the bones of the truth, which is more than others have any right to expect. It is the bald truth of exactly what happened that single afternoon. No one has asked about your past association with the man, have they?" She eyed Clair. "They have? I see." Althea considered her friend. "My dear, if you do not wish to be bothered by prying and impertinent questions, why do you not ask that Jason take you home?"

Clair's eyes lit up. "Home . . ." The light faded and she drooped. "How can I? He is worried about the coming battle. He wishes to help . . ." Her eyes widened. "He actually suggested he might enlist and only when I cried would he promise he'd not. Althea, he does not wish to return to England."

"But you do."

"That is not important," said Clair, waving a hand as if at a pesky fly.

"Is it not? I wonder . . ."

Althea had almost reached the door when Clair called after her, "I forbid you to say one word to Jason. I will never speak to you again if you do."

"Speak to Jason? My best of friends, the notion had not crossed my mind," said Althea quite truthfully—and then quickly, before Clair could forbid anything else, she closed the door behind herself. She traced the dowager Lady Lambert to her own room where the lady mended some fine lace she did not trust to her woman.

"I am sorry to intrude," said Althea, "but there is something I must discuss with you." She explained about Clair's unhappiness.

The dowager nodded. "I too have noticed something wrong with the child. I hoped it was that she was in the early stages of a pregnancy, but you say not?"

"That possibility had not occurred to me. It is possible and if her unhappiness is exacerbated by that particular condition, then what I have to suggest is, I think, still more important. I believe you should develop qualms about remaining in Brussels, my lady."

The dowager cast her a quick look. "*I* should have *qualms*?"

"Yes. Clair has forbidden me to speak to Jason about her feelings. I suspect she would be equally angry with *you* for suggesting she needs to go home. On the other hand, if *you* wished to return to London or perhaps to Andover Place? The country would soothe her, would it not? Clair loves country life more than city life where she must share Jason with everyone in the government, the army and, of course, socially."

"I believe you malign my daughter-in-law, Althea. She hasn't a jealous bone in her body."

Althea smiled. "I know. But she truly prefers the quiet life and if she is *enceinte*, then it is important she feel relaxed and content."

The dowager nodded. "Yes. With that I agree." She closed her eyes for a moment, her lips tightly compressed, and then she nodded. "Very well. I will, over the next day or two, develop qualms. We should be off by the end of the week."

Althea had heard more and more rumors concerning the imminence of battle and hoped it would be soon enough. Once the war actually began, travel was likely to become difficult.

Val arrived soon after Althea's *tête-à-tête* with the elder Lady Lambert. "I thought we meant to ride this afternoon," he said, surprised to find her in morning dress.

Althea drew in a deep breath and let it out in a huff. "I have been so preoccupied with Clair's problems, I forgot."

"Forgot," he said mournfully. "I see."

She cast a look his way and found him eyeing her. A weariness hung about him that she did not understand.

"It is time, is it not?" he asked, his voice harsh.

"Time?" she asked, bewildered. "For what?"

"To end this farce of an engagement. Very well," he continued before she could speak, "I shall look about me for a suitable ladybird and . . ."

Althea felt panic rise within her. "No!" she interrupted.

"No?" he asked.

"It is too soon. Much too soon," she said, and desperately searched for a reason to delay what he saw as the inevitable break between them. She clutched at a notion she thought might do. "I cannot face a new scandal on top of the one that is still upon us."

Ah, if only I were brave enough to demand he wed me, brave enough to tell him how much I loved him, that I no longer care if he is a rake, if his reputation is not exactly as one would wish.

He eyed her thoughtfully, wondering what was causing her such anguish. "You do not think that it would be easier getting it all over with at once?"

There was even a shade of humor in his voice and she relaxed a trifle. "I can't face it, Val. Not now."

"Very well," he said. "Will you tell me when you are ready?"

She hesitated a moment too long.

"Ah. You do not feel you can make that decision, either?"

She felt panic return.

"So," he said, and after a moment nodded. "Very well. At some point I will find a bit of muslin and do what is necessary without informing you. That way you can be properly surprised and disgusted and—" Again that harsh note she dreaded was heard. "—*you* will do what you must do." He bowed and turned on his heel and left her.

Althea barely made it to her room before she burst into tears. That had not gone well. She had made mistake after mistake. Why could she not be honest with him? Why not trust him with her feelings? Her love?

Worse, now she would never know when he felt it time to end it all. He would show himself, perhaps in the park, with a bird of paradise on his arm and the whispers would begin and some *kind* soul would inform her what went forward and she would be expected to . . . to break it off with him.

"Well, I won't" she muttered into her damp pillow. She sat up, a militant look in her eye. "*I won't do it.*"

For the next few days Althea was much preoccupied with helping Clair and her maid pack. She saw very little of any of the men, except at meals, which were erratic, invitations pouring in for the Lamberts the instant it was known they meant to leave Brussels.

Althea had a long talk with her mother and was relieved the older woman was not ready to depart, her cicisbeo having arrived and the two of them seemingly unaware that a war was about to be fought, possibly on their doorstep. If Althea had not already decided she meant to wed Val come hell or high water she would have done when she saw how happy her mother was, how content, and how obviously she anticipated her own nuptials—although nothing had been admitted by either herself or Sir Robert.

In any case, it was with a lighter heart Althea waved off the coach taking the Lord and Ladies Lambert along with Jared Lambert to the coast. Jared had insisted he must cross the Atlantic at once, but it was argued, successfully, that he should take this opportunity to learn something of his family's history and ancient home.

Clair, of course, would prosper once they reached Jason's estate. Althea had heard the two planning changes to their suite, the building of a new walled rose garden, and other such things. Clair glowed and Jason obviously doted on her. It was good.

Now it was time to settle her own future. She recalled something her mother had once said. Life had been comfortable. There had been no reason for change. But that peace had fled. Her mother had revealed her wish to rewed. Val had suggested he'd leave for parts unknown. Life would never again hold any comfort.

Had that been another reason she'd refused Val's proposals? That she, like her mother, was comfortable and did not like change? But that was nonsense!

I have to find the courage to cut the knot and make things right. Unfortunately, finding courage seemed impossible.

Althea devoted as much time as possible to Val. They rode together, attended parties, joined large numbers of people attending the increasing number of military revues, and in every way her conventional soul allowed, tried to show Val how much she wanted to be with him.

"If one did not know," he said, the irony clearly there to be heard by the densest soul—which Althea was not, "one would actually believe you loved me."

"I seem to recall a day when you claimed I did," she retorted. Then she wondered how she'd had the nerve to refer to that kiss, that day when she had thought all would be well between them, that he had realized she had given her heart and soul to him . . .

"You have loved me for a long time, my dear," he said, his voice dry as the dust rising from the parade ground where a cavalry unit was showing off intricate maneuvers. "Unfortunately, it has not convinced you we should wed."

"I wonder . . ."

He cast her a quick look and she lost her nerve.

". . . if Lady Babs *will* wed her soldier. Look," she said, nodding to where the two appeared to be arguing heatedly.

"Blast," said Val. "I thought I had convinced her that Charles is not one on whom she can play off her tricks!"

"Tricks?"

Val sighed. "Babs, despite what one might think, is inse-cure. She has a need to test a person's love for her, to see how far she can push him—and then she is heartbroken when he will not put up with it, proving to her he is false."

"How nonsensical."

"I suppose we all have our little quirks."

Althea thought of her own, her inability to admit to him she did not want to break off their engagement, that she wanted to walk down the aisle and meet him at an altar, wanted to exchange vows, wanted to leave the church and begin their life together—whatever that might bring.

She sighed.

"Yes?" he asked.

"We all have quirks, do we not?"

"You believe you know mine, of course," he said politely.

"I was thinking of my own," she said.

"Yours?" His brows arched. "But my dear Althea, you are the most clear-eyed, clear-headed woman I know. To what could you possibly refer?"

"Hmm? Oh . . ." Again she found her tongue frozen, that she could not speak the words she longed to say. She sighed. "I don't know."

"Or do not trust me enough to tell me. Very well. Are you ready to leave this *mêlée*? I find the day too hot. What I want more than anything is a nice little *café* where I can rest in the shade of a canopy and sip a nice cool glass of wine. Shall we interfere in whatever is between Babs and Colonel Audley and see if they will join us? For propriety's sake?"

The four had their horses saddled and cantered back to-ward Brussels, stopping at the first small suburban *café* to which they came.

As the days passed, it seemed to Althea that Sir Valerian grew more and more nervy, jumping at unexpected sounds, and off in some sort of daze from which, sometimes, she found it difficult to draw him. She feared the day would soon arrive when she would be forced to face her fears and *do something*.

About then, her worse nightmare began. She noticed people looking at her, some with speculation, some with pity, some slyly, some with an I-could-have-told-her look. Val, it seemed, had begun appearing in public with a black-haired beauty hanging on his arm.

Lady Barbara arrived early one morning and demanded Althea's presence. "At once," she said, storming into the salon before the footman, who Lord Lambert had left behind for the Bronsen's comfort, could open the door for her. When Althea arrived, the tall redhead was storming from one end to the other of the long room, her habit slung over her arm in such haphazard fashion a bit of stocking above her boot showed.

"Lady Babs?" said Althea, drawing her guest's attention.

"He does not have that chit in keeping. I swear it," said Babs, swinging around and dropping the skirts to her habit. They swung across the floor and, when a faint cloud of dust rose an inch or two into the air, Althea made a mental note to get after the maids who were supposed to see to such things. "You must believe me," continued Lady Babs earnestly. "He loves you to distraction. I do not understand what he *is* doing, but don't you dare to think he is being false to you!"

Althea smiled at her ladyship's vehemence. Then she sighed. "I know exactly what he is doing and I know he isn't, wouldn't, won't . . . oh, I don't know how to put it. It is all a sham and I don't want him to do it and I haven't had the courage to . . . oh, blast." Althea, who had been unable to sort out her thoughts into a coherent stream of logic, shut her mouth.

"What do you mean a sham?"

"He . . . we . . ." Althea turned away.

Babs swore with the fluency of a trooper, which brought

Althea around to stare at her. Babs, seeing her look of surprise, barked a laugh. "Sorry. There are times I cannot control my temper. It doesn't mean anything, you know. Or not
usually. But right now I am very angry. What do you mean a
sham?"

Althea bit her lip.

"Come, Althea. You may trust me, you know," said Babs
with rough kindness.

Althea swallowed. "The engagement was a plot to throw
that awful cousin of Lord Lambert's off stride. Andover was
trying his best to throw a rod into the wheel of Lord Lambert's
marriage, breaking it up. The other cousin, the real heir, explained it to us. He thinks his half brother did the same thing
once before."

"The same thing? You are not making sense."

Althea realized she had not explained and, silently, berated herself for turning into a widgeon, which she was *not*.
"He broke up a marriage back where he lived before, split
them apart, and then—or so it appeared—the man commit-
ted suicide for despair at losing his beloved wife. And then
Andover took over the man's fur trapping area. It seems men
have some sort of agreement about where they will trap and
there are problems if one man intrudes into another's territory. That happened to be a particularly rich source of excellent furs." She shrugged. "We think he meant to do the same
with Clair and Lord Lambert's marriage—killing Jason but
making it look like suicide and then he, as heir, would become Lord Lambert with no one suspicious."

"Good heavens." Babs stared. "Then *Wellington* lied about
what happened that day?"

"Oh no. It was exactly as we said. The real Jared Emerson
Andover confronted his bastard half brother. They had had a
fight last year which ended with the older brother pushing
the unconscious younger brother into the river where he should
have drowned . . . but didn't."

"What an evil man."

"Very."

Babs thought about it for a moment and then shrugged. "But that does not explain what Val is doing showing that doxy to the *ton*."

"It was all arranged. Once we had Andover under control— we did not mean *dead*—we would break it off. I would . . . would . . ."

"Jilt him." Babs nodded. "Such a ridiculous notion. Why would you do such a thing?"

Althea felt the strain pulling her facial muscles into taut lines. "I . . . don't want to."

"So?"

"I cannot tell him."

Babs blinked. "Why not?"

Again Althea hesitated. "I . . . don't know."

"You are just going to let him go? You are going to embarrass the both of you? You are going to live with the knowledge that everyone will call you a jilt?" Babs was about to lose her famous temper once again.

"No."

The stiffening went out of the angry woman. Once again Babs blinked those obviously darkened lashes. "No? Just no?"

Althea laughed at the bewilderment Babs revealed. "They are in the park?" she asked.

"I think they'd still be there," said Babs, still confused. "I saw them, heard the speculation, and—" Red touched her ladyship's cheeks. "—turned away from my party and rode directly here." She looked a trifle dismayed. "I wonder if my groom managed to follow and catch my horse!" She strode to the window, looked out, and saw the lad holding both his and her horses. "Well. That's all right then."

"But they should still be in the park?" insisted Althea. "Why?"

"I . . . don't know."

But she did. Somehow she had to cut the lines fouling

their understanding of each other. She had to find the courage and find it now.

"I believe," she said slowly, "that I must take a walk in the park."

"Ride and I'll ride with you."

"No. I'd have to change. It would take too long." Althea, her mind made up, went to the door and asked the footman to call her maid. Soon she was ready to walk out. "Lady Babs, I am not certain if I thank you for coming. On the other hand, someone or something had to prod me off the fence on which I've been sitting. Good day," she said, holding out her hand.

Babs, guessing at what Althea meant to do, ignored it. She gathered up her skirts. "I'll ride ahead and see if I can locate them. If I do, I'll find you and tell you where they are."

Althea nodded. She had wondered how she was to come up with Val. Inside, something cringed at the notion of facing him this way, but, sternly, she pushed it down and, her maid following along behind, strolled down the street twirling her parasol as if she had not a worry in the world.

Inside, where no one could see, she seethed and boiled and worried and wondered what she would do when she did find the couple for whom she searched.

What *could* she do—as a proper young lady?

She laughed a dry little laugh. Perhaps it was necessary that she not be quite so . . . proper?

CHAPTER 19

Fifteen minutes later she saw them and wished with all her heart she were home in bed with her head under the covers. Feeling particularly craven, she very nearly turned on her heel.

Instead she forced herself to watch the approach of Val and the ladybird he escorted. The young person was a small woman with dark eyes that flashed and rounded hips that no lady would admit to owning. Or, if she did, would do her best to hide rather than showing off in such a fashion as this young thing managed with every step.

Was this the sort of woman Val admired? If so, then perhaps she was wrong. Perhaps he truly did want her to give him his *congé*. No. That was too mild. *She was to jilt him.* Jilt him? A muscle jumped in Althea's jaw and anger strengthened her will. Her mouth thinned. *Jilt him?*

When he was everything she wanted in all the world? No. She would not.

Seeing a mist of red before her eyes, Althea marched toward the couple. She saw Val stiffen. Saw in his eyes a depth of pain . . . and, seeing it, her anger faded. He did *not* want her to play the jilt. He was doing this only because he'd made a bargain.

A bargain.

Bargains could be unmade as well as made. It was time this particular bargain was laid aside forever.

Althea forced a smile to her lips. "Good morning, Val," she said, pleasantly. "A new friend?" She cast a pitying look over the flashily dressed bird of paradise. "My dear, I fear you have made a grave error," she said softly so that only the three of them heard. "He is mine, you see, and I will not give him up."

As Althea spoke she searched blindly in her reticule for a small knitted purse she'd placed there only the day before. It had the month's housekeeping money in it, and, although it was quite a lot, she hoped it was enough payment for services, er, *not* rendered!

"I think," she said, still smiling, "that you were asked to do a job of work?" She felt sorry for the young person, who stared at her as if she were quite insane. *Perhaps I am*, she thought. She stole a glance at Val and saw an unholy gleam in his eye that would have made her blush if she hadn't had to concentrate so hard on saying just the right thing. "I think this will compensate you for the time you will *not* be spending in his company," she finished, holding out the purse.

Althea's gaze held the harlot's bemused glance. Slowly, the girl—she was no more than that really—held out her hand. Althea dropped the purse and rather grubby fingers closed around it, the wrist sagging just a trifle at the unexpected weight of it.

"Good-bye, my dear. You run along now," said Althea, keeping her tone to that firm but kindly note with which one spoke to slightly naughty children. "You should use what you've earned wisely, you know, and not waste it on frivolity."

When no one moved she sighed. Reaching out, she attempted to remove the chit's hand from Val's arm. It took a bit of prying until the girl realized what was happening and opened her fingers. She lifted her hand and backed a step away.

"Very good. Now, good-bye. Val?" Althea asked, turning her gaze up to meet his. It took every ounce of bravery she could muster to hold his look. And then, when his lips twitched, she relaxed slightly. "Shall we go?" she asked softly.

His gaze softened still more and he smiled, allowing her to relax ever so slightly more. "Go?" he said in a voice that must have carried well beyond the three of them. "My dear I will go to the ends of the earth for you."

"No, no . . . unless you mean to take me with you?" she asked—perhaps a trifle pertly.

Soft clapping came from somewhere nearby. Val and Althea turned. "Well done," said Lady Barbara, softly, lifting her crop to her forehead in a sort of salute. "Well done indeed."

Val, when Althea's hand on his arm urged him in that direction, walked up to the rider. Althea looked up. "Thank you," she said.

"Very glad to be of service. You only needed the least little hint, you know," said Babs, grinning. She sobered, looking over their heads to where several officers on horseback rode together. "Now if I can only manage to tell myself to do what I know needs doing . . ."

Suddenly she nodded to them, kicked her mare, and rode off—but not toward Colonel Charles Audley and the other men as Althea had assumed she'd do.

"Will they manage to come to an understanding of each other?" asked Althea.

"Only time will tell," said Val. "I have something else on my mind. Have *we* managed to understand one another?" he asked, smiling down at her.

"I have come to my senses," admitted Althea. "I have known for some time what I wanted—I just could not find the courage to tell you."

He chuckled. "Well, when you do find courage, you find a great deal of it. Would it not have been easier in the privacy

of—oh, say, the back parlor when no one else was around?"
He made a rather subtle gesture toward where any number of
people ogled them.

Althea did blush then. "I suppose it was necessity that
drove me to it. I might have gone on in my wishy-washy
fashion forever if you had not decided to bring our play acting to an end."

"But it is not acting in a play, is it? Not now?" he asked.
There was just a hint of an anxious note to that. "We are
truly engaged? We will wed?"

"Oh yes."

"Soon?" he asked. "I know where that curate lodges . . . ?"

Althea's eyes widened. "Is it possible? Would one not
need a license?"

"There are exceptions. When one cannot come up with a
bishop for a license, and it is something of an emergency,
then there are ways."

She frowned, ignoring a group of young women who
were trying very hard to catch her eye. "Is this an emergency?"

"My dear, can it be anything else?" he asked, humor returning to lighten his tone. "Do you think I can wait until we
return to England and then wait still another three weeks
while the banns are called before I give in to this most in-
credibly urgent of urges I feel? One demanding I take you
into my arms and never let you go?"

"You are not used to waiting, are you?"

"No," he said—but then laughed. "Unless you count the full
three years I've waited to hear you admit you will wed me!"

"Three years . . ."

He sobered. "Once I fell in love with you, Althea, no
other woman would do."

He spoke so simply she had to believe him. But then that
old insecurity arose to make her bite her lip.

"What is it?" he asked softly.

"Val—after that kiss, the one in the vicar's garden, why
did you laugh?"

"Laugh? I *laughed*?" His surprised faded. "Ah! I remember." He glanced around to assure himself no one was near enough to overhear him and then spoke softly. "My dear Althea, do you have any notion how rare it is for a man to find that not only is a woman the woman of his heart and mind, but that she will also fulfill all the needs of his body? I never dreamed that, with all else perfect about you, you would also be capable of such passion."

"Passion." She walked on for a ways. "Is that what it was? Those . . . sort of hot melting feelings I had?"

He smiled and nodded.

"They scared me half to death," she said. "A lady should not . . ."

"I wish," interrupted Val plaintively, "that whatever fool decreed that it was unladylike to admit to the passions of the body might be boiled in oil for all eternity. Have you any notion how many marriages would be improved a hundredfold if the wives would only allow themselves to *feel*?"

It was Althea's turn to glance around, but again no one was near. In fact, she decided, everyone was giving them a wide berth—as if it were obvious they needed time alone. "I wonder if our mentors have not confused the notion of moderation in one's daily dealings with . . . with . . ."

"What goes on between a man and woman in the privacy of the marriage bed?"

"Val, you must not embarrass me."

"Too blunt for you?" He cast her a teasing look. "But, my dear, I was careful to use the most tactful phrases."

She cast him a rueful glance. "I have no desire to know what you'd have said if you were *not* tactful. Val," she went on, firmly changing the subject, "I wonder if we should return home and tell my mother that we mean to wed in the very near future."

"Tomorrow?"

"Val!"

"Ah well." He grimaced. "One can always hope, can one not?" And then he cast her a look of pretended horror. "I suppose I need time to convince Loth that our marriage will change nothing between him and myself—or if it does, it will be his fault. He has not stopped grousing since we first announced we were engaged."

In the end and not until they returned to England, it was Althea who discovered how to get Loth to accept the marriage. She had a long talk with Loth's lady love, hired the woman as housekeeper for their new establishment, and by her perceptiveness, had Loth concluding there was not a better woman in all of England—after his love, of course.

". . . and anyone," he was prone to say when he'd hoisted a mug or two or three of ale, "who thinks to argue the point can just step outside where we'll not be disturbed!"

But that was later. Months later.

"Mama," said Althea, when she and Val walked into the salon after leaving the park. "We have come to inform you that we must expeditiously get my trousseau together. Sir Valerian is impatient to have us wed, but I have told him I will not, under any circumstances, come to him in only my shift—"

She smiled at her mother's gasp at that particularly unprim locution. It was, she decided, rather fun to rid oneself of some of the prudishness that had ruled her for so long now.

"—so he agreed that I may have just a little time to do things up in something approaching a proper manner."

She watched her mother mouth the phrase, "in her shift!" and laughed. *Oh how good it is to laugh*, she thought. *I wonder why I ever forgot how?*

But she knew.

Falling in love with a gazetted rake was a terrible thing to happen to a young woman convinced she was far too sensible to ever do anything so ridiculous. She had been forced to portray the most prim and proper lady she knew how to be in order to compensate for such ill-judgment!

When, she wondered, *did I first realize that Sir Val is not the rake he is purported to be?*

It mattered not. The exact *when*. Not really—except that the realization had freed her.

Laughter was only *one* benefit of that new freedom. She looked across the room, her heart in her eyes at the most important one, which was Val himself.

Althea busied herself with calculating just how quickly she and her mother could manage to acquire the needed trousseau. Val, on the other hand, calculated how quickly he could convince her it was unnecessary. They'd acquire anything she needed once they were together.

In the end no compromise was necessary. Napoleon stole a march on Wellington and the battle that followed was not only the bloodiest of twenty years of bloody war, but left everyone accepting that there were times when the conventions ruling society must be set aside. When one could hear the fearsome booming of artillery in the distance, time had run out. With very little discussion, the convenient curate was located by a grumbling and mumbling Lothario Bitterhouse, was brought to the house, and not only Althea and Val wed, but Lady Bronsen set aside her reservations concerning a second marriage and wed her Sir Robert as well.

And then the two couples, horrified by the wounded pouring into Brussels, put aside all thought of marriage journeys and opened the house to total strangers. During the next several weeks they did what they could to alleviate pain and suffering, everything from changing bandages and feeding men who could not feed themselves to writing letters for those who had family they wished to contact.

As Val said in one of the rare moments the two managed to have together. "We've the rest of our lives, Althea. We've waited years already. We'll wait just a little longer to begin the adventure of our life together."

And he'd given her one of those long drugging kisses she'd come to wish would grow and become so much more . . . but she went back to work, this time scolding a recalcitrant sergeant who insisted—although he was missing one leg and had his arm in a sling—that he must go look for his men, must see how they were faring.

"Val!" she called, holding the man down by sprawling across his chest.

Val, she knew, would calm the soldier and soothe him, and charm him, and then do his best to help him. His help, on this occasion, took the form of sending Bitterhouse to track down the information the sergeant fretted to know.

Val would always do what he could to help others—as he always had. Gradually, diffidently, friends and acquaintances dropped by to give congratulations and best wishes, and to tell Althea tales of the things he'd done for them. And then, looking around to see that Val was occupied elsewhere, demanded she not reveal to her new husband that they had told of good deeds he insisted should not be bruited about among the *ton*.

"Why," she asked at one point, "did it take me so long to discover how wonderful you are?"

"Why did we waste three years?" he asked—and then smiled. "I suppose because my pride would not allow me to reveal to the world that my reputation is nothing but a *façade* covering a bruised ego that actually healed years ago."

"Ah. You mean it was *your* fault?" she teased, her lips twitching.

He didn't smile. "My refusal to explain was part of it. Another problem was an equally ridiculous feeling that insisted I shouldn't have to explain. That you should *know* I was not the man the world insisted I must be."

She moved into his arms. "But I did know."

"You did?" He stared down at her, bemused by her glowing face.

"Yes. In my heart. I would never have fallen in love with you if you had really been the man my head insisted you were."

"*You love me.*" It was not a question. It was a statement of wonderment—to say nothing of satisfaction.

"*As you love me,*" she responded softly, and gladly lifted her face to his when his fingers put light pressure under her chin.

This kiss was gentle, exploring the softer side of love—until another demanding groan penetrated their hearing. This time it was a very young soldier who, when they went to investigate, embarrassedly ordered Althea to go away, that Val would help him.

Val and Althea exchanged a glance over the man's cot.

And Althea went away. Quickly. And didn't despair. She knew that, before very long, she would never have to leave his side again. She longed for that day to come.

It did of course.

Napoleon was once again under Allied control so, instead of returning to England, the couple took several months to travel around Europe. Althea satisfied her curiosity about a great number of the places she'd once told her horrified mother she meant to see.

Surely it is needless to add that Val also satisfied her other curiosity, that concerning what went on between the sheets. Never, when they retired to their room for the night, would he allow her to remember that, as a properly brought up young lady, she should keep a firm restraint over her passions.

"Not," he always insisted, "when we are in bed together!"

Dear Readers,

I sometimes think that living down a reputation one has acquired either by accident or during a time of life one would rather forget must be very difficult. My rake was never quite so rakish as gossip made him, but he didn't worry about it until it interfered in his pursuit of the one woman he would love forever. Of course, she had her own problems, her own reasons for not wanting to believe him!

My January book is titled *An Acceptable Arrangement*. For those of you who have followed my writing from the very beginning when I published three volumes with another company, this will not be a new story. My current publisher is generously bringing those three volumes out in paperback for the first time so that many of my readers who never saw the hardbacks will have a chance to read them. This story is one of a man and a woman who are tired of avoiding the silken traps set during the Season for eligible unwed men and women. Both decide it is time to marry and each contrives a similar plot. Servants gossip. They will use this in the search for an acceptable arrangement. They will, each independently decide, have their personal servants seek out information about various eligibles until they find exactly the right one.

Needless to say, the plot thickens nicely, with problems arising now and again, but the end, as is usual in my tales, results in Mr. Right meeting and marrying Miss Perfect. (Well,

not *perfect,* perhaps—no one is perfect—but the woman fo
him, nevertheless.)

Wishing you happy reading,
Jeanne Savery

PS: I love hearing from my readers and may be reached b
snail mail at P.O. Box 833, Greenacres, WA, 99016 or b
email at *JeanneSavery@earthlink.net.* Please enclose an SASI
for a return snail mail response.